Critical Acclaim for *Iron Shoes*

"This is storytelling at its best. Molly Giles's readers are blessed.
Spread the word."
—Amy Tan, author of *The Joy Luck Club*

"Prepare to be appalled. Prepare to laugh and cry and cheer.
The story is irresistible and bewitching."
—Susan Trott, author of *Crane Spreads Wings: A Biggamist's Story*

"*Iron Shoes* is a terrifying work, terrifying because
Giles dares to investigate the banal, the base, the hateful and
petty parts of her characters, the places we do not wish to visit.
Her triumph is that she makes the visit such a pleasure."
—Joanna Smith Rakoff, *San Francisco Sunday
Examiner & Chronicle Book Review*

"As taut as a well-turned short story . . . emotional
bloodletting, as Giles shows in this subtly moving novel,
can be as purgative as it is devastating."
—Mark Rozzo, *Los Angeles Times*

"Beguiling . . . Ida is a tour de force of a character. . . . *Iron Shoes*
is full of candor and humor."
—Pam Houston, *Elle*

"While a less-gifted writer could have sugarcoated this tale of
domestic woe and family misunderstandings,
Giles's mordant and mature wit shines on every page."
—Bay Anapol, *Albuquerque Journal*

". . . [a] dark and piercingly funny book . . ."
—Donna Rifkind, *The Baltimore Sun*

"Molly Giles proves that she can take the hard-won epiphanies
of her short-story characters and bring them to even greater
emotional depths in a full-length novel . . . polished prose and
dialogue that rarely misses a beat."
—Kristen Iversen, *The Denver Post*

"Molly Giles brilliantly straddles the line
between comedy and tragedy."
—Colleen Kelly Warren, *St. Louis Post-Dispatch*

T0114150

Also by Molly Giles

Rough Translations
Creek Walk and Other Stories

Molly Giles

Iron Shoes

a novel

SCRIBNER PAPERBACK FICTION
Published by Simon & Schuster
NEW YORK LONDON TORONTO SYDNEY SINGAPORE

For Hannah

SCRIBNER PAPERBACK FICTION
Simon & Schuster, Inc.
Rockefeller Center
1230 Avenue of the Americas
New York, NY 10020

First Scribner Paperback Fiction edition 2001

SCRIBNER PAPERBACK FICTION *and design are trademarks of*
Macmillan Library Reference USA, Inc., used under
license by Simon & Schuster, the publisher of this work.

For information regarding special discounts for bulk purchases,
please contact Simon & Schuster Special Sales at 1-800-456-6798 or
business@simonandschuster.com

Designed by Karolina Harris

Manufactured in the United States of America

1 3 5 7 9 10 8 6 4 2

The Library of Congress has cataloged the
Simon & Schuster edition as follows:
Giles, Molly.
Iron shoes : a novel / Molly Giles.
p. cm.
1. Women—Fiction. I. Title.
PS3557.I34465 I7 2000
813'.54—dc21   00-021778

ISBN 0-684-85993-9
0-684-85992-0 (Pbk)

Acknowledgments

W h y a book that only takes a few hours to read (less if you skip this page) took over seven years to write is beyond me, but I would be writing it still if it were not for the refuge/residencies kindly offered by Nell Altizer, the Bruemmers, the MacDowell Colony for the Arts, Villa Montalvo, Milt Wilson, and Yaddo, and for the help and support of the following readers: Sarah Baker, Paul Bendix, Toni Brown, Jo Carson, Marcia Clay, Alan Dressler, Betty Hodson, Ellen Levine, Leo Litwak, Amelia Mosley, Charlotte Painter, Kate Pelly, Paul Pruess, Bridget Shupp, Carol Houck Smith, Terese Svoboda, and Debra Turner. Thank you all and extra heartfelt thanks to my wonderful editor, Marysue Rucci.

Forgive me.
(Pause. Louder.)
I said, Forgive me.

SAMUEL BECKETT, *Endgame*

One

K a y hurried down the hospital corridor, trying to balance the bag of gifts in one arm and the bouquet of flowers in the other. Her shoulder purse banged against her hip as she half-walked, half-jogged toward her mother's room, and her hair spilled out of its pins, wispy against her flushed face. Hastily she rehearsed the rules she had set for this visit: she would be light and charming; she would not complain about her husband nor brag about her son; she would not cry—as she had after the last operation when she saw what was left of her mother's leg—and she would not tell a single lie unless she had to. She checked the number inked on her wrist to make sure she had the right room, tucked her bunched blouse back into her skirt, and raised a hand to knock. The bag immediately slipped, tore, and spilled out of her arms. Not fair! Kay thought. The hangover she had been fighting all day kicked in and her throat watered with savage longing for a cigarette. She gathered the things, straightened, took a deep breath, and knocked again.

Ida, propped on pillows in a gold satin bed jacket, did not turn.

She was staring out the window. "You took your sweet time," she said.

"Sorry." Kay tried to think of an excuse that would work. There was none. "I left work late. There was a lot of traffic. I got lost."

Ida turned and looked at her over the tops of her glasses. "You got lost coming to the hospital?"

"No. I got lost in the hospital. Don't look at me like that. It's a big hospital."

"You've been lost all your life."

"Sorry," Kay repeated, adding, "How are you?" which was the wrong thing to say. She braced herself, expecting to hear, "How do you think I am? I just had my last leg cut off. How would you be if you just had your last leg cut off?" But Ida only said mildly, "Fine. Except it seems I've caught bronchitis."

"Can you 'catch' bronchitis?"

"I don't know. One of the surgeons was sneezing all over me. Oh what are we talking about? Come give me a kiss. Christ! Don't sit on the bed."

"I wasn't going to."

"You most certainly were. You were going to knock me off balance."

"No, I was . . ."

"I have no balance at all. I roll around like a papoose. How would you like to be me?" Ida stared at her, glittering. How beautiful she was, Kay thought. Even now. Those huge eyes, dark as the sapphire on her clenched hand. The creamy skin. Cleft chin. Valentine mouth. The heavy diamond earrings were in place, only three days after surgery, and the surgical cotton dabbed with L'Heure Bleue was secreted somewhere inside the silk bed jacket; the whole room reeked of it.

"I would not like to be you," Kay said.

"Right. Do you know what Francis calls me now? Humpty Dumpty. Can you believe it?" Ida's eyes were full of tears and something else, some lit and sparkling secret life. Laughter, Kay thought, shocked. "I better not fall off any walls," Ida said gaily.

"A wall ought to fall on Dad."

"Oh he can't help it. I wish he'd call though. I haven't heard from him all day. What did you bring me?"

"Just these." Kay unfolded the sheath of flowers. They looked battered; not the brave flags she had seen in the florist's window, nothing but a bunch of bent and broken stalks. She tried to smooth them straight. "Gladiolas," she apologized. "They reminded me of you."

"They're lovely, darling. What color would you call that?"

"Orange?"

"Let me see. No. Bring them closer. I can't come to you. You may not have noticed, but I don't have any legs. And not in my face! I'll get pollen up my nose! Can you believe this? Bronchitis? Did you bring a vase?"

"I'll ask a nurse."

"I wouldn't if I were you. The nurses here are all dykes."

"Maybe there's one in the bathroom."

"Oh they're all over."

"I meant a vase."

"There might well be a vase in the bathroom. I wouldn't know. I can't go to the bathroom, Kay. I can't walk. Remember?"

"Yes, well, I'll go down the hall and find one. Here, Nicky made you a card. And I made macaroons. And here's a new novel from work I thought you might like."

Ida picked up each item and studied it closely. "There's been a mouse in the pantry," she said, shaking the cookie bag. Kay licked a crumb from the inside of a tooth and shrugged. I'm forty, she thought. I need to eat. She watched Ida examine Nicky's card. It was one of his nicer ones. Or was it? She leaned forward. Oh-oh. It showed a little boy with no hands running from a house on fire. "Don't Be Scarred" was crayoned on top. "I wonder why you let him use gilt," Ida said. "It makes such a mess."

Kay looked at the festive salting of gold and silver that had fallen from Nicky's card onto her mother's hospital sheet and let her eyes finally move past the lap to the two short lengths of thigh and then to the flat empty place where the rest of Ida's legs ought to be. There. She had looked. A roar of pity thundered in her ears. She had loved her mother's legs, their angles and curves, the saucy way they kicked out when Ida danced, the way they dovetailed together when she arced off the diving board. She had loved the sheen of the ivory-colored skin after shaving, the hard knees with their freckles, the strong square toes with their bright red polish. It had been hard to accept the loss of the first leg, a year ago, but this second loss was worse. Oh, what was the matter with Ida? Why couldn't she follow the diets, quit the cigarettes, do the exercises, forgo the martinis? Why did she have to lurch out of the wheelchair, slip in the bath, fall off the commode? Every time she hurt herself she got gangrene and every time she got gangrene she had another amputation. It was endless. "Mom," she said, "oh Mom."

Ida, ignoring her, picked up the novel and studied the author's photo on the back. "She's about my age, isn't she? Maybe even older. And this is her first book? Well! There's hope yet!"

"There's always hope."

"Easy for you to say." Ida set the book down. "Do one thing for me? Bring the phone a little closer? Just in case Francis calls while you're out finding that vase?"

Kay moved the phone as far as the cord would stretch and escaped.

Ida watched her leave. Then she rubbed her sapphire ring against the sheet to make it shine and rested her head back against the pillows. This morphine was stronger than the last time. She felt about

again. The horse was still there. Mr. Know-It-All. Bright blue. He
had spent the morning advising her on flight. How it would feel,
how she would do it. She would want wings, nothing fancy, the
horse had said, but serviceable, strongly feathered wings; her own
arms were too puny. She would have to strap the wings on, wheel
herself to the window, and hoist herself out. Once out, she would
fall—not far—a floor or two, and then she would rise. She would
ride a wind current home. It would be hard sweaty work but she
had never minded hard work and she would soon see her own
house, tucked like a glass castle in the green folds of the mountain.
She'd knock on the skylight and Francis would look up from his
crossword puzzle and smile at her the way he used to, as if she
were the most delightful creature in the universe. And then she'd
settle down with Coco barking welcome and she'd float through
the front door. And once I'm home, she hissed to the horse, you'll
be gone. And once you're gone, I'll be all right.

Francis heard a knocking at the skylight and looked up from his
crossword. Bird suicide number 241. You'd think they'd learn, but
no. Birdbrains. He tapped out one cigarette, lit another, penned in
a two-letter word for a three-toed sloth, and rattled the ice in his
drink the way Ida did when she wanted a refill; it made a forlorn
racket in the empty house. That was how Ida's ghost would sound,
when she came back to haunt him.

    Not that he needed to think of her ghost just yet. Jim Deeds said
she was making record recovery this time around. Her only problem was her cough, and everyone coughed. Francis coughed a little
himself, finished his drink, remembered they were low on Scotch,
and rose to put it on the list. He paused for a minute in his stocking feet to feel the late afternoon sun slanting through the windows. He'd designed this house for light, forgetting that light, like
everything else, is full of grit and scurf and flecks of filth. He put
his hand out and watched dust motes touch and drift off his wed-

ding ring. This must be how Greta, their so-called housekeeper, spent her day. In some Teutonic dream, batting at sunbeams. She didn't vacuum, clean, or cook. He should have let her go the first time she served sauerkraut with cocktail weenies. Kay could come up once or twice a week and do the same work for free.

He wrote "booze" on the notepad, then "fire Greta," then went to check the freezer for Coco's ground sirloin. Coco skittered to her feet as he approached but even though the door to her kitchen cage was open, it was clear she wasn't coming out; she was having one of her "in" days; the vet called it stress and Kay called it "the vapors" and Victor probably thought it was Possession by the Devil, but poodle psychosis was what it was, plain and simple, and a sad thing to observe. "Nut case," he said as he passed. Coco's black eyes trembled and teared beneath her tangled curls; she whimpered and thumped her expensive stick of a tail, then howled as the telephone rang.

And rang. Six calls in two hours. Two from Sunny-at-the-Office, one from poor Nealy Mouth, and the rest from Ida. Ida felt better today, no doubt about it. Problem was, he did not. His back ached and he was tired, tired the way he always was when he took an afternoon off work, as if there weren't enough time in the entire world to catch up on his rest.

"Francis?" Ida's voice, sounding dangerously close, recorded itself on the answering machine. "Francis, are you on your way over here, I hope? I need that round silver mirror. And could you bring some Vaseline? My lips are dry as a monkey's. Oh I hope you'll get here soon. What are you doing, anyway? Tell me"—she paused to cough—"are you just standing by the phone listening to me?"

"Why would I do that?" Francis mouthed. He poked through the packages in the freezer; there was plenty of sirloin; Coco would be fine through the weekend, unless her anorexia kicked in.

"To make me mad." Ida coughed again. "I have enough to make me mad. I've been seeing that blue horse again. And Kay brought me the kind of flowers you send to an enemy's funeral."

Good-o, Francis thought, padding back to his chair with the last of the Scotch in his glass, Kay's there. Maybe she'll make herself useful. Do something right for a change. Last week she'd shown up in baggy jeans, hair all over the place, two hours late to take Coco to the vet's. If anyone saw her like that they'd want to know what had happened to the prodigy girl, the first prize winner at the Music Conservatory. And Francis would have to say he didn't know. And he didn't. One minute you had a daughter who was going places and twenty years later you looked up and there she was, still standing in front of you with that same expectant look on her face. What happened to girls? Was it sex? Did sex make them stupid? Victor had never been bright, but Victor was doing all right, still married to Stacy, holding his own at the Ford dealership. Victor was slow but he got there. Kay—smart as a whip—could read music before she was five, and look at her. Dropped out of college to run off with a Gypsy, who in turn ran off with a waitress, went on to have her heart broken by a string of other jerks too numerous to name, worked one menial job after another, never saved a cent, never learned a thing, and now here she was, stuck in a hut in the woods, working at the smallest branch of the county library for peanuts, married to a dreamer as foolish as she. All those lessons. All that talent. Thrown away.

He settled back into his chair and picked up his crossword. His gold pen caught the late afternoon sun and flashed a swift wand of light around the room as he filled in word after word. He could feel night coming on—the great weight of the dark massing up from the mountain—but for a second, pen snapping and sparkling, he felt as though he could still keep it back.

The nurse at the desk was a young Filipina with an engagement ring who gave Kay a plastic container for the gladiolas at once. "You're Mrs. McLeod's daughter?" she asked.

Kay nodded, prepared for a curious look. People either liked

Ida or they didn't—there were no in-betweens—and they often
studied her brother Victor and her as if looking for clues to their
mother. Victor was easy, as long as he didn't start witnessing about
Jesus; he had Ida's dark blue eyes and cleft chin. Kay was harder to
pinpoint. Grocery clerks sometimes asked for her ID when she
filled her cart with jug wine, but that, she thought, was probably
because her face still broke out. No one but Nicky thought she
was beautiful, though Neal used to say she "looked fresh" and her
glamorous friend Zabeth said she had "an old-fashioned face,"
whatever that meant.

"Your mother is an amazing woman," the nurse said now.

"Yes," Kay agreed.

"And your father!"

"Yes."

"Devoted."

"Thank you."

She dawdled down the polished hall, reluctant, after her great
rush to get there, to return to Ida's room. She had always secretly
liked hospitals, their jangle of bells and intercoms and footfalls,
the underrush of Muzak and the occasional startling moan of human need. She liked the cool chemical smells and the bland wafts
of hot food. Like home, she thought, like all those drafty glass
houses Victor and I grew up in. "The Famous Francis," she remembered another architect telling her years ago, at one of her
parents' drunken parties, "can design prisons and palaces but he
sure can't design a place for people to live in, can he." She wondered now what had happened to that man; she had slept with him
later, partly out of pity for his jealousy of Francis and partly out of
gratitude for his contempt, and he'd been an eager, tender lover—a
surprise—who wanted to keep seeing her, but she'd met Neal by
then, and had broken it off. She had not had a lover since. Unless
she counted Charles Lichtman. And how could she count Charles
Lichtman?

Still, at the thought of his name, she shivered, rose on tiptoe, and hugged herself in the hospital corridor. Charles Lichtman always arrived with both names in tow, the way they looked on his library card, and though he was sometimes in the library, in her fantasies, reaching to pull her down to the fake bearskin rug in the Nature Nook, he was more often up on the ridge above West Valley. He appeared in walking shorts, no shirt, a rose-colored bandanna around his curly black hair. He drank from a canteen and rested on his bike, waiting for her to catch up with him. And the one time she had—what a disaster. Why had she just glared at the ground and pretended not to know who he was? How could she have pretended not to know who he was when she had been obsessing about him for months? And when he called to her, "Hey, Library Lady," why had she just waved as if batting a deerfly and trudged on? She didn't deserve to have a lover. She wasn't good enough to be an adulteress. They'd have to sew a big red *D* for Dud to the front of her dress. And anyway—"Library Lady"—he wasn't interested in her. He must have a hundred girlfriends. And she had Neal. And Nicky. And Ida, waiting for this vase.

Ida studied the horse. Say he was right. Say she could somehow get to the window. Say she could somehow open it—say she could even strap the damn wings on by herself. Then what? It was ten floors to the ground. Did he want her to die? Did everyone want her to just give up and die? Well they had a second think coming if that's what they wanted. "Nice try," she said to the horse. "But no deal." She was not as good at jokes as Kay and Francis but she tried one. "I'm not *falling* for it," she said to the horse. She heard a soft, uncertain footstep and followed the horse's bulging eyes to the door but there was no one there but Kay, unsteady as a twelve-year-old in high heels and cheap hose twisted at the ankles. "If God would give me my legs back, I'd even settle for ones as shapeless as yours," Ida said.

She winced at the hurt look that flattened Kay's eager face, closed her eyes, said, "Just kidding," and held out the novel. "Read to me?" she asked.

An hour later, Kay closed the book. A best-selling love story set during the Civil War, it had seemed a good choice for Ida, but already, by page 50, the hero had lost an arm in battle and his young wife had died in childbirth in a hospital with the same name as this one. "Sorry," she said.

Ida, still frowning out the window, said, "That's all right. Get my purse and find my lipstick, will you?"

"Where is your purse?"

"How should I know? Honestly. Use your eyes."

I am, Kay thought, and crossed them. Ignored, she searched the room until she found the navy blue pocketbook under a pile of magazines. She opened it with distaste. The stained silk lining stank of L'Heure Bleue and tobacco and the zippered compartments were crammed with loose pills and grimy candies. She stopped to look through a photo folder containing pictures of Nicky as a baby and Coco as a puppy, four of each. Ida's driver's license, expired three years ago, showed her in a turban and cat glasses, looking mean. Three $100 bills fell out of a dog-eared copy of The Prophet and a fortune cookie fortune ("Never apologize, never explain") was tucked inside the cellophane of a package of Merit 100s. "Hey," Kay scolded, "you're not supposed to smoke anymore."

"Oh good!" Ida brightened. "Hide them, will you? Here, by the bed so I can reach them later? Dr. Deeds will give me hell if he sees me."

"If I can quit, you can," Kay said as she put the cigarettes in a drawer in the nightstand.

"You're a better person than I am."

Kay looked up, surprised, but Ida was staring out the window again. She handed her the lipstick. The same red Revlon shade Ida had always worn, "Fire and Ice," worn to a beaky point. Ida took it without looking. She had thrown off the sheet and was flexing her thigh. It rose and fell, thickly bandaged in bright white strips.

"Is that a cast?" Kay asked.

"Of course not."

"It's bigger than your other one."

"That's because it's swollen, dum-dum." Ida lifted it up and down, up and down; she might have been working out at a gym. "Have you ever felt as if you've gotten half a BM out and not the rest? Because that's how I feel now."

"Probably a reaction to the anesthesia."

Ida nodded. "Like the horse."

"What horse?"

"Oh this horse who's out there talking to me. You don't have to look so understanding. I know he's not real. He's blue."

"Sounds pretty."

"He is not pretty." Ida took the lipstick, uncapped it, and without a mirror applied two swift red strokes to her lips. Kay watched, her own lips parted.

"I can never do that."

"Of course not. You don't even wear lipstick. Anyway, it's just a question of knowing where your mouth is. You do know where your mouth is, don't you?"

"Sure. I just look for my foot." Kay held her breath, waiting for Ida to say, "Look for mine too, why don't you," but Ida was rubbing more color on her cheeks and frowning. Kay pulled a small stiff brush out of Ida's purse and walked to the side of the bed, careful not to bump it. "Here, let me brush you out." She tugged as gently as she could through Ida's curls, shaping and fluffing. The tips were soft and blond but the roots were grey and damp with sweat. "You're so hot. You feel like you have a fever. Have you been taking . . ." Kay started, then stopped. Aspirin, she had been about to say. Have you been taking aspirin? You've just endured a major amputation, you're sick on anesthesia, you have bronchitis, you're hallucinating horses, and I want to know if you've been taking aspirin. She bent and lightly kissed the top of Ida's head. "There. You look gorgeous."

It was true. Ida's light hair haloed out around her heart-shaped face and the bright red lipstick which should not have looked good looked very good indeed. Ida flashed a thanks and continued to flex. Kay studied the new stump. She was used to the old one. Shaped like a slim beige sausage, tied at the tip in a neat knot, it often poked from beneath the hems of Ida's silk dresses. This new stump, though, was rawer. Ruder. More butchered-looking. Meat, Kay thought. That's what we're made of. No wonder Neal won't touch me. She licked her own dry lips. "Did the therapist tell you to exercise so soon?"

"Oh the therapist," Ida said. "The therapist is a Nazi."

Kay waited. Sometimes Ida liked Nazis.

"She picked me up this morning and threw me into that chair in the corner. As if I were some old pillow. And then she went to a staff meeting and left me there alone. I screamed," Ida said. "I screamed and screamed and screamed. Finally an orderly came in and I told him what had happened and he said, 'Here I think you and I can do better than that,' and he wheeled me over to the side of the bed and I clawed and scratched and pulled myself in. I did not stop crying for two and a half hours."

Her eyes on Kay were fierce and satisfied, and Kay could not look away. She could see it vividly: Ida like a maimed cat clawing her way back into the bed. I'll have to find the administrator in charge, Kay thought, her heart sinking. I'll have to make a complaint. She bit at her cuticle, stalled with dread. Then quietly it occurred to her that her mother might not be telling the truth. Things like this had happened to Ida before. She insisted she'd been blackballed from college sororities years ago, snubbed during her modeling career, dropped from dance troupes, and excluded from country club committees by jealous women who hated her. Just two weeks ago, she had locked herself in the bathroom to storm because a neighbor's wife had not smiled when they'd passed on the street.

"Did you talk to Dad about it?" Kay asked, her voice careful.

"Francis is useless in situations like this."

"Did you talk to your doctor?"

"You bet I did. Jim Deeds was absolutely shocked. No one should touch you, he told me. And when Morey Schoenfeld came in and I told him, tears came to his eyes."

"What happened to the therapist?"

"Oh she's biding her time. She'll probably try to get me tonight, when she thinks I'm sedated."

Kay nodded, silent, and stared glumly at the table where she'd set the flowers. There weren't as many bouquets as usual. Ida's friends must be getting used to her hospitalizations. There were some yellow asters from Victor and Stacy, with a plastic crucifix stuck in the middle, a basket of ferns from Peg and Pete Forrest, and two dozen long-stemmed red roses so dark they were almost black. "Who sent these?" Kay asked, smelling them. Beautiful things, but no odor at all.

"Aren't those spectacular? Glo Sinclair sent them. Duffy's widow."

"Remind me: is Duffy Sinclair the one who got electrocuted in the hot tub?"

"No, that was Darcy Lavin. Duffy Sinclair is the one who committed hara-kiri in his bathroom during *60 Minutes.* Glo was devastated. He used her best knife. Don't laugh, Kay. It's not funny."

"It's not unfunny," Kay said. She reached behind the roses and pulled out a small handsome house plant. It had a name she couldn't quite remember, though she'd seen one like it at the nursery last week when she'd gone in to buy tulip bulbs. She read the card, looked more closely at the plant, and frowned.

"The mystery plant," Ida said. "It came yesterday and neither your father nor I could figure it out."

"It's from my friend Zabeth. You met her last summer. I had

her to dinner right before you were supposed to leave for Greece."

"Oh. Right. The night I fell."

"One of the nights you fell."

"What?"

"Nothing."

"I hate it when you mutter. We never did make it to Greece, as you know. Now Francis is talking about going to India."

"With you? How?"

"I don't know. He thinks he can hire a bearer or some fool thing. Maybe he wants to stick me on a corner with a cup to beg."

"Mom."

"I don't know what he thinks. I just know it's late and he hasn't shown up yet. I remember Zabeth. Thin and tan and very flirty. Not your type."

"You've never liked my friends," Kay reminded her.

"Well you haven't had that many and most of them have been whores. Oh where is he? This is ridiculous. Yesterday he hardly stayed at all. What time is it now?"

"It's almost four. Most of my whore friends are just waking up."

"He gets so restless here, well, who can blame him. Yesterday he paced and paced, I thought I'd go crazy. I asked him to bring the sheepskin pad from the bed at home and do you know what he brought instead? The bathroom rug! He didn't even wash it! Oh look at you. You're still mad about that Zabeth person?"

"I like her," Kay said. "And she liked you. She thought you were beautiful and brave."

"Honestly," Ida said. "She doesn't even know me." Still she smiled, pleased, and started flexing again. A wiry swatch of grey pubic hair poked out from beneath the sheets as she lifted one stump after another. The old flasher, Kay thought. Ida had always been an exhibitionist, a breast barer, a skinny-dipper. The less you wanted to see, the more she wanted to show you. Just last week Kay had caught Nicky in the bathroom with her, dutifully peeling her nylon panties down so she could go to the toilet. "I'd do it my-self," Ida had snapped, one hand holding a highball glass, the other waving a lit cigarette, "if I could, but I can't. Besides, Nicky's six; children in France help their grandparents pee all the time."

"No they don't."

"How do you know. You've never been to France."

Nicky, who was, Kay knew, fascinated, had started to say, "I'm seven, not . . ." but Kay shooed him out. "Poor Gramma," he had said, as he left.

"Grandmère," Ida had corrected. "And there's nothing poor about me."

"Do one thing for me?" Ida asked now. "See if the phone is off the hook? Sometimes I don't put it back correctly."

"It's on."

"Are you sure?"

Kay picked it up, listened, put it back. "Yes."

"He must be on his way. So. How's Neal?"

"The same." Kay wondered if there was anything amusing or interesting she could say about Neal. Nothing came to mind. "He's been working hard." What had he said last night just before he had fallen asleep? Oh yes. *Another wasted day.* "Today's our an-niversary," she added, "and he forgot."

"That slug. I always said he was too old for you. Well at least you have your music. I wish I had something. How are the re-hearsals going for your concert?"

"It's not my concert, Mom. It's Walt Fredericks's concert."

"But you have an important solo."

"One piece. Yes. I wish . . ." She stopped. I wish I could play better, she thought. The first notes of the piece she was to play be-gan to sing in her head and she tapped her fingers on her lap, too fast.

"And the concert hall has wheelchair access?"

"It's not a concert hall. It's the West Valley Community Church. And, yes. It does."

"Good. Because I am going to be there." Ida drew the sheet up, smoothed it down, and fixed her eyes firmly on Kay. "I am going to be there if they have to carry me in on a stretcher. Tell me again what day it is."

"November something. Still a few weeks to get ready. By then maybe we'll be worth hearing. But right now . . ." Kay thought of Walt Fredericks and shook her head. Walt was a large, tremulous, excitable man with tiny hands and feet who liked to say that he had "discovered" Kay after he heard her playing on the old upright at the library last summer. He insisted he "knew talent," yet in rehearsals he never noticed when Kay's playing was all passion and slop or when it went tick-tick-tick like a mechanical pulse. He looked at her with his hot eyes brimming no matter how well or how poorly she played and that scared her to death. Someone else to let down. "I need to practice," she said. She rose. "I ought to go."

"Do one last thing for me? Phone Francis? I have this feeling he's home. Just a feeling. He won't answer for me. But he might answer for you."

Kay dialed her parents' number, a number she knew better than her own, and waited. Nervous, she twisted a strand of hair between her fingers and tugged; when she looked down she was not surprised to see the frizzy strand in her fingers was grey. She heard Ida break into a trill of dainty laughter and glanced over her shoulder. Tall, good-looking Dr. Deeds stood in the doorway and Ida leaned toward him, dimpling.

"Who is it now?" Francis started out of his nap, blinked back a bad dream, and picked up the phone as Coco howled.

"Just me, Dad. Your daughter. Kay? Sorry to bother you. Mom asked me to call but now it looks as if the doctor's here so she can't talk after all."

"Too bad," Francis said. "Goodbye."

"Dad? Don't hang up! Just wait a second. How have you been?"

"I'm fine. It's your mother, you know. She's the sick one."
Francis hugged his elbows and yawned. The golden light had left
the house and the air had cooled. Winter coming, he thought.
Time to order firewood soon. What was the name of that fellow
he'd used last year? Hippie fellow, lived out near Kay, in the
boonies.

"Now you're supposed to ask me how I've been," Kay
prompted, her voice faint on the other end.

"You're fine," he said. "Aren't you? Still have your part-time
temp job at the smallest library branch in the county?"

"Yes."

"Still making four cents an hour?"

"Something like that."

"And when exactly are they pruning your particular twig?"

"That's up to the voters. It's a good little library. There's a bond
to save it."

"Right. And the car? Running all right?"

"Fine. The radio doesn't—"

"That radio was always lousy. How are the brakes?"

"The brakes are good."

"I had those brakes relined, you know, before I sold you the
Lincoln. Gus down at Sergio Brothers said they'd be good for another three years."

"Yes, I know, I remember, and thanks, they're—"

"And Nicky? Doing brilliant work in third grade?"

"Second. His poster was chosen for the Halloween contest
and—"

"Good, and Neal? Old Neal still framing frames at the frame
shop?"

"I don't really know what Neal does at the frame shop . . ."

"Good. Good. Nothing like mystery in marriage. He still taking
all those vitamins?"

"Vitamins, minerals, acidophilus, antioxidants, algae. Yes."

"Well. I owe him a phone call. Tell him I've been busy. I'll get to it tomorrow. There was something else I wanted to ask you, Kay . . . but can't think of it now. Ta."

"Ta. But Dad? Hold on. I think I solved the mystery of who sent Mom that house plant. It was my friend Zabeth. You met her last spring."

"Oh yes," Francis said. "The sex fiend."

"She's not a sex fiend. She's a licensed masseuse."

"A rose by any other name, Kay."

"Dad! She's putting herself through law school."

"As well she should. Anyway, it's not much of a 'mystery' is it. It wasn't who sent that plant that puzzled me. It was what kind of plant it was in the first place."

"It's a bleeding heart."

"Can't hear you."

"I'm whispering because I don't want Mom to hear. It's called a bleeding heart."

"Catchy," Francis said. "Takes me right back to me carefree Catholic childhood."

"Kay," Ida called, "is that Francis?"

"It's odd, you know, but I can hear your mother's voice more clearly than I can hear yours," Francis said.

"Well I've been whisperi—"

"*Francis!*"

"The voice of my master. Better put her on."

"Okay. Nice talking to you, Dad."

"Not at all."

Kay was sweating as she handed Ida the phone. Talking to Francis was hard work. "How can you stand it?" she wanted to ask, but Ida was flushed and sparkling, her red lips pressed into a firm pretty line as she said "You rat" into the receiver. Kay bent to kiss her goodbye. "I'll call you tomorrow," she promised as she headed toward the door. Behind her she could hear Ida saying, "What do

you mean you don't think you'll be coming tonight? I need you
and I need my round silver mirror and I need"—here she gave Kay,
in the doorway, a mischievous look and dropped her voice—"my
G-I-N." She blew Kay a kiss and Kay waved back, dismissed. She
was halfway out the door when she heard her name and turned
back. Ida, the phone cupped with one hand over the receiver,
leaned toward her. "He's checking the liquor cabinet," Ida said.
"But before he comes back—I've been wanting to ask you all
day—where did you get that smashing outfit you're wearing?"

Kay looked down at the wrinkled white blouse and pleated
plaid skirt with its terrible fringe held in place with a tarnished
brass safety pin. "You gave it to me."

"I did?"

"You bought it in Scotland."

"I thought it looked familiar. It was extremely expensive. But
itchy."

"How do you know? Did you wear it?"

"Oh, you know how it is when you're traveling, you get so sick
of your own clothes. But Kay? Thank you. I'm glad you wore it today and I'm glad you came to see me."

"I'm glad too," Kay said, helpless with the truth of it, stuck in
the doorway.

"I love you darling, now . . . What? Francis? Well if you can't
find any G-I-N, look for some V-O-D . . ."

That wasn't so bad, Kay thought as she backed out to the hall.
Not fun exactly. But survivable. I had an actual three-and-a-half-
minute conversation with my father. And Mother said "Thank
you." She tried to work up a small glow of accomplishment as she
stepped into the elevator, but the glow faded as she realized she
had entered a service elevator by mistake. Two doctors moved
aside to give her room; both were dressed in paper caps and
smeared smocks and Kay saw too late that the wet stuff dripping
to the floor was human blood. She stared at the door until the elevator stopped and they filed out. Their blue plastic booties left

dark footprints and she decisively turned in the opposite direction down an ill-lit hallway lined with pipes. Her steps boomed on the concrete floor and she heard the sounds of machinery somewhere in the distance. She came at last to a heavy corrugated door marked EXIT and pushed it open with relief only to find herself standing outdoors in the cool autumn twilight, completely enclosed in a cement courtyard ringed with loading docks. The door clicked shut behind her. She was alone and—she tried the handle—locked out. She looked up. The hospital rose in tall walls of windows above her. Ida was behind one of those windows and could probably look down and see her. "Francis!" Ida would cry on the telephone, "Kay is trapped and turning in circles."

"Nothing new there," Francis would point out.

Kay shook the Merit 100 she had stolen from Ida out of her cuff and put it to her lips. Too bad she didn't have a match. Then everything would be perfect.

Two

It was dark by the time Kay got home. She could smell West Valley as soon as she turned off the freeway—the damp woodsy kick to the air, the whiff of dead skunk, the undercurrents of horse manure and wild blackberries. She walked up the cottage path with the groceries—lamb chops and raspberries, rosemary and cream. She would make a feast tonight for their anniversary, she would trick Neal into celebrating. In the bag too, a fifth, not a gallon, of good, not cheap, red wine. She would be a better wife, a better mother, and a better alcoholic.

Nicky met her at the back door, swinging the stuffed animal he was too old for. "You're in trouble," he sang. She nuzzled his hard little head and breathed in his day—the dinosaurs he'd drawn instead of writing down the spelling words in his workbook, the butterfly he'd watched instead of the ball on the soccer field, the long dreamy route he'd taken along the creek instead of coming straight home.

"Stop gloating," she told him. "Where's your dad?"

"He gave up on you."

"He what?" Kay grabbed for her son but Nicky giggled and wiggled away. She caught him, kissed him, and gave him the bag of groceries to unpack in the kitchen. He tore through to the bottom, looking for cookies. He had quick clever hands, long-fingered, like Francis's. He had Neal's thick bangs, Victor's pink cheeks, Ida's clear voice. Nothing of hers. He'd be all right.

She looked up as Neal came in. "Don't tell me you're still buying that poison," he said. She looked down at the innocent carton of milk in her hands and tried to remember the article Neal had made her read in *Prevention* magazine. Cow's milk damaged bones, teeth, skin, and, if she remembered correctly, caused a form of liver disease not unlike cirrhosis in children.

"It's low-fat," she offered. Neal shook his head. He measured something dry and green from a box in the refrigerator, stirred it vigorously into a glass of purified water, and swallowed it down with his face squinched up. Pitiful, Kay thought. You'd think someone who valued their health so much would like their life a little more. She handed Nicky a box of animal crackers under the counter and watched him tiptoe backward out of the kitchen. "I thought we could have a nice dinner," she began, but Neal shook his head again.

"Maybe tomorrow night. But it's too late now. Nicky had cereal and I'd just as soon fast. I read this new study. You're not supposed to put anything on your stomach after six."

"But it's our anniversary," Kay protested.

Neal looked at her, genuinely astonished. "It is?" His voice wavered in its reedy censure, broke. "Oh babe. Why didn't you remind me?"

"I thought you'd remember."

"No." He stared down at the scummy residue in his glass. "No, I didn't."

Kay reached in her purse and pulled out a card. "Well, I didn't do much about it either. All I got you was this." Self-pity spasmed inside her as she turned to the sink and started to rinse Nicky's cereal bowl. Neal stood silently behind her. She knew he felt bad. He

had always given her something on their anniversary: jewelry, or
new sheet music, or dinner out. They used to toast each other with
champagne cocktails at Le Petit Jardin and then order garlicky es-
cargot and melt-in-your-mouth sweetbreads and lovely gold and
green purees of baby thises and baby thats; they'd hold hands and
make plans for trips they'd take, remodeling they'd do, gardens
they'd put in. But all that was gone now. All this last year, Neal
had been distracted. At first she'd believed him when he said it was
business worries that weighted him down, made him too tired to
go out, or talk, or make love. But his mysterious weariness had
gone on for month after month and finally she had to face the
truth: He didn't love her anymore. She'd been a fool to think anyone could. Maybe her skin exuded some invisible chemical repellent. Maybe she was repellent, heart and body and soul. Neal
wouldn't tell her what was wrong and when she stormed he said
she was "spiraling" and "insecure." Well who wouldn't be insecure? She sniffled, wiped her nose with the back of her wrist, and
watched the evening's first tears splash effortlessly into the sink.
"What's happening to us?" she asked.

Neal came up behind her, placed his hands on her shoulders,
and leaned close to her cheek. "Nothing's happening," he said as
he always said. "We're fine. I'm worried about the shop is all."

Kay thought of Neal's shop: Sorensen's Art Supplies & Framing, a dusty high-raftered storefront in a reconverted stable in
downtown West Valley. She had always loved the big room with
its clutter of brushes and paints. Prints and posters swung from the
ceiling in bright banners and old photos and oil paintings lined the
walls. It smelled good in Neal's shop, like sweet chalk and turpen-
tine and charcoal, and the acoustics were great. The last time she'd
gone in, Neal had been blasting the World Series, but he also had
tapes of her playing Beatles songs, with Nicky singing along in a
brave off-tune voice. The shop didn't make much money, barely
enough to live on, but Neal had never cared much about money;
that was one of the best things about him.

"Is there something there I could help you with?"

"What could you do?"

"I could do whatever you want. Frame. Mat. Charm the customers."

"No."

"Just no?"

Kay looked down as his hands trembled along the length of her arms, carefully avoiding contact with her breasts. She had never liked Neal's hands; they had always reminded her of rat paws, with their glaze of fine white hairs and deep-set narrow nails. But she had liked other things about him. The way his eyes closed up when he smiled. His gentle fussy kindness to children and animals. His niceness. Neal was—used to be—the nicest man she'd ever met. She touched an age spot on the back of his hand she had not seen before. "This is Kay's *old* old man," Francis had said, introducing Neal to some friends at a cocktail party at his golf club. "I'm just her father." She remembered Neal's eyes darting toward her, his smile faltering as the other men laughed. He had seemed frightened then, and he seemed frightened now. She brought the age spot to her lips and kissed it.

"Things will get better," Neal promised. "I know right now is bad. I'm preoccupied at work and you're under a lot of pressure too."

"The concert," Kay nodded.

"No, I meant your mother. Her dying."

"She's not dying." Kay pushed back, puzzled. Didn't Neal know Ida at all? He didn't seem to. When he'd first met her parents he had turned to her, eyes shining, and pronounced, with conviction, "Your father's a genius and your mother's a sweetheart." She should have known then that Neal could never help her. "Mom will live forever," she explained. "Dr. Deeds says she's got the heart of a twelve-year-old. She'll be in a wheelchair for life, but it's going to be a really long life."

"Oh babe." Neal sucked in his breath. Kay stood silent, stubborn. After another second, he released her. "Well," he said, "happy tenth."

"Ninth."

"Really? Seems longer."

"What do you mean by that?"

"I mean . . . oh forget it."

Neal trudged back to the living room and Kay threw the sponge into the sink. Charles Lichtman bicycled through her brain, shot her a heart-stopping smile, and disappeared, his rose-colored bandanna fluttering behind him. She sighed, fished the sponge out, and finished rinsing the dishes—thick brown and white dishes Neal had used during his long stint of bachelor life. She soaped and rinsed the flatware Francis and Ida had given her when they bought a new pattern. The griddle she wiped down on the Wedgwood stove had belonged to Neal's mother. In fact all the appliances in the kitchen had belonged to Neal's mother; she had lived in this cottage until the night Neal told her he was getting married, whereupon she had a quiet, tactful stroke and died. Kay folded a dish towel and hung it back on the rack, then refolded it and hung it a bit straighter. She often caught herself doing things like that for Mrs. Sorensen's approval, and sometimes when the house settled she imagined she heard a heavy step and felt Mrs. Sorensen's round eyes in steel-rimmed glasses rest dimly upon her. She had liked the old woman and didn't mind trying to please her ghost. It was child's play after years of trying to please Francis and Ida.

Still, some willful displeasuring was in order once in a while, wasn't it? She opened the bottle of expensive Bordeaux, poured a full glass, and drank, frowning at the faded plaid paper on the walls. She had taken the ruffled curtains down long ago and repainted the cupboards; she had refinished the dining room table and bought a new bed for their bedroom. She had transformed Mrs. Sorensen's sewing room into a music room; it was just big enough for her baby Baldwin, and with the door closed and his earphones on, Neal could watch television without having to hear her practice. Nicky's room was redone, with dinosaur decor wall-to-wall. But most of the cottage was as it had been in Mrs. Sorensen's time, a warren of low-ceilinged rooms with a musty stench to them. The best thing about the place was the wide front porch that looked out onto the street, and the creek and woods in back.

She saw Neal enter the back yard now. She narrowed her eyes, wondering how she would see him if she didn't know him. A tall man with bad posture and a thick grey ponytail in a faded Jefferson Airplane tee shirt—someone's bachelor uncle, gentle and solitary. From this distance you couldn't see the gold lights in his eyes or hear the catch in his voice when he said "Oh babe." Curious, Kay watched him pause under the porch light to pick mint leaves and drop them into his pocket. He would take them to the shop tomorrow and boil them on his hot plate and make a piss-colored tea which he would sip as grimly as hemlock, pausing only to take his pulse. When had this unwholesome fixation on his health begun? When the fertility doctors told them his sperm count was so low that Nicky's conception must have been a statistical miracle? He had taken that news with his usual stoicism, had promised her they'd adopt when they could afford it, and had refused to talk about it since. When his biggest client died of a seizure he had become a vegetarian, and when the owner of the shop next door died of pancreatic cancer he had started taking massive vitamin supplements. But he hadn't really started to proselytize about nutrition until Ida's second or third amputation. Her illness made him ill, Kay decided. His fear of it. She refilled her wineglass. If Neal ever had to live a day in Ida's body he'd get a lesson in courage and endurance that would probably kill him.

Oh what was the matter with him? with her? with them? Other couples didn't live in silence or go for months without sex. When was the last time they had made love? Labor Day? Victor and Stacy prayed together, hand in hand, every night in front of their waterbed before tumbling into the missionary position. Zabeth and her lovers soaped each other up with chocolate guck and licked each other off in her candlelit shower. Even Francis and Ida were sexual; Kay had grown up to the rhythmic squeal of their bedsprings. Every morning when Francis left for work Ida tipped her face up and he kissed her goodbye on the lips with a sweet little smack that rang through the house like one of Chopin's trills, and every night when he came home he whistled to her from the front door and she whistled back.

Neal and I should move, Kay thought. She turned from the window and dried her hands. We should sell this house and his shop and go away. Start over in Oregon or Colorado. Get away from all these role models and family ghosts. Nothing's keeping us here, not really. Mother needs help but she doesn't need my help specifically. She has Dad on the weekends, Greta during the week. "I don't know what I'd do without you"—Ida had always said that, but it didn't mean anything. She said it to everyone. She could get an ad out tomorrow, Kay thought, and replace me. *Wanted: Dum-Dum for Grande Dame. No Skills Needed.*

She filled her wineglass again and began to leave the kitchen. As she reached for the light, she saw Neal's card lying on the table where he'd left it. It was a silly card—a picture of a prince embracing a princess over a slain dragon. The prince had a familiar weight-of-the-world slump to his shoulders, the princess was hamming it up, clasping her hands and batting her lashes, and the dragon had one eye slyly open: the whole effect was meant to be lighthearted, but it fell flat. Kay was ashamed of it and ashamed of the sentiment inside: "To My Hero. You Saved Me." It wasn't true. Never had been. If she had any hero, besides the Jamaican laundress who had finally let her out of the hospital courtyard, it was still, for some stubborn, perverse, unimaginative reason, her father: Francis X. McLeod. She wondered why, after all these years, she believed she could call him from jail, from Mars, or from the bottom of the sea and he would come to her rescue. He had not even come to her wedding. Ida had been in Emergency that day with a cracked tailbone from a fall during her tango class, and Francis had been at her side, practicing his putts on the floor.

The kitchen phone rang and she picked it up, nuzzling the receiver under her chin as she tore the card in half. A deep voice said, "Sis?" Oh-oh, she thought, Victor. Victor never phoned unless he wanted something. She pulled the stool over and perched on it. It was best to sit when Victor spoke.

"Yes?" she said. "What can I do for you?"

His salesman's laugh, not yet perfected, rippled out and ended a note too short. "I just wanted to say hello and give you some good news. Mom's coming home from the hospital Sunday."

"So soon?" Kay scanned the calendar on the wall. Two days away. Ida would need lots of care—she always did when she first came home—and now, legless, she would need even more. Greta was a housekeeper, not a nurse. Had Dad hired a nurse? He always said he was going to, just like he always said he was going to fire Greta, but he never did. Usually, Kay had to come up and help. "That really seems soon."

"Doesn't it? Just great. So here's the thing. Stacy and I were thinking we should all get together and give her a welcome home dinner. Like if we all go up to their house Sunday night and have a real gourmet meal."

"And who's going to cook this 'real gourmet meal'?"

Victor hummed a scrap of hymn and said nothing.

"Stacy?" Kay suggested.

That salesman's laugh again. "Stacy's got Bible class all morning and, frankly, between you and I, she just doesn't get it, about food. And I'd like to, you know that, but it's hard on Sundays with church in the morning and the lot until six."

"All tied up, huh. So what were you thinking?"

"Cassoulet."

"Right. With the goose confit and the boned rabbit? The one that takes four days to make and costs a hundred dollars and still tastes like baked beans?"

"That beef bourguignon you do is always good too. Or plain old coq au vin. There was too much salt pork in it, remember, last time I think I told you, but I really liked what you did with the little pearl onions."

Kay pulled the phone pad toward her, poked through a kitchen drawer until she found a pencil stub, doodled a second, and finally wrote "pearl onions." What was the use. She'd been feeding Victor ever since he'd been born; she'd given him his first bottle of formula and his first spoonful of mashed banana. She'd learned to bake before she was six because he liked her egg custards, and by the time she was ten she was frosting the six-layer coconut birthday cakes he requested. So what was one more meal? One more time? She cooked for her parents practically every Sunday anyway. And at least, unlike her husband, they ate what she served. "Have you talked to Mom at all?" she asked.

"I did." He paused. "She sounded a little strange."

"I'll say. I think she's hallucinating on the morphine. Did she talk about a horse?"

"The thing about Mom is, she needs Jesus. I keep telling her and telling her. She really needs Jesus." Victor's voice dropped, then boomed loud and false again. "So we're all set for Sunday. Terrific. And oh hey I meant to tell you, there's a sale of late summer peaches at Gladstop's."

"No pie. Forget it. You bring dessert."

"Nothing is better than your warm peach pie."

"You . . . bring . . . dessert."

"Hey! No need to bite my head off."

Kay swallowed the last drop of wine in her glass and tried to remember if Victor had been this awful before he turned Christian. He had been a frightened child with fastidious habits who hoarded money. He'd been slow in school and poor at sports and almost invisible at home. Neither Francis nor Ida seemed to expect much from him. He'd been free to eat and watch TV all day. Kay had read to him, helped with his homework, taught him to drive. After she left home, he had a breakdown she still felt guilty about, but what could she have done? She was with Biff and having a breakdown herself. He'd done a lot of drugs, gone in and out of rehab, and then he'd met Stacy and the two of them had gone to a Bible meeting and found Jesus and now he was a militant Christian who believed everyone who wasn't should be shot.

"I'll see what I can do about a pie, Vic," she said now, and he, relieved, said, "I knew you'd come through."

She hung up the phone, dumped the rest of the wine into her glass, and went into Nicky's room. "Ready for your story?" She could hear her voice, how thick it sounded. Last week she had started to hiccup in the middle of reading; the week before that she had passed out and he'd had to wake her up. She steadied herself on the back of a chair.

"Not a story, Mom," he reminded her. "This." He raised the stuffed animal he called Pokey and pointed to the same thick green book, *Dinosaur Facts and Figures,* that she had been reading to him for months. She made a face but settled down beside him, the book propped open on her knees. She had just read the dimensions for the tail span of the tyrannosaur for the umpteenth time, trying not to slur, when the phone rang. "That will be your uncle again," she said, sliding off the bed. "Asking us to bring homemade ice cream with the pie." She picked the phone up.

But it was Ida. Her voice was small and clear. "I want you to stop it right now," she said.

Kay laughed. "Stop what?"

"Killing me."

"What?"

"I want you to stop killing me."

Kay leaned into the receiver. "Mother?"

"I mean it," Ida said. "I am not kidding about this. I have had it up to here with you two." There was a sudden clatter, the sound of something falling. "Goddamn you to hell," Ida screamed. The phone dropped and went dead.

. . .

That was a mistake. She would surely pay for that one. Sometimes the penalty was worth it though. Ida waited until the horse finished laughing. His tongue was wet and fat and his teeth were small, stained, and oddly human. Everything about him was wrong, off kilter, like one of her own paintings. She had probably made him up from parts of old enemies. That smug abortionist in Oakland. The art teacher. The redhead at Ransohoff's. She closed her eyes. When she opened them again the horse was gone but Kay was there.

I know I owe you an apology, Ida thought. And you'll get it. A big one. But—she closed her eyes again and feigned a deep sleep—not right now, it's too complicated, I can't even start. She felt Kay bend over, stole comfort from her smell of soap, red wine, and sweat, the brush of her hesitant lips, her rabbit breath—she must have driven like the wind to have made it over here so quickly—and then fell into a real sleep at last. The dream, if that's what it had been, did not follow. Kay and Francis did not tumble naked onto her bed, mocking her while she lay beside them helpless, pinned beneath the horse's sharp hoof.

Three

"It's an interesting accusation," Zabeth said. "I can see why you panicked."

"You can?" The white breath of Kay's voice disappeared into the mist. It was eight o'clock on Sunday morning and she was jogging after Zabeth through the woods. They had only been out five minutes and she was already winded. She pushed back a cuff on her baggy sweatshirt, felt it relapse bit by bit down her arm, wiped the sweat off her neck with her wrist. She was more out of shape now than she'd been two months ago, when they had started these weekly runs. She watched Zabeth's narrow hips pump decisively up the path and groaned as she chose the steepest trail, the one leading through the laurel and scrub oak straight to the ridge. "So you don't think I was an idiot to jump in the car and drive straight to the hospital?"

"No, I think you were an idiot not to put a pillow over her face when you got there and found out she was still alive."

Kay panted and ducked under a spray of poison oak. The hospital room had looked different at night, eerier, like the cabin of a spaceship. A dim green lamp had lit Ida's halved body, making her white skin and golden hair gleam above the crosshatch of empty shadows below. A cloud of L'Heure Bleue had hung about her along with another scent, sweetly chemical, maybe morphine, maybe those black roses, fragrant at last. But Ida herself had been sound asleep, the telephone crouched on her table, innocent as a sleeping cat. "I thought this physical therapist she'd fought with earlier might have come back for revenge. I totally forgot that she used to say 'Stop killing me' every time I asked for my allowance or needed a ride to a piano lesson. In that same insane voice. Sobbing."

Zabeth laughed, a loud series of linked ha-ha-ha's that sounded like slaps. "Exactly!" Zabeth said. "That's what I love about old Ida. She's so B-movie."

Kay thought about this, Ida as Garbo coughing into a hankie, then discarded it. Ida's pain was real. She had been ill or injured as long as Kay could remember. "You're the one who looks B-movie today," she said, to change the subject. Zabeth had dressed for their jog in lime green Nikes and black spandex tights topped by a leopard-skin print sports bra. A gold spangled chiffon scarf snaked around her throat, silver bracelets banged up and down on her arm. Despite the relentless pacing of her little feet, it was clear she had been out partying the night before. Huge rusty earrings still poked through the frizz of her perm. She hadn't washed the thick lines of green kohl around her eyes, she reeked of musk and spermicide, and she had a large purple hickey on her neck.

"Blue movie," Zabeth corrected. "But getting back to Ida—why do you let her pick on you?"

"Mom's first fall was my fault," Kay explained. "I left some toys at the top of the stairs and she tripped over them and broke her back. Dad had to give up a big commission in New York and come home and take care of her."

"And you were how old then?"

"I don't know. Three."

"Ha-ha-ha! Do you still have the name of that shrink I told you about?"

Kay flushed. She knew, of course, that that first accident had not been her fault and she didn't need anyone named Dr. Tanya Tamar to explain it to her. Still—she felt guilty. *You did this to me. How often had Ida said that? You made me a cripple.*

Zabeth looked over her shoulder and grinned. "I only met your mother once and I wanted to kill her. I bet your father thinks about it. If he were single he could have any woman he wanted."

"He could?" Kay pictured Francis, slight, skinny, his hair parted low and combed over his bald spot, looking, despite his little British brush mustache, like a frail boy in the bow ties and striped shirts he always wore. She liked his looks, of course, but then he was her father, and she had no choice. "You think he's attractive?"

"Yep. Plus all the extras: Famous. Smart. Funny."

"Funny?" Kay grimaced. "He's sarcastic. That's different." She shook her head. "He's no fun to live with. Sits in his chair and does crosswords all day. Lectures when he talks and doesn't listen when anyone else does. Says no before you finish asking a question. He's a lot like Neal, actually."

"Ha-ha-ha. They say we marry our fathers."

"I hope not."

Neal had slept on the couch last night. He'd never come to bed at all. Oh she didn't want to think about Neal. She scrubbed her wet palms on her shorts, picked up her pace, and fixed her eyes straight ahead. Beethoven was good to jog to. "Ode to Joy." Thump thump thump thump THUMP THUMP THUMP THUMP. What was poor Beethoven's idea of joy anyway? She tuned the beat to her footfalls, and tried to focus on becoming as thin and trim as Zabeth.

Not that a Sunday workout could do that. Zabeth was light years ahead of her. When Kay first met her, last spring, Zabeth had been dating a Colombian drug lord's stepson. She sat in the back row at the one and only AA meeting Kay had ever attended, and the first thing Kay had noticed, as she sat down beside her, was that she was dressed entirely in black leather and creaked when she moved, like parts of a harness. The second thing she noticed was that she was sipping tequila from a Wonder Woman thermos. Kay took a few sips herself; they went straight to her head in delicious crescendo and when a melancholy woman stood up and said, "Hi, I'm PattiAnn, I'm an addict-alcoholic and I'm your treasurer," she had giggled. Zabeth, looking at her with interest, had said, "Right. Let's go." They had gone to an Indian restaurant, where they ordered dal and daiquiris, and talked for hours about men, and music, and yes, even then, their mothers.

"It's not just you," Zabeth said now. They had come to the ridge top, to the grassy turnout where they always stopped to catch their breath. West Valley spread out beneath them, grey brown in the autumn mist. Sweat and mascara ran down Zabeth's face as she turned to Kay. "Your mother puts everyone through changes. I'll never forget that dinner last summer."

Kay flushed. "That dinner last summer" had been the worst night of her life. One of the worst nights of her life. Zabeth didn't even know how bad it had been. For two days, Kay had worked to prepare a gala going-away-to-Greece meal for her parents. The shish kebab, avgolemono, and dolma had been perfect. But the people! Stacy arrived fresh from a right-to-lifers march clutching a baby doll bloodied with catsup; Victor tried to sell everyone a used Taurus; Neal kept turning the TV on to check the game; Nicky had a fit when he was asked to help set the table; Francis and Ida had been drunk when they arrived; and Zabeth, in some Sheba, Queen of the Jungle outfit, had wanted to talk about the relevance of Greek myth to modern-day relationships. She had learned enough Greek in grad school to sprinkle her talk with slippery words full of *x*'s, and every time she opened her mouth, Ida's eyebrows lifted, her red lips tightened, and her jeweled knuckles clenched on the rests of her wheelchair. Kay knew the signs. She watched Ida's jealous mood darken and when she saw her hand hook out for something to throw—a knife, a fork, a wineglass—she covered the hand so hard with her own that Ida shrieked and spat out.

"She thought you were flirting with Dad," Kay said now.

"I *was* flirting with him. So what? We were talking about Medea and suddenly your mother calls me a small-town slut and bursts into tears."

Zabeth laughed her bracing ha-ha-ha and Kay turned aside. "That was the night she fell out of her wheelchair," she reminded Zabeth as they started to jog back toward the trailhead. "She tried to go for a midnight swim when they got home and somehow she crashed onto the cement by the swimming pool. That's what hurt her leg. That's essentially why she had to have this last amputation."

"Serves her right," said Zabeth.

They ran in silence for a while. "So how have you been all week?" Kay asked. "While I've been commuting dutifully to the hospital. Where'd you get that hickey, for instance?"

Zabeth grinned over her shoulder. "Jealous?"

"Yes. You know what Neal's like."

"No, and promise you'll never tell me."

"Neal nibbles—"

"Stop!"

"—but he never nips."

"Well, Garret nips."

"Garret? The soccer player?"

"No, the pharmacist."

"The one you said was 'medium height, medium weight, medium everything'? I thought you hated him."

"No, I hate the soccer player. Garret's good. Medium good. Yesterday was our two-week anniversary and he gave me a briefcase made of Peruvian duck skin filled with red lace panties, a tab of LSD, and three love poems he wrote himself."

"Poetry," Kay repeated, jealous.

"I don't know if it is poetry, exactly. It's more like pornography. But it's very effective. You know? I like that. I like to be wooed. Don't you?"

Kay remembered Neal's first gift to her—a boxed set of Brahms symphonies. "Nothing can match the music inside you," he'd written on the note. And his last gift? A fly swatter. "Just don't get married," she said darkly.

They slowed as they came out of the jogging trail onto the road where they'd parked, Zabeth's new Saab pulled close to Kay's Lincoln Town Car with its peeling roof. Kay realized that Zabeth had probably had to roll out of a warm water bed filled with a hot lover to keep this jogging date today, and felt contrite. She was lucky to have any friends, let alone one as brave and spicy as Zabeth. "Thanks, Zab," she said as they bent to stretch. "You're good to come all this way just to help me get a heart attack. And the plant you sent Mom!" She flushed. She had completely forgotten the bleeding heart. Smashed upside down on the linoleum floor, it had been the only clue that anything at all had happened in Ida's hospital room that night. It looked like Ida had thrown it straight against the wall. "It's beautiful. She loves it. To bits."

"She does? Well, good. I wanted to send something, just to let her know I was thinking of her. I mean the thing about Ida is, she's a total witch but you've got to admire her." Zabeth grinned up at Kay. "Feel better?"

"Yes. Still no runner's high but I always feel better after I see you. Would you do me a favor though? Don't tell."

It was a mistake, and Kay flushed, steadying herself for Zabeth's astonished "Don't tell who?"

"My parents. About me going back to the hospital at night. I mean, you probably won't even see them again, but if you do— Mom isn't going to remember calling me, I'm sure, and Dad doesn't know, and I'd just like, I don't know . . . I don't want to give them the satisfaction."

"Of knowing they can jerk you around whenever they want?"

"Something like that."

Kay waited for the ha-ha-ha but Zabeth was silent. "I am going to see Francis, actually," she said at last. "We're having lunch on Thursday."

"You're having lunch with . . . ?"

"Your father."

"Why? I mean," Kay caught herself, "where?"

"Calm down. It's no big deal. He phoned and ordered this prescription from Garret while I was there and I just thought it would be more fun to deliver it in person. He's not that easy to talk to on the phone, is he?"

"Where?" Kay repeated, bending to tighten her laces. "What restaurant?"

"I don't know. Where do you two go?"

"We don't."

"His office is only *how* close to the library and you don't go to lunch with him? Kay! I had lunch with my father every week when I lived back East, and once a month we went to the movies."

"He liked you," Kay said. "My dad doesn't like me."

"You ought to get to know him, Kay."

"There's nothing to know," Kay said. "And anyway, every time I try . . ." Her voice trailed away. Had she ever had a real talk with Francis? She couldn't remember one. In fact, she couldn't remember a single pleasant exchange. Had he ever even touched her? Well yes—Indian wrist burns, Dutch rubs, knuckle raps. He used to flick her with a tea towel when she did the dishes. When she kissed him he squinched his lips up. When she told him she loved him, he said, "Ditto."

"You ought to get to know him," Zabeth repeated. "Before your mother dies."

"My mother is not going to die."

Zabeth touched her shoulder and looked her in the eye. What bloodshot little eyes she had, inside all that kohl. "Are you all right with this, Kay? It's just a lunch."

"Of course I am. Why wouldn't I be?" But Zabeth didn't answer this very good question, nor did she invite Kay to join them on Thursday. Instead, she squeezed her shoulder again, hard, waved goodbye, and drove away. Alone in her own car, Kay groped through the glove compartment for the emergency aspirin; when she couldn't find it, she emptied the entire contents of the glove compartment onto the floor. That felt good. As she sat up, her elbow grazed the stack of Chopin tapes and she knocked them off the seat with a swift smack. That felt good too. Then she shoved the library books onto the tapes. Then all the empty cardboard and Styrofoam fast food containers. Then she pounded the steering wheel with her fists and that felt good too. But not good enough. Her head was throbbing and crazy words were going through her head, like *He's my father. Mine. You can't have him!*—and what sense did those make? She punched the leather seat beside her three times, four times, felt the car flood with yellow light as the sun finally broke through the morning mist, then almost immediately darken as a shadow fell over her hand. She glared and looked up.

Charles Lichtman, leaning on his bike, smiled in at her. She gasped in horror. All she could focus on was the bandanna tied around his dark curly hair; it was the same rosy pink as his full lower lip. "You all right?" he asked.

"Oh yes," she mouthed. "Fine. Just. You know. Throwing a fit."

His eyes, brown as syrup, poured over the mess inside the car and returned to her hot face. "Good luck," he said. He waved and rode away.

She could not stop shaking all the way to the Fredrickses' house. The image of Charles Lichtman bicycling away trembled before her eyes. How long had he watched her tearing the car apart? Had he noticed that the library books she had tried to karate chop were the same books he had just returned? Was he wondering, even now, what interest she had in Van Gogh's let-

ters, John Wesley Powell's trip down the Colorado River, or
Japanese joinery? Did he know she had only taken those books
hoping to find some note or message from him tucked between
the pages? Did he think she was insane? Was she insane? She
eyed a bar sitting sunny and silent on Main Street: the White
Oak. Not open. Too bad. Not that she would go to a bar on a
Sunday morning, alone, when she was supposed to be at rehearsal—it was just an idea. For a minute, imagining what it
might be like: the boozy secret dark, the long mirror, the candy-
colored lights of the jukebox in the corner, a good idea, yes. But
not one she would ever pursue. She had never gone to a bar
alone. She wasn't like Zabeth.

Zabeth! Those little red eyes! *He could have any woman he
wanted.* And what about that LSD? What kind of present was
that? Dad ought to know better, Kay thought, her lips pressed together. He ought to be ashamed. What does he think he's doing?
The old fool. And Mom. Poor helpless Mom. Oh where was that
card with Dr. Tamar's number on it? Who would trust anyone
named Dr. Tamar?

The Fredericks lived in a large tract house at the edge of town,
near the freeway, and the other musicians had already arrived by
the time Kay drove up. She could hear Walt's voice as she hurried
up the walkway; he was well into his weekly pep talk.

"You know what a genius is?" Kay let herself in the front door
and glanced around at the others, ducking her head in apology at
being late. Walt sat on his yellow velvet pillow in the center of the
living room floor in lotus position, warming his tiny fat hands
around a teapot. "A genius is someone who dares. Haydn dared to
compose great music and we dare to play it. So what does that
make us?"

He twinkled at Lois Hayes, who said, "Excuse me, Walt, but I
have to be back in an hour."

"Of course. Of course. We all have places to go and people to meet and things to do. And why is that? Barry?"

Barry Morris, a volunteer fireman who played the cello, looked at his diver's watch and said, "I don't even have an hour."

"No of course not, you're busy, we're all busy, we're involved with life and we're involved with life because we dare to be. Isn't that right? Zipper?"

Walt's son Zipper ran his hand over his shaved head and said, "Sure. I guess." Zipper was seventeen and the most balanced of the group—Lois looked wild-eyed already, bouncing her viola case against her knee, and Barbara Billings, who clerked at the shoe store, was making little cluck-cluck sounds to herself, bird calls maybe. "Remember what Haydn said," Walt continued. He closed his eyes. His face was cheeky as a toddler's. His tongue flicked between his plump lips. "'God will forgive me,'" he quoted, "'for having a cheerful heart.'" His wife came to the doorway; she wiped her hands on her apron and peered around the room, making sure everyone was paying attention to Walt, then she stepped forward, knelt as before an altar, whisked his teapot away, and left.

"Geniuses," Walt breathed, opening his eyes and clapping his hands, "have cheerful hearts. So let us commence."

Everyone reached for their instruments with relief. Kay, shaking her wrists out, walked across the room toward the piano. Walt, still on the floor, feinted for her ankles but she sidestepped him, smiling thinly. Every week he made the same pun about her jogging shoes, called them ReBachs instead of Reboks; today he sang a bar of "O Sole Mio" as she tugged them out of his grasp. She pulled out the piano bench, sat down, and opened her music.

She had not practiced regularly this week and she could hear the rushes, fakes, and sloppy phrasing as she began the first movement of the Haydn. She wondered if Walt could hear them too. She glanced up from the keyboard, expecting censure, but he was bent over his violin, intent, eyes closed. She refocused on the music, trying to force a cheerful heart. The Haydn bored her, though, so vigorous and busy; it just made her more tired than she already was. She enjoyed the second movement more, but still could not concentrate. She finished playing and looked up. "I need a lot of work," she said. No one contradicted her.

The third movement was a nightmare. Lois hissed to herself over her viola, Barbara's timing was off, Barry flubbed bar after bar, and Walt had to stop playing to rub his wrists, which were swelling with bursitis. Only Zipper, eyes open, fixed on nothing, played well, and he stopped when he saw them all watching and dropped the flute from his lips, a smile becalmed on his face. Walt called, somewhat mechanically, "Bravo, bravo! Now on to the Chopin."

Kay sat still on the piano bench as the others disbanded. Don't be nervous, she told herself. Don't think about your mother, your father, your friend, or your husband. Don't think about Charles Lichtman. Don't think about anything but the music. She hit the first notes and was startled when Walt's "Lovely, lovely" brought her back to the present. She had played the whole piece the way she so often drove, in a dream, head down, flying through black-out. Now as she lifted her hands off the keyboard Walt planted a wet kiss on her forehead. "I don't deserve it," she warned him.

"You can tell she's not used to praise," Walt said to the others. And that at least was true. She was not used to praise.

Four

"Oh no." Neal stood in his wrinkled shirt cradling a jar of beet juice against his heart as he stared at the tumble of tapes and books spilled onto the floor of the Lincoln. "A thief broke into your car."

"Not exactly."

"You got rear-ended?"

"I did it myself. I had a tantrum." Kay opened the back door of the car for Nicky, watched while he fastened his seat belt, and then carefully set the peach pie down on his lap. "Sure you want to hold this?" she asked. "Yes," he whispered back. She closed his door and straightened. The smoky autumn night had an edge of cold to the air. Neal stood backlit by the pistachio tree that still held sunset color in its leaves. His face sagged, tragic, rumpled with grief. She felt a throb of alarm. Something was wrong with Neal, something she ought to know about and fix. Sighing, he bent and began to pick Chopin tapes off the floor of her car. She wondered if he'd ask why she'd had a tantrum, if he'd show any curiosity at all, but all he said was "Oh babe," in that same tearful voice, as if he knew far too much already.

She opened the passenger door, cleared a space, and eased the pot of boeuf bourguignon onto the floor so she could clamp it steady between her feet as Neal drove. The mandarin collar of the brown brocade dress her parents had brought her from Hong Kong bit at her neck as she pulled on the seat belt. "At least when I lose my temper I don't hold it in," she said. "I act out." As if that were anything to be proud of. As if that were even true. She turned and stared out the window.

"I just wish you were happier," Neal said, and then, to Nicky, in the same funereal voice, "All right, son? Ready to face your mother's family?"

"It's his family too," Kay said.

Neal said nothing. Kay watched the junky, comfortable, tree-shaded clutter of their neighborhood empty into the half-deserted downtown of West Valley, then thin and disappear into the free-way. She wished she could show Nicky what this county had looked like when she was a girl. She could still see the fields of live oaks and lupine where the strip malls were now. She could remember how she and Victor had tobogganed on flattened cardboard boxes down grassy hills now terraced with condominiums. The orchards had been torn down for tract homes; the duck pond had been filled in with concrete and turned into a strange buzzing enclave of radio transmitters, the meadows had been bulldozed for uneasy-looking hotels and office buildings. The new cinema complex floated in glassy splendor on what once had been—and surely would be again—marshland, and Manzanita Heights, which Francis had designed and developed on the east side of the mountain, rose confidently over a lava bed. There were still a few reminders of the old county: the library where she worked still nestled beneath an ancient acacia tree; Le Petit Jardin still sent rich winey smells to the streets of Rancho Valdez over its gated brick walls; the community college where Ida took class after class was still an oasis of white paths winding through clipped green lawns.

Neal's hand reached for hers across the front seat and she

pressed it, grateful, but then his finger probed the place she had burned on her thumb while browning those little pearl onions Victor liked so much and she winced as he rubbed it back and forth. Neal doesn't know, she reminded herself. It's just a gift he has. "Honey," she said, "that hurts." Neal withdrew, his profile no more stricken than it had been all day. Some people have a secret life, she thought. Neal has a secret death. "Do you think my father has a mistress?" she asked.

"Your mother's his mistress," Neal answered. "She runs him ragged."

"Um. So that's what mistresses do. I always thought some black lace was involved." She waited a minute, then, "Zabeth would make a good mistress, wouldn't she? Don't you think Zabeth's attractive?"

"Who's Zabeth?"

"Help."

Neal was silent for a while then, "You'll be good?" He frowned as the old car coughed in its climb to the Heights. "None of your tricks?"

"What tricks?"

"Smoking," Nicky said from the back seat.

"You don't smoke anymore, do you?" Neal glanced at her, astonished.

Kay thought of the battered Merit she was about to slip back unsmoked into Ida's purse and said, "No." She reached back through a crack in the seat and grabbed for Nicky's knee; he giggled and hollered, "Yes she does."

Neal, intent on driving, ignored them. "I was thinking more of the way you upset her," he said after a while.

"I? Upset her?"

"Just watch what you say. Every time we leave, Ida's in tears."

"That's not my fault."

"Grandmère cries over everything," Nicky agreed. "Once she even cried when my Go-Bot got broken."

Kay remembered the Go-Bot, Nicky's favorite plastic superhero toy, the way its jointed leg had snapped off at the knee when Victor got excited at dinner one night and bent it too far back. "That was because Grandmère's left leg had just been amputated the first time," she reminded him, turning to talk over her shoulder. "And try not to stare tonight, Nick. Her other leg is gone now too."

Nicky nodded gravely as he balanced the pie. "I know," he said. "She's in a lot of pain and she's very sad."

"I know."

"Do you really think I make Mom cry on purpose?" Kay turned back to Neal and waited, convinced as always that at some level Neal knew more than she, saw things more clearly. But Neal said nothing more. He turned the car through the brick gates with the wrought iron arch that Francis had designed in twenty seconds—or so he said—and passed the big houses with their big garages, came to her parents' driveway at the top, and parked. All the lights were blazing and from somewhere inside they could hear Coco's sharp bark. God, I don't want to be here, Kay thought, and she stood in the twilight, clutching her pot of hot food, swaying on her high heels, breathing in the familiar smells of chrysanthemum and cypress from the garden, chlorine from the swimming pool, creosote from the redwood deck, dog poop from the long slate walkway. Nicky walked close to her side, holding the pie, eyes on the swimming pool—he had not gone in the pool since last summer when they had both seen a rattlesnake swim across it, undulating slowly, its wedged head alert, held high, not unlike the way Ida swam, Kay had thought, the same regal sweep. Neal followed with the rest of the groceries as Kay led the way to the door. All three stood, taking a communal deep breath; then Kay raised the heavy brass temple gong and rapped as jazzily as its weight would permit.

"Now who's come to bother us?" Francis caroled through the door, and Ida cried behind him, "For God's sake Francis, get the dog!" Then the door opened and there was Francis himself, in corduroy pants and a striped shirt, peering at them over the tops of his glasses. He pointed his gold pen at Nicky. "Well now," he said, "who invited you?"

Nicky glanced up at Kay, uncertain, and just at that second, Coco, a blur of blond fur and bulging black eyes, raced toward them and leapt. Ida screamed from the living room, Nicky closed his eyes and bravely raised the pie, and Kay collared the dog just as its nails ripped the length of one of her stockings. "Hi, Dad," she said. "Hope you're hungry."

"Oh, I haven't been hungry since 1934," Francis said, taking Coco from her, "and then it was only because of the Depression. It passed. Most things do pass," he said to Nicky, as Nicky opened his eyes again. "You're not afraid of a little old poodle dog are you?"

"Coco's not a dog," Kay said. "She's a fiend from hell."

"I didn't drop the pie, Mom," Nicky said.

"I'm glad it passed, Francis," Neal said behind them, his timing, as always, impeccable. "I brought you and Ida some fresh-squeezed beet juice and some of that Vitamin B complex I was telling you about to help it pass even smoother."

"More smoothly," Ida's voice corrected from the living room.

"Your mother," Francis said to Kay as he dragged Coco off to her cage in the kitchen, "has been waiting for you since four."

Kay walked over the polished tile floor of the entry hall, Nicky holding the pie out before him. Their footsteps made hard, hollow sounds and the mirrored walls glittered with recessed lights. She could hear the low roar of the football game Francis had been watching in the television room and she could smell the meaty aroma of Coco's dinner, simmering on the stove.

"You kept me waiting thirty-six hours before you were born," Ida sang out, her voice already hoarse from the determination to be gay, tears already edging each word, "and you haven't changed a bit." She sat in her wheelchair, positioned in front of the empty black vault of the fireplace; she was flanked on either side by tall unlit candles set on the hearth. She suddenly smiled her beautiful lipsticky smile and lifted her hands, palms up. She was wearing a new dress of flowered pink silk and had a mink blanket over her lap. "Come give me a kiss."

Kay bent down and kissed her mother's cheek. She tasted rouge, powder, felt the rough brush of a diamond earring against her lips. Ida's small head was hot, her hair damp at the roots—she must still be having that afternoon fever. She coughed, laughing, against Kay's shoulder, and her cough smelled of whiskey, tobacco, perfume, that sweetish hospital medication, and something else, just a whiff of something grey and fetid. "We're not that late," Kay soothed. Ida clutched the blanket against her waist with one hand and reached for Nicky with the other.

"What a lovely pie you brought for my dinner," Ida said to Nicky. "Did you bake it yourself?"

"No."

"Did you at least pick the peaches yourself?"

"No."

"Then what good are you?"

Nicky, confused, looked up at Kay. She steadied her fingers on his shoulder, thinking of the poster she had hung in his room. A CHILD DOESN'T HAVE TO BE SOMEBODY, the poster said. A CHILD IS SOMEBODY.

"He's very good indeed," Kay said.

"Oh I know that," Ida said. "I'd hold you in my lap," she added to Nicky, "if I had a lap. But it's gone. The doctors took it away."

Nicky's eyes dropped frankly to the space beneath the blanket and Kay looked just as hard at the empty glass by Ida's side. How long had she been drinking? She seemed to have passed the *toujours gai* part of the cocktail hour and slipped into the darker humor of her late night drunks. Why did Dad let her do it? The drinks he mixed her were enough to stun an ox. Didn't he know better? Or did he do it on purpose? Ida lifted the empty glass as Neal approached and jiggled the ice at him.

"Why don't we all hold off and wait until dinner," Neal said. "I brought you some nice juice."

"Neal. Take this goddamn glass and go in the kitchen and get me a goddamn drink. Thank you. Now. Nicky. Give me a hug. Come close. Closer. Don't be scared. Ouch. Watch out. You stepped on my toe! Ouch ouch, you hurt Grandmère's toe."

"You don't have a toe," Nicky said.

"Yes I do! You just can't see it! I have a phantom toe! And now, oh ouch, it's having phantom pain."

"So could we just feel phantom guilt about stepping on it?" Kay asked, guiding Nicky off toward the safety of the kitchen.

"Why should you feel anything about it? It's my problem, isn't it." Ida sniffled loudly and covered her face with her hand. Maybe she'll pass out, Kay prayed. "You've got to ignore Grandma when she gets like this," she whispered.

"It's Grand*mère*," Ida called eerily behind her, "and all I ever am is ignored."

The acoustics, Kay mouthed to Neal. *The acoustics in this house are Satanic.* She set Nicky up on the high kitchen counter to draw dinosaurs as she unpacked the salad makings and slipped the casserole into the oven to reheat.

"I'm waiting," Ida called in an unsteady voice.

"Your drink is coming, Grandmère," Neal muttered.

"I'm not *your* grandmère. I'm not *that* old."

Nicky giggled and Kay had to grin too. She is awful, Kay thought. But, as Zabeth said, you had to admire her. Fresh out of the hospital and as impossible as ever. She waited until Neal left to take the heavily watered Scotch he had made to Ida, then she opened her purse, extracted the rumpled cigarette, and started to slip it into an open pack Francis had left on the counter. It didn't want to go in. It bent and buckled. Oh just smoke it, Kay thought.

She picked up a kitchen match, murmured something about needing a clean dishtowel to Nicky, and stepped into the laundry room off the kitchen where she could hide. She struck the match

against her shoe, leaned against the dryer, and inhaled deeply. The
Merit didn't draw well, but by the third drag the tobacco finally
announced itself: stable hay, sharp as summer sex with a stranger.
It made her feel nauseated and excited, evil and doomed. Her heart
beat more quickly; her fingertips and toes went ice-cold, her throat
burned. She felt scared as a teenager and when the side door
banged open and Francis stepped in from the garage, she acted like
a teenager, quickly turning to run the cigarette under the laundry
sink tap.

"Gotcha." Francis held a library book under his elbow—the
Civil War romance Kay had brought Ida in the hospital. Had he
been reading it out in the garage? She remembered last Fourth of
July when she had seen him out there, tipped back in the bucket
seat of his Porsche, sound asleep. "I thought you were going to set
us a good example," Francis said now, "and quit that vile habit."

"I have quit," Kay said. She managed a weak, stupid smile. "It's
just . . . sometimes."

"Bad for you," Francis said. "Very, very bad for you." He
reached into the cupboard over the dryer and brought down a new
quart of Chivas Regal. "In case you ever want to know where the
good stash is," he said, "look up here. Del down at the booze boutique gives me a deal when I buy cases. Just don't tell your mother.
She'll get Greta to bring her bottles in bed. Speaking of not-telling-
your-mother"—he reached past Kay and turned the tap back on so
the water sounded loudly in the sink—"there's something else I
don't want her to know."

Kay prepared for his confession. Zabeth, she thought. He
knows I know he's having lunch with Zabeth. And now he's going
to ask me not to mention it to Mom. She crossed her arms and set
her jaw, waiting. But Francis raised clear, tired, innocent eyes. "Jim
Deeds and his boys at the hospital found spots," he said.

"Spots?" Kay stopped, confused.

"On Ida's lungs. They think she may have TB."

"On top of everything else? That's awful. Can they treat it?"

"Oh sure. They can treat anything these days. Just not very well."

Kay said the first thing that came into her head. "Poor Dad."

"Not at all. I'm fine. No spots on me. Yet." He reached into his shirt pocket and pulled out a cigarette. As he bent to his lighter Kay saw his growing baldness. His scalp beneath the strands of stiff grey hair was rosy and freckled and tender as trout skin. She wanted to reach out and touch it, comfort him, if she could, for growing old and having so many worries to deal with. But what could she do? She'd only make things worse. Her hand curled and dropped by her side as he looked up. "Your pushy friend Zabeth," he said, "wants to meet me for a drug deal on Thursday but that's the day I have to take Ida in for more X-rays. Think you could call her and cancel? Or I could get Sunny-at-the-Office to do it if you can't."

"Sure," Kay said. She hid a smile of relief. If he won't even call Zabeth himself, it must not be a "date." It must be no more to worry about than the "spots." Tuberculosis was curable these days after all; Ida would be fine. "Do you want me to reschedule?" she asked brightly. She felt like Francis's loyal, hardworking secretary, Sunny-at-the-Office herself.

"Hey." Francis turned the water off and cocked his head as Coco yipped from her cage. "I do believe the Lion is telling us that the Christians have arrived. Repent. While there's still time." He led the way out of the laundry room and Kay followed him into the kitchen. "Well now, looky," he crowed. "Sister Stacy and Brother Vic."

Stacy, her arms wrapped around Nicky at the kitchen counter, tipped her head and giggled, her tongue curling up. She was dressed, as Kay was, in some awful ethnic outfit Francis and Ida had brought back from their travels, but the Swiss dirndl skirt and peasant blouse suited her, emphasized her curves and softness. Kay tugged again at the mandarin collar and resolved to give the damn dress to charity tomorrow. Stacy beamed and swung Nicky back

and forth. "What a cutie," she said. "And getting sooo tall."
Nicky squirmed, thrilled, ducking away as Victor came up to give
him a feint to the belly. Victor laughed, flushed and handsome, the
one with the looks in the family, his gold hair and blue eyes from
Ida, his small nose and long lashes from Francis. He and Kay ex-
changed cold grins, then he turned to Francis and shook his hand.

"How's it going, Dad," he said. "You holding up okay? Just
saw Mom out there in the living room. She looks great as ever."

"She keeps getting shorter," Francis complained.

"Sure. But hey. What a constitution, you know? Just back from
the hospital? Old Neal couldn't take it. He's white as a sheet.
Watching the football game."

"He is?" Kay reached for the wine and poured herself a glass.

"Yeah. Mom was telling him about the doctors and stuff and he
just got up and went into the TV room. But Mom's cool about it."

"She's super," Stacy said.

"She is indeed," Francis agreed. "Runs on blood, guts, and al-
cohol."

"Unless Neal makes my drinks," Ida called from the living
room, "then I run on tap water. Someone bring me a real drink?"
She shook the ice in her glass.

"Coming, dear," Francis said, tiptoeing backward.

"Smells delish," Stacy said, moving to make Ida's drink for her.

"Not bad," Victor agreed. "What kind of wine did you use with
the beef?"

"Same kind I drink."

"Yeah? Night Train?"

"Children," Francis said. "Don't forget: you're not anymore."
He disappeared into the laundry room and Kay heard him open
the back door and pad into the garage. He still had the book, she
remembered. And the quart of Chivas. And—her eyes scanned the
countertop—the pack of Merit 100s. He could sit in the Porsche
and read and drink and smoke in peace until dinner. A real family
man. Not as macho as Neal though. Actually getting up and walk-

ing away while Ida told him about her operation: that was extra-ordinary. That took passive-aggressive to a whole new level. "He doesn't have enough fire for you," Ida had said the first time she'd met Neal. And she was right. Charles Lichtman had fire. But Charles Lichtman would probably never speak to her again.

"Want to help?" she asked Victor. "You could set the table."

"Better get Stacy to do that. I haven't really had a chance to talk to Mom yet."

"Amazing." Kay watched him walk out of the kitchen carrying the fresh drink Stacy had measured and poured. "Does he help you out at home?"

Stacy giggled, her tongue pink through pink lips. "He's sort of traditional," she admitted. Then, "Look at you."

Kay looked. Terrible dress, torn hose, terrible shoes. "What?"

"Cute."

"Cute?"

"Really cute."

"Thank you." Kay wondered when, if ever, she and Stacy would have a real conversation. Perhaps it was impossible. Yet she knew there was more to Stacy than this weird little female imper-sonator she appeared to be: She had survived gonorrhea and a conversion to Christianity so total that she and Victor had torn up their marijuana plants by the root and written a joint letter of con-fession to the local papers, recanting their past lives as "helpless hopeless hippies." She taught Sunday School, helped edit a right-to-life newsletter, and read the Bible to blind people once a week.

"Let's get the table done together," Kay suggested. "I'll do the silver if you'll get the napkins."

They used crystal and linen and hand-painted china. Some-one—Francis?—had set the banged-up bleeding heart in the center of the table. Kay lifted it off, set it outside on the deck to die, and replaced it with red leaves she quickly ripped off a Japanese maple in the dark by the swimming pool. All the Sunday dinners as far back as she could remember had been this formal, with candles

and monogrammed napkin holders and the salt and pepper
clogged inside the old silver shakers. She straightened a corner of
the lace tablecloth, then hurried back into the kitchen to slice the
French bread, make the salad dressing, unwrap the butter. Sometimes she felt as if she were on roller skates here, or in some old
movie, jerkily zipping from chore to chore like a silent actor. She
poured more wine into her glass, drained it quickly, and poured
just a touch more. She started to slice tomatoes into the salad bowl
but jumped when Francis came in from the garage. He pointed at
the cut she had just given herself, right above the burn on her
thumb.

   "Anything in that salad," he asked, "besides blood?"

Five

"I could eat a cat," Ida said, as Victor wheeled her to her place at the head of the table. "I've never been so hungry. They don't feed you in the hospital. Do you know what people die of in the hospital? Nicky? Do you? Malnutrition!" She lifted one arm and plucked the loose skin. "I'm malnutrified. Do you know what size this dress is? Kay? Do you? Six. Size six. I haven't worn a size six since I was nineteen."

"You were nineteen for five years," Francis reminded her.

"Oh joke, joke. Now I'm the same size as Glo Sinclair."

"Mrs. Sinclair's a two," Stacy said. "But you're cuter than her."

Ida's smile faltered, then flew through the candlelight. "She," she corrected. "I'm cuter than she." She paused, delighted with herself. "I really am, too, aren't I?"

Stacy laughed and patted the chair next to her for Nicky, who slipped into it shyly. Francis said, "What's this? Eating again? I thought we ate yesterday," and wandered off down the hall. Victor stared into the candle flames, silent. Kay raced back and forth with the salad, bread, plates of steaming bourguignon, a special platter

of lentils and steamed vegetables for Neal. She set it down and
went to see where he was; he might still be watching the football
game. But then she heard his voice in the hall, talking to Francis,
which was odd, because after the first few attempts, he and Francis
had settled into silence years ago. But now he was going on and
on, using that monotone she hated so. It must have irritated Francis too, for she heard him say, impatient, "Not now, later, come
into the office and we'll talk about it next week," and then the two
of them appeared, expressionless, and took their places. Kay tried
to catch Neal's eye—what was going on?—but he ignored her. She
hoped it wasn't about money. She had made him promise years
ago never to ask her parents for money.

She sat down, shook her napkin out and touched her fork, waiting for Ida to take the first bite. But Ida sat with her head bent, not
moving. So did Stacy, Victor, and, after a second, Nicky and Neal.
Kay appealed to Francis but Francis only shrugged. Scowling, she
bent her own head. They had never said grace when she was growing up.

"We thank you Dear Lord," Victor intoned, "for returning my
mother home safe from the hospital after her successful leg treatment and we celebrate her return to good health with the fruits of
Thy bounty. Amen."

"Amen," said Ida.

"Leg treatment?" Kay stopped at Neal's warning look and tried
not to laugh. This was probably what he meant by her "tricks."

"When can we hear your concert?" Stacy said, after a minute.
"Ida says you're going to play with an orchestra."

"It's not a real concert." Kay reached for her wine and took a
deep sip. "And it's not a real orchestra. Just some people from
town. We sound pretty awful so far." She watched Victor cut a
piece of meat and chew it, intent. "I have more formal training,
with my one year at the conservatory, than anyone else in the
group," she added. "If that tells you anything."

"The director's in love with her," Neal said.

"Well of course," said Ida. "Who wouldn't be? You big fool," she added under her breath.

"You used fresh thyme," Victor announced.

"Yes." Kay waited.

"It makes all the difference." Victor continued his slow, thoughtful chewing. "Where'd you find it?"

"I grow it."

Victor nodded, swallowed, said, "Good." Kay sat back, ridiculously relieved, and took another sip of wine. Ida, beside her, ate with quick inept greed, her knife scraping back and forth on her plate, food falling off her overfilled fork.

"Oh damn," Ida said, tearful. "I've gone and spilled on my new size six. Nicky, *mon cher,* would you do me a favor? Come here and tie a bib around my neck?" Nicky glanced at Kay, who nodded. He stood up slowly. "You always think I'm going to bite you," Ida complained. She handed him her napkin. "Now just tie it around my neck as if I were a baby." She opened her mouth wide and flapped her hands. "Waaaa," she cried. "Waaaa. Waaaa." Nicky bent his head and tied. "That's good," Ida said. "You're a good baby bib tier."

"Now you can spill as much as you want to, dear," Francis said from his end of the table.

"It's too good to spill." Ida looked directly at Kay. "You don't know how hungry I've been."

Her voice was flat and factual and Kay, held by her darkened gaze, paused, hearing the truth. Every so often she saw her mother's life as it really was, stripped of its glamour and clownishness. Just the hard, quiet, bare-boards life of an invalid. Tomorrow, Kay thought, while we're all out in the world, she will still be in that wheelchair, alone, in pain, and she will still be there the day after and the day after that. She will never walk or run again. She's stuck. It's real. And it's terrible! Terrible! She looked away.

"Speaking of spilling," Ida said loudly, and laughed, for Nicky just then tipped over his milk. Kay hurried to the kitchen for a sponge. When she returned, Ida was saying, "Sticky Nicky, Sticky Nicky"; Neal was saying, "That's what happens when you give kids milk"; Victor was saying, "Our church raised four hundred dollars to buy dry milk for children in Tanzania"; Stacy was saying, "They sent us the cutest thank-you letter"; and Francis was saying, "Kay used to throw her milk out the window to get rid of it. Don't know why she thought we wouldn't notice the hydrangeas turning white."

Victor gave his insincere salesman's laugh and cleared his throat. "I remember I threw a fried egg out the window once and Dad brought it back inside on a garden trowel and made Kay eat it."

"Why did *she* have to eat it?" Nicky asked, interested.

"I don't know," Victor said.

"It was filthy," Kay remembered. She looked up from the table-cloth she was sponging. "It had dirt all over it and it was greasy cold and it was Victor's egg." She turned to Francis. "Why did I have to eat it?"

Francis shrugged and pushed his plate back. "Don't ask me. I had to go to work, remember. I couldn't hang around the house all day checking up on who threw whose hard-earned food out the window."

"Anyway," Victor said, "payback came when I got punished for picking the gold letters off the piano—which is something *you* did, Kay."

"But I didn't," Kay protested.

"You're both liars," Ida said evenly. "Thieves and liars."

"Peasants," Francis agreed. "Your mother and uncle," he added, turning to Nicky, "were very bad children."

No we weren't, Kay thought. She carried the milk-sodden sponge back into the kitchen and rinsed it out. We were good: much better than we are now. Obedient, quiet, eager to please. I got straight A's and came home every day to practice the piano for two and a half hours. Victor was a Boy Scout. I did all the house-work. Victor mowed the lawn. And what were they doing all that time? Mother was either at dance lessons, tennis lessons, ceramic lessons, painting lessons, French lessons, meditation lessons, aqua ballet, or flower arranging; Dad was either at work or playing golf. When we came in to kiss them goodnight they'd be propped side by side in their huge bed, Dad with a murder mystery, Mom with some homework assignment, both of them with a lit cigarette in one hand and a nightcap in the other. They'd look up as if they'd never seen us before. We should have worn name tags. She remembered the friends she'd brought over who'd asked to leave in the middle of dinner; the friends Victor had over who cried for their own beds at midnight.

She poured some Scotch and drank it straight from the jigger. I don't even get drunk anymore, she thought. She began loading the dishwasher, tried to fool Coco into eating a pearl onion, and downed a second jigger.

She returned to the dining room and sat back beside Stacy, who was cutting the last of Ida's meat so she could eat it more easily. It was peaceful to watch; even Stacy's hands and wrists were curvy. The candle flames flickered on the cutlery, the Scotch made another flickering flame inside her, and she could feel a smile loosen on her face and a comfortable ringing begin in her ears: oh good, she thought, a buzz, I'm getting a buzz on at last. She sat back and looked into the living room where Nicky was sitting on the floor playing with an old mah-jongg set that Ida kept on the coffee table. Behind him the piano gleamed against the black bank of windows facing the mountain. Someone had picked those gold letters off to make it read ICK instead of CHICKERING, but it had not been her; that at least was one joke she had not made. She rose to begin serving the pie and coffee when Ida's voice stopped her.

"Big eyes," Ida had just said to Stacy, and Kay turned, warned by the tone that Ida's mood had changed. She glanced at Stacy, but it was too late; Ida's hand had shot out and was gripping Stacy's smooth arm. "Big eyes on my sapphire all night," Ida was saying. "Well, missy, you can forget it. My ring may look better on your pretty hand but I am not dead yet. Not by a long shot so don't even think about it."

"I wasn't," said Stacy.

"Oh yes you were. I saw you."

"Excuse me." Stacy left the table and crouched down to play with Nicky. Kay heard their whispers and hushed, intimate laughter. We should all go home now, Kay thought. Before things get worse. But for some reason she couldn't move. The candlelight still threw a deceptive cozy glow that held her. She looked at Ida sitting erect and righteous in her wheelchair. "You know Stacy's not like that," she said. Her voice felt slowed and slurred.

"I don't care," Ida said loudly. "I get sick of her staring. It's her working-class background, I guess. I don't know. Not that I'm prejudiced. I almost married a plumber. Jerry Solinsky. He went down on his knees and asked me twice."

"Not again." Kay turned away

"And Jerry Solinsky," Ida continued, "came home from the war with a trunkful of medals, put himself through law school, and now he's a senator. I could kick myself."

"Not any more you can't." Francis appeared with two *lit* cigarettes, one of which he handed to Ida.

"If I'd married Jerry you'd certainly be different, Kay." Ida gave her a level look behind an exhalation of smoke.

"She'd have a bigger nose," Francis agreed.

"She'd have more than that. All Jerry's children have made something of themselves."

Kay knew it was no use waiting for someone to say, "But Kay has made something of herself too." Neal was watching clips of the football game, Victor was finishing the leftovers in the kitchen, Stacy's back was turned to all of them, and Francis had already started to wander away. Besides, she hadn't made anything of herself. She wasn't the concert pianist her parents had groomed her to be, nor the well-adjusted happy wife and mother she had tried to become on her own. "If you'd married Jerry I wouldn't have been

born," Kay said. It was a child's argument but it was the best she
could do.

"You almost weren't," Ida said.

"What do you mean?"

"We tried to abort you," Ida said.

"Oh dear." Francis disappeared into the kitchen.

"Don't try to get out of it," Ida called after him. She looked
down at her still full dinner plate. "He always runs away."

"Why would you want to abort me?" Kay asked.

"Why do you think? We didn't want you."

"You didn't know me."

"Wouldn't have made any difference," Ida said. "Frankly." She
touched her lips with the hem of her bib. "This was just a delicious
dinner, darling." When Kay kept staring, she said, "Francis and I
had it all arranged. We found a doctor in Oakland. Francis borrowed a car from Ansel Lipscott; we had the money from Peg Forrest—"

"Peg lent you money to abort me?"

"Oh Kay, don't be such an ass. It was three hundred dollars.
Where on earth were we supposed to find three hundred dollars?"

"But Peg," Kay repeated. Peg Forrest had called her Buttercup,
had taught her to read music, had taken her to her first symphony.
"I thought Peg liked me."

"I guess she liked me more," Ida said.

"So," Kay asked, "what went wrong? Why am I here?"

Ida ignored the sarcasm and only said, "The doctor. I had a
slight cold and I sneezed once in his office and that was that; he refused to operate on me. These days they just haul out their chain
saws and whack your legs off but in those days they had scruples.
Or something."

"So you went home?" Victor, eating salad from the bowl,
looked scared; well he should be. He would have been next. Kay
could feel her own eyes straining wildly from her head. She hoped
Stacy wasn't listening to this; she'd have a fit. She reached for

Francis's cigarettes lying on the lace tablecloth, pulled one toward her, reached for a candle, and lit it.

"We didn't go straight home," Ida said. "We went to a steak-house down on the waterfront and drank quite a lot of whiskey as I recall. The next day your father found a job."

"Been working ever since," Francis said from the kitchen. He came to the doorway. "I was always against it," he said to Kay.

"Oh you big coward," Ida said.

Kay watched him shrug and head out toward the garage. Now he'd be gone for the rest of the night. Well, let him. She inhaled sharply, glaring down. "There's nothing like the truth, is there?"

"No, there really isn't." Ida put her fork down. "I used to go to Peg and weep. 'Why doesn't Kay love me?' I'd ask her. They say a fetus can hear you in the womb, you know. You probably heard every word I said."

"Of course she did," said Stacy. Oh-oh. Her sweet slow voice was outraged. "Fetuses can even hear what you think." Nicky, on the floor beside her, continued building his pyramid of bone white tiles with that quiet, liquid-eyed concentration that promised at least one nightmare later tonight. Kay wanted to bend down and put her hands over his ears. That's probably how she had looked in Ida's womb, little monkey, hear-no-evil, humming, blocking out the voices.

"Yes. Well." Ida dismissed Stacy and turned to Kay. "I always thought you held it against me. Did you?"

"Of course not."

"Then why were you so cold to me?"

"I wasn't."

"Every time I came near your crib you cried."

"I was a baby."

"Oh yes, but if Francis came near you, you lit right up! You cooed and got cutesy. What's the first word you said?"

"I don't know. How would I know?"

"'Daddy.' What's the first sentence you said? 'How was your

day at the office, darling?' Who's the first person you crawled toward? The first person you walked to? Francis. You've always
loved your father," Ida said, "and you've never loved me. When I
fed you pudding you spit it back out! But when Francis fed you:
gobble, gobble, gobble. Oh! Did I tell you I lost a filling last
night? Do you know what that means? Kay? Do you? That
means I'll have to go to a dentist. And do you know how I'll get
into a dentist's chair? I'll have to be lifted. I'll have to be lifted
like a rag doll. I am helpless. Do you have any idea what it's like
to be helpless?"

"Yes."

"*Liar!* Francis? Francis, get in here. Right now!"

"Coming, dear." Francis reappeared, pulled the wheelchair
back from the table, and wheeled Ida down the hall toward their
bedroom.

Kay stubbed the cigarette out. "Help."

"There's something called Intervention." Victor stepped forward, looking pale. "Our pastor told us about it last week. You
can call AA and they'll come out and talk to her."

"AA? Do you think Mom's an alcoholic?"

Neal entered, the remote control still in his hand, and laughed.
"What a question!"

But Kay and Victor looked at each other.

"I don't know," Victor said.

"She had three or four highballs," Kay said, counting. "But she
didn't finish her wine. And she never drinks before lunch."

"Of course she's an alcoholic," Neal said. "Both your parents
are alcoholics. Ida takes drugs on top of that. And they both
smoke like . . ." He looked sadly at the new cigarette Kay had just
pulled out of the pack and at the glass of Ida's wine she was lifting
to her lips. "Hon? What are you doing?"

"I don't know. Being their daughter?"

"It's going to kill you."

"No it's not. I escaped my own abortion, remember."

"Your own murder," Stacy corrected.

"My mother," Kay said, deepening her voice, "had an unsuccessful womb treatment." She struck the match and inhaled.

"Oh babe," said Neal.

"'Oh babe,'" Kay mimicked as she rose to clear the rest of the table. For some reason she was madder at Neal than anyone. What gave him the right to come into her family and label everyone? His family hadn't been so great. Francis and Ida were awful people, it was true, but they were her awful people. She slammed the dishwasher door and punched it on.

"Careful, careful," Francis sang, padding into the kitchen in his socks. "Leave some plates for the next meal."

"Is she still crying?"

"You know your mother. She likes to cry." Francis poured out two brandies and handed one to Kay. She took it, puzzled. Was he going to have a companionable after-dinner drink with her, after all that had happened? He'd never done that. She gripped the stem fearfully, not sure if she was ready to accept a toast—To Your Survival, My Daughter, May You Prosper—but all Francis said was, "Here. Take this to the poor old thing. She wants to say good night to you."

"What if I don't want to say good night to her?"

"Just skedaddle on in there. Now."

The snifter was overfull and Kay shielded it with her hand as she walked slowly to the bedroom, stopping once to lick her fingers. She pushed the door open with her foot and peered in. "Mom?"

At first she couldn't see her. The bedroom was enormous and disordered. The drapes had been pulled back unevenly; the tall windows were wet, black, and reflective, doubling the tables, the lamps, the dresser. The king-sized bed with its twelve hard tasseled pillows was rumpled but empty. The television in the corner was on, turned low, and it took Kay a minute to finally see Ida beside it, sitting silently, erect on a plastic commode. She was wearing a white nylon gown with straps that had slipped down. The table beside her was crowded with medications. Her jewels sparkled in the dim light, and her eyes sparkled too, with silver shadow and tears. Her two stumps, the old one, the new one, still thickly bandaged, stuck straight out. Hacked, Kay thought. Here is a person who's being hacked to pieces. She placed the brandy glass by Ida's side and Ida gripped her strongly and drew her down to sit on the edge of the bed before her.

"Look at me," Ida ordered.

"I am."

"No. Really. Look at me. What do you see?"

"You."

"Not a monster?"

Ida held her gaze until Kay, weary, looked away. She listened to the sounds of the house: Coco's yip, Nicky's questioning laugh, the creak of a madrone branch outside the window. She could hear the hum of Ida's bowels and one small plop. She willed her nostrils to close against any smell.

"You're too human to be a monster," she said.

"I promised myself years ago never to tell you about that abortion."

"That's all right."

"It had nothing to do with you. Who you are."

"I know that."

"It was just that we didn't have any money. And I had a chance to be in a play. They had offered me this part . . . oh it sounds so silly now . . . I was going to play a college girl named Rosalyn, some comedy, who knows—anyway the theater company went bankrupt before our first performance. I can't believe I let myself hurt you."

"I'm not hurt."

"I have often thought what my life would have been like if that doctor had gone ahead and cut you out that day. How lost I'd be. How alone. I don't know what I would have done without you,

Kay. You have been such a gift to me. Your beauty. Your talent. Your sympathetic heart."

Kay looked up, opened her mouth, shut it again. She was deeply, dangerously pleased. She had heard all this before and still longed to trust it. Kiss/slap, she reminded herself. Come here/go away. But if only it were true! If only she were loved, valued, honored. The wanted child of parents who adored her! Barely breathing, she dropped her eyes again.

"I've been having so many dreams," Ida continued. "I don't even know what's real anymore. Half the things I say are from the horse anyway. But one thing you must know and that's that I'm so very sorry. Here. I want you to have this as an apology." Ida drew her hand from Kay's and tugged at her sapphire ring.

"Oh no." Kay looked at the ring with dismay. She had never liked it. As a child she had thought of it as Ida's third eye. It was the same shape, the same color, had the same cold gleam. "I don't want it."

"Yes. Help me get it off."

Reluctantly, Kay slid the ring to Ida's first knuckle; it would go no further, and, glad, she slid it back.

"Sorry. You're stuck with it." She folded Ida's hand inside her own. "But thank you for the thought."

"I have so little to give you. You deserve so much and I give so little. All my life I've been so selfish. Such a bad mother!"

"Shh." Kay put her arms around Ida and patted her shoulder. Ida's back was surprisingly muscular, and her grip on Kay's neck was strong. Victor opened the bedroom door and peered in, blinking. "The Pietà," Kay said, embarrassed, as Ida clung to her. Victor, somber, nodded and closed the door again. He's done that before, Kay realized, as she rocked Ida back and forth. He's surprised us before, Mother and me. All those nights when Mother would careen upstairs with her accusations and apologies and collapse by my bed and Victor would come to the door, half-asleep in his pajamas, scared, holding his tennis racket for protection, and then he'd see it was just Mom, nothing unusual, and he'd go back to bed. And the next day none of us would say a word. Dad because he didn't know about it, Mother because she wouldn't remember, and Victor and I because we took it for granted. It was just something that happened at night—like the thermostat clicking on and off or the cat scratching at the window to come in.

"You weren't ready to be a mother when I was born," Kay said now. "That's all. You were too young."

"Yes," Ida sniffled. "I was so young."

"Only nineteen," Kay teased, kissing her lightly.

Ida giggled. "For five years." She blew her nose, her eyes fixed at a point behind Kay on the wall. Kay, curious, turned slightly and met their two reflections in the vanity mirror. Her blood chilled. Learn, she thought to herself. Learn.

"Have you been watching yourself this whole time?"

Ida didn't answer. Then, defiant, "From this angle I look like I'm whole."

"You are whole."

"Yes. Well. Ha-ha. Thank you for bringing the dinner, Kay. Now please tell your father I can't do more potty."

"Do you want me to lift you back into bed?"

"No. Just tell him to get the hell in here. Good night, Kay."

"Mom? Are you crying again?"

"Wouldn't you be? If you were me?"

Kay stood up and let herself out of the bedroom. As she passed the dining room table she saw the open pack of cigarettes still lying there. She shook three out and slipped them into her purse. Francis was nowhere in sight. Neal and Nicky were gone too—they must already be in the car. Victor and Stacy were waiting for her in the living room, standing hand in hand. "I feel about a thousand years old," Kay said. "And she's still crying. Where's Dad?"

"Asleep in the guest room."

"Come help me then. We've got to wake him. Mom's stuck on the commode and can't get to bed without him."

"I'm not going to wake Dad." Victor crossed his arms. "He wakes up swinging. Last time I woke him he gave me a black eye. Besides. The guy's worn out."

"I know. But we can't just leave them." She imagined the house after they all drove away, Ida staring at her reflection, the ash on her cigarette growing longer and longer, Francis passed out down the hall. She shivered. "Victor?"

"They'll be fine."

"Victor?" Kay repeated, but he and Stacy were already halfway out the front door. She walked slowly down the loud tiled hall, pausing at the wide ramp that led upstairs to Ida's studio. Francis would not be up there, but she walked up anyway, hit the light, and looked inside. There were all Ida's paintings, some slashed, turned to the wall, others shrouded with sheets. There was the file cabinet crammed with first drafts of short-story and novel manu-scripts, and the electric typewriter frosted with dust. French and Spanish language texts jammed the bookcases and the *Greek for Travelers* workbook was still open on the desk. A ballet bar ran the length of one mirrored wall and the old yoga props were piled in the corner. Sewing machine, knitting basket, potter's wheel—all still here. Maybe soon—in a month or two—Ida would be back here herself, frowning in unhappy concentration over some brand-new project. She had been talking about getting a computer, taking a correspondence course in world religions, learning to play the harp. Kay imagined her here, caught up in a hard new enthusiasm, and felt the familiar rattle of envy and irritation. She turned the light off, descended down the ramp, and followed the hall toward the guest room.

Francis lay on top of a twin bed, eyes closed, his glasses still on. His face looked pale and beaky. His hands were folded across his chest, his stocking feet were crossed at the ankle. Afraid to touch him, Kay said, loudly as she dared, "Dad?"

"Run along," Francis said, his eyes closed.

"You sure? Mother's still up."

"Not at all."

"You can get her to bed?"

"Absolutely."

"She's on the commode."

"Righto."

"Well. Okay. I'll call Zabeth, and I'll call you, you know, later this week, about the TB tests."

"No problema. Look forward to it."

She noticed his bathrobe hung over one chair, his slippers on the floor, an overflowing ashtray on the table beside him. He must sleep here often, she thought. When it's too cold to spend the night in the Porsche.

"Dad!" she said louder. "I'm not going to leave until you get up."

"Kay?" His voice was mild and even. Eyes closed, he groped across the table for his cigarettes, lit one, inhaled. "Why don't you mind your own goddamned business?"

Fine. That was fine. What was her business? Two drunk parents, one stuck on the toilet, the other smoking in his sleep, but they'd made it this far without her, they could make it a little farther. She turned and walked to the door, then stopped and turned back. "This is how Mom falls," she warned. "This is how she hurts herself. She'll try to get herself to bed and something else will break. A rib. Her hip."

Francis sat up and Kay took a step back. The look he gave her was small and direct, a straight shot of pure dislike. She raised her chin, said, "Well, good, you're awake, I'll leave then," and, heart thudding, backed out the door.

Neal and Nicky were sitting in the warm car, listening to the radio. Nicky smiled and hugged her neck when she settled into the front seat, but Neal stared straight ahead. "Sorry," she said, kissing and releasing both of Nicky's hands. "But it's hard to just leave them like that."

"Got to leave them somehow," Neal said. He kicked the gas

and backed out the driveway with a rough twist of the wheel. He aimed down the dark hill, taking the curves with a squeal of the tires. Kay leaned her head against the seat and looked out. If he wanted to kill them that was fine with her. "You know what?" she said to Nicky.

"What."

"We forgot to eat the peach pie."

Nicky considered this. "Well," he said at last. "It wasn't really a dessert night."

"No. It sure wasn't."

Six

" Notice how I do it," the horse instructed. He reared, brought his front hooves together, and waltzed unsteadily on his two back legs. "*One* two three *one* two three."

"I'm not going to notice anything." Ida lay still as he lurched and lunged around the bedroom. Either two hours or two nights had passed since Francis had come in, lifted her off the commode, made her blow her nose, tucked her in bed, and passed out beside her. "Go ahead and make a fool of yourself if you want to." She turned her head on the pillow but after a minute shot a look to see if his penis showed. It did. God. Was it blue? It was. And huge. "You better not wake Francis though. You know how he gets."

The horse laughed. Sparks flew from his hooves, bright sprays of gold and silver that flared like little fires. It smelled like fire in here. Ida turned her chin to her armpit and inhaled. That was it. Her own stinky, sweaty, food-stained self. Fever, and then she'd been smoking too much; she smelled like a barbecue pit. She turned to look at Francis; he was lying like the saint he'd been named for, his two hands templed on his chest, his nose pointed toward the ceiling, his lower lip fluttering as he snored.

"I know how he gets," the horse breathed darkly. "He gets pos-i-tive-ly pug-il-is-tic."

Ida narrowed her eyes. How did the horse know that? Had he been observing them privately for years? Did he know other things about Francis as well? He probably knows more about that little architectress in New York than I'll ever find out, she thought. Francis will never confess. He always says I make things up to make myself miserable. Still, I know he slept with her. And I know he slept with Peg Forrest. And no matter what he says, I know he'd like to sleep with Mimi Johns, Sunny-at-the-Office, and stupid little Stacy. She studied the horse. "Where did you come from?" she asked at last.

"Where do you think?"

"Hell?" She waited. "Is there a hell?"

"That's for me to know and you to find out."

I had better get baptized then, Ida decided. Just in case. Francis had been baptized Catholic and although he hadn't gone to church in fifty years he always bragged he had his "ticket punched." If he was going to heaven she'd better go too. You never knew.

"No, you don't," the horse agreed. "Look out," he added, "company's coming."

She covered her eyes with her arm just as the two demons arrived, plunging down on the bed beside her and starting to pump into each other as if she didn't exist, didn't matter, never had. They were sobbing, but what good did that do? They were sorry, but so what? Her own body rose and fell with their heavings and her ears rang with the sickening smack of their flesh upon flesh, but her eyes stayed closed, the damn horse could torture her until he was blue—even bluer—in the face but nothing could make her look. She lifted both arms and pushed.

· · ·

Francis felt a push on his shoulder and woke up punching the air with his fist. It was already five-thirty on Monday morning, lots to do, no time to waste, up and at 'em. He groaned, sat up, and thought, Well what do you know: I'm still dressed. His belt was buckled, his watch was on, there was change in his pocket. Not the best way to start the week but nothing a shower, some coffee, and a total blood transfusion couldn't fix. He pulled his glasses down off his forehead, picked up the notebook he'd left by the bed, and reviewed the day's list through tired eyes. He had a meeting with a tribe of rich Iranians at eight; that would be easy, give them a design that faced East with a bell tower or two. He yawned, put down the notebook, and peered over at Ida. She always slept pretty. Here she was with one arm thrown up, hospital bracelet still on, her eyelashes spiky with last night's war paint, looking like a little rose. Who had she gotten to cry last night? Besides, of course, herself? Stacy? Kay? Hard to keep track. Today should be good; she'd have Greta to push around. Old Ida, he thought. The Scourge of the Suburbs. "Wild thang," he mouthed.

He said it again when he saw his own face in the bathroom mirror. Zabeth was getting him some of that Swiss stuff—Eterna-Something—it was made out of Novocaine, guaranteed to keep you looking young, should that be your cup of tea. The young people he had observed last night, Kay and Victor, were pretty sad examples of the species. He turned his face from side to side as he clipped his mustache, yawned again, and stepped into the shower. Zabeth was supposed to bring something else too: some wonder drug her pharmacist friend had cooked up, something to help Ida when the time came to help Ida. He'd have to sell some stocks to pay for a quart of that stuff. So, he thought: Call my broker.

Soaping, he continued to add to the day's list in his head: meet with Jim Deeds, pick up Coco's Elizabethan collar at the vet's—she was biting that hot spot on her back again—take Ida's Volvo in for an oil change, figure out something to tell Neal when he saw him. Neal looked like a man who had heard "No" before. Poor guy.

But what could you do? He wanted to turn downtown West Valley into the boutique center of the world or something, who knew? Neal was a dreamer, plain and simple; he had no more idea of what it took to develop property than a giraffe did. Even if he had an ounce of business sense, it wouldn't work. It was a bad idea and a bad idea was a bad idea.

Francis stepped out and pressed into the towel, disliking, as always, that second of darkness as he dried his hair. His brother Mick used to lassoo him like this, catch him off guard, hold him down, and slap his nuts for being—what was the word Mick had used?—stuck up. "You think you're so smart?" Mick would ask. "You think you're better than me and Kip and Harry and the rest of us?" Well yes. Anyone would be. "I'll teach you respect," Mick had promised. But Mick, poor Mick. Couldn't teach a dog to piss. Respect, Francis thought. Put that on the list.

"Francis?"

"Be right there. Hang on to your horses."

The low thick laugh lurched into a cough. "That's exactly what I'm trying to do."

Kay felt Neal lift the sheet and edge back into bed. Sex? she thought. Now? After seven weeks and two days? To what, she wanted to ask, do I owe this great honor? What's the fucking occasion? Keep your mouth shut, she counseled herself. She forced herself to swallow her giggle and lie still, pretending to sleep.

Neal was still damp from the shower and his hair, as it brushed across her nose, was wet enough to make her sneeze. "Bless you," he said, and his voice, too deep, too kind, was a giveaway; he must already have a hard-on; he did; she could feel it bob and poke against her. Something thrilling must have happened in that shower. If only she could feel a thrill about something herself. All she felt was hungover. Her headache pounded, her eyelids were crusted, her breath reeked of last night's meat and tobacco. She bit back a bubble of bile to see if it would stay down; it did. So, she thought, go with the flow, get it while you can, *caveat emptor*—no!—*carpe diem*—no!—*mea culpa*. Trying to shield Neal from her breath, she slipped her leg up and over his damp hip and nestled close. "Do we have time before you open the shop?" she whispered.

"Fifteen minutes," he assured her.

Fifteen minutes. Wow. They could do it three times. Stop. Be nice. He drummed his fingertips along her spine in a brisk marching cadence, then lay still. End of foreplay. She knew he could lie there for the full fifteen minutes; he could even fall asleep—he had done that before—if she didn't act now. Follow-through was her job. She reached down and touched him. His erection was a sleek bouncy thing, much nicer than the rest of him, simpler, with a friendly, happy attitude. She loved the way it fit in her hand, alert and amiable. Neal nuzzled her neck and shivered. He smelled aggressively of toothpaste but when he smiled that blind, sweet, trusting smile, he was Neal, her beloved buddy Neal, gentle friend and helpmeet.

"Want to come in?" She opened and lifted. She wasn't ready but she probably wouldn't be, at this rate, perhaps because she was frigid or perhaps because she was out of practice or perhaps because they only had fifteen minutes. It didn't matter. She'd be ready once he got in. If he got in. He was still bumping bone. She guided him once, twice, and at the third knock he entered. "Oh I love that," she smiled. "Hi, honey, I'm home."

Neal nodded but didn't answer. He didn't like talking. It spoiled his concentration. Neal needed total concentration. His strokes were long and deep but difficult for her to catch; as soon as she adapted to one rhythm he changed to another; oh well, they were both lousy dancers. After a few false starts he stopped altogether and began to fumble for her clitoris with his hand. Now how could he miss it so often? It was like when she told him there was food on his chin, and he wiped it off and it was still there. Still, he was trying and even though he wasn't succeeding, even though he was in fact failing, it felt good, to be held. She remembered to lie still as the bed rocked and creaked. Neal had abandoned the clitoral hunt and was coming in to the home stretch. Any movement from her, he once confessed, "made it worse." Bouncing limply up and down on her back, she wondered where the velvet spread had gone to. Neal had kept it in his back room, at the shop, a thin stained soft thing they used to stagger toward and fall upon, in the old days, when they first met. How long ago had that been? Only twelve years? How she used to come on that red velvet spread, all of her naked and open and hot. How she wished she could come now. She should touch herself like the books said, she shouldn't just let him go on without her. But it was already too late. "Oh boy," he was saying, and then, a second later, in that same surprised, faintly outraged voice, "Oh boy," and that was that, and even though her own body felt quiet, her crotch humming to itself like a child left to play alone on a swing, still it was good, to hold him close another minute, and today there was a little shiver, not exactly an orgasm, but a little shiver of almost-there before he slipped out and sat up.

"That was a treat," she said.

"Was it? You felt sort of far away." Neal was already reaching for his clothes. "You had a wild night last night."

"I did?" The bubble of bile rose again and tasted, when it popped, of blood. Neal left her, padded into the bathroom, closed the door, and stepped into his second shower. He can't even go to work with my smell on him, Kay thought. He has to wash it off. She grabbed a pillow and hugged it tight, then raised it up and punched it hard.

"Hon? My comb?" Neal came in with a towel around his waist. He was smiling down at her as if he had a funny secret. "Did you take my comb again?" Clutching the pillow, she watched him rummage through her purse and extract the old white comb with its three broken teeth. "Second time this month," he said.

"But who's counting." Kay swung her feet to the floor and stood up. He very carefully did not look at her naked. He was smelling his socks; the same socks he'd worn the day before and the day before that. She watched him slip them on. Another day, she thought. Another dolor. The phone rang.

"That's your mother." Neal looked at his watch. "She's late."

Ida usually phoned at seven, "But I slept in," she said gaily. She wanted to thank Kay for a wonderful time. It was so nice having all the family together. Wasn't it? It was good for Francis to see everyone and have a chance to visit with little Nicky. He was such a dear child. Wasn't he? Even though Greta was not being paid to put mah-jongg tiles away. And speaking of putting things away! That pie! Greta brought a big piece for breakfast on her bed tray and it was the best thing she had ever tasted in her life! And guess what! It had given her a bowel movement! A big fat yellow one! The second in two days!

That was Monday.

Tuesday Ida was blocked up again.

Wednesday she called to say she couldn't talk. She'd fallen out of her wheelchair, stupid thing to do, but it was Francis's fault for making martinis for the Junior Bentleys and Jim Deeds was going to be furious when he saw her on Thursday.

Thursday she called from the hospital, in tears, she was sick of these damn tests, it wasn't fair, everyone treated her like a white rat, and it wasn't more X-rays she needed for Christ's sake it was a decent dentist and some human contact not that she'd ever gotten anything like that from her own, her only, daughter.

On Friday she called three times. Once to say she was sorry she had shouted the day before and to please forgive her; the second time to shout that she would shout if she wanted to; and the third time she simply cried for five minutes, while Kay, cradling the phone against her shoulder, tears running down her own cheeks, took late fees at the return desk at the library.

On Saturday she asked to speak to Nicky and when he took the
receiver from Kay she shouted *Boo!* so loudly Kay could hear it
across the kitchen as she was making Nicky's breakfast. "Halloween's not until tomorrow, Grandmère," Nicky said politely.

"I may not be alive tomorrow," Ida said, and hung up.

On Monday she called to say she'd been prophetic. She had
cancer.

Kay was at work. She stood at the back office of the library
watching raindrops bead and necklace across the top of the window. The hills were dark khaki against an olive-colored sky. The
old orchard behind the library, like everything else, had recently
been sold to developers. The library was slated to be sold soon
too. She watched a crow rise from a parked tractor and flap to a
bare tree standing alone in the field made mud by construction.
Her eyes burned, either from studying instruction manuals all
morning so she could explain the new computer system to her su-
pervisor, Mrs. Holland, or from lack of sleep. Last night had been
bad. She'd awakened to Nicky's nightmare screams and by the
time she'd rocked him back to sleep, she'd felt wildly awake and
had sat on the couch in the dark until dawn, worrying about her
smoking and her drinking, and her marriage, and her mother. The
word "cancer" seized her now with a cold thrill. It seemed a word
she'd been waiting for. She felt her lips part in a terrible smile and
pressed the phone to her ear. "What?" she said.

"I'm not going to say it twice."

"You have cancer?"

"I mean it, Kay. I'm going to hang up if you don't behave."

"Where is it?"

"Everywhere. You name it. My lungs. My lymph glands. My
bones. And—get this—my brain. Which at least explains the damn
horse."

"I can't believe this," Kay said. She backed into a chair and
sat down, the phone to her ear. Her heart was beating very fast.
She felt alert, excited. What is this? she thought. Am I happy?

Tell me the truth, she heard Zabeth say. *Don't you want her to die?*

"I know." Ida was silent. "It's the limit, isn't it."

"It really is."

"They say it's because of cigarettes."

"You mean if you hadn't smoked you'd be all right?"

"No I mean if I hadn't smoked I wouldn't have cancer. Do you have your thumb in your mouth, Kay?"

"Sort of. My cuticle's bleeding."

"Well don't let it get infected. Do you have any antiseptic there at the library?"

"Yes. Mom? Are they going to . . . can they operate?"

"Nope. I'm inoperable."

"Chemotherapy?"

"What's the point. Are you there?"

"Yes. How do you feel? Aren't you in pain?"

"No. That's the strange thing. I feel better than I have in eight years. I slept like a baby for ten hours straight without a single hallucination, and this morning"—her voice lifted—"I had seven little BMs, like seven little . . ."

"Dwarves."

"Yes!"

"So they're not going to treat you at all?"

"Of course they're going to *treat* me, Kay. I'm starting radiation therapy at one-fifteen tomorrow. What, Francis? Oh yes. Francis wants you to know that tomorrow's the Day of the Dead, ha-ha."

"No it's not. Tell him it's All Souls' Day."

"No it's not. It's All Saints' Day, dum-dums, both of you. Oh hang on a minute, Greta's leaving. Bye, Greta. Are you coming back tomorrow?"

"Of course she's not coming back," Francis's voice answered, as Greta's tinkle of assurances petered out and their front door slammed. "It's a big holiday, remember?"

"She'll be sick tomorrow," Ida predicted, back on the phone.

"Holidays take their toll on Greta," Francis agreed in the back-ground.

"She didn't come back for a week after Christmas," Ida remembered.

"And when she did come back," Francis finished, "she had a tan."

The two of them laughed, merry as wolves, Kay thought, with their sharp teeth glinting. "About the radiation," she began.

"Oh darling, look and see what she left for our dinner," Ida interrupted, calling to Francis. "I just hope it isn't that dreadful Wiener schnitzel again," she said in a lower voice to Kay. "Coco was sick for two days after we fed it to her."

"So at one-fifteen . . ."

"Yes. At one-fifteen tomorrow, think of me."

"Of course I'll think of you!" Kay promised, but Ida had hung up.

At one-fifteen the next afternoon Kay was sitting in a small restaurant with Zabeth, thinking of nothing but lunch. She was just about to open her mouth and give her order when Zabeth, with a jangle of earrings and bracelets, snatched her menu away and said, "Forget it. No chicken salad."

"I like chicken salad."

"I'm ordering for you today. You're having grilled anchovies, steak tartare, garlic bread, and a martini."

"I am?" The table at the Dark Moon Grill tipped when Kay crossed her legs and the floor felt as gritty as the floor of a movie theater. The dabs of light falling from the stained-glass windows made polka dots of green and amber on the backs of the chairs. "Why?"

"Because your mother has cancer."

"I don't see how my having a martini is going to help her with that."

"Not her. You."

"I'm fine."

"Sure you are." Zabeth gave their orders to the waiter and returned to the appetizer she had already ordered for them, forking some fresh mozzarella onto a tomato slice and handing it across the table to Kay. Zabeth's nails weren't clean, but her black suit was fashionably padded at the shoulders and cinched at the waist and her hair had just been blunt cut and dyed—"Only you would say 'dyed,'" she had groaned when Kay said she liked it. Her direct eyes regarded Kay through the chaos of colored mascaras that fringed them. "If you're so fine, why are you sitting there wringing your hands."

Kay unknit her hands and smoothed them on her lap.

"You know if she dies you'll be free."

"She's not going to die," Kay said. "And I've always been free."

"Ha-ha-ha."

"My problems are my own," Kay recited. "I can't blame my mother for them." She lifted the martini the waiter brought; it looked lethal. When she brought it to her lips, it tasted lethal too. A sharp oily hit like an eel bite. She could feel her blood slow and chill. The restaurant around her, however, instantly lightened. It seemed cleaner, cozier. The few diners left at the other tables looked less intimidating and the Vivaldi in the background didn't annoy her so much. "This seems like a good place to meet for an affair," she said, and then, almost in the same breath, just to get it over with, "Is this where you had lunch with Dad?"

"No. We never did get together. I went by his office and gave the stuff to his secretary."

Kay dropped her eyes, relieved. "What kinds of prescriptions does Garret give him anyway?"

"Swiss vitamins. A new kind of painkiller."

"Oh." Kay's relief increased. "He's been so secretive about it I thought it was polar bear sperm or something."

"Ha-ha-ha. Now there's a job for you to look into when your library closes. Jerking off a polar bear."

"I do have to think about looking for work. What could I do?"

"You could do anything."

"You think so?"

"Anything where you took orders," Zabeth said wickedly, "and ran around trying to please other people all day."

"And failing," Kay agreed. She sipped her martini. Forty years old and no idea what she wanted to be when she grew up. She'd had a hundred jobs. But a real career to commit to? She loved the little West Valley branch library, but you couldn't make a life out of a place that was doomed to close soon. She thought of her morning at work—she'd read Henny Penny to a class of preschoolers, led Mrs. Holland through six trial Web searches, fixed the Xerox machine, handed a Kleenex to the homeless man sneezing behind the *Wall Street Journal*, cleaned out a cache of Kentucky Fried Chicken bones some teenagers had picnicked on in the Nature Nook, helped old Mr. Giddings find a magazine article on kickboxing, pinned autumn leaves and cutouts of Thanksgiving turkeys all over the bulletin boards, reshelved a cartload of murder mysteries, and fed the goldfish. None of that seemed like work. She looked at her friend. Zabeth was a licensed masseuse who ran her own business, partied hard, studied law six hours a day, and planned to take the bar exam in a few months. "What made you decide to go back to school?" she asked.

"I love the law," Zabeth said. "You get to wear great clothes and send people to prison. Plus, you know, my Dad always wanted me to be a lawyer. What did your Dad want you to be? I know what Ida wanted you to be—her favorite flunky. But what did Francis think you'd become?"

"Who knows? Nothing." Kay ran her finger around the rim of her glass, licked it. "I don't think he was as serious about my so-called concert career as Mother was. He never paid any attention to the classical stuff. But he used to sing when I played pop songs. 'Darktown Strutters' Ball' was his favorite. And 'Pennies from Heaven.'" She smiled, remembering Francis's sweet tenor swinging up from its hiding place in the deep leather chair, lilting through the newspaper he held in front of his face, joining her, on the piano bench, in a covert coupling of beat and rhythm. Ida would sometimes try to join in, but she never could carry a tune, and Francis and Kay would continue to soar around, beneath, above her. They would finish together on a rapturous high, Francis's loafer stopping its polished bounce precisely at the moment when Kay took her hands off the keys, the rattle of ice in Ida's highball glass their only applause. "He had a beautiful voice. But he hasn't sung with me in years. Not since I left school and ran off with Biff."

"I always wanted to run off with a Gypsy," Zabeth said.

"Oh Biff wasn't a Gypsy. He was from Cleveland. It's just that he wore an earring." Kay closed her eyes. She could no longer remember Biff's face but she could still see his narrow shoulders and strong wrists poised over the keyboard, the way he fell forward into the music. "He was a genius," she said. "The real thing. I hope he's all right."

"He ruined your career, broke your heart, and you miss him."

"He was really a good pianist," Kay protested. "I was crazy about him."

"So you did the right thing. You met a boy, fell in love, and followed him. You needed love then."

"I still need love." Kay suddenly noticed Zabeth's wrists were circled with bruises. "Ouch. What happened to you?"

Zabeth grinned. "I need love too." She saw Kay's look and laughed. "It's nothing. Rope burns. Garret and I started bondage. He ties me up."

"Why?"

"Why rope? Or why bondage? Well we don't always use rope. Sometimes we use handcuffs. And it's not all one way. I tie him up too."

"Really?" Kay focused on her food. She didn't want Zabeth to see her face; it was twitching with condemnation. She remembered the glimpse she had had once of Zabeth's bedroom—dark unpol-

ished furniture, the walls hung with scarves and masks and feathered hats, an unmade bed, a shelf of antique dolls. The heavy
scents of marijuana and oranges; the *I Ching* open on top of a
stack of law books piled on the floor.

"It's sexy," Zabeth said.

"Yes? Well. Then Neal and I ought to try it. We don't do much
that's sexy."

"What is the matter with that man?"

"I don't know. It's me too. It's my fault too. I've been unin-
spired."

"It's this hard time you're going through. You'll be fine once
this is all over."

"Once what's all over?"

Zabeth shook her head, then gestured to the waiter to bring
them two fresh martinis.

"Oh no," Kay said. "I can't drink another. I have to pick Nicky
up from school."

"I'm sure they're used to parents reeling in drunk at school.
Anyway, it's my treat."

"No it's not, Zabeth. You can't afford—"

"Yes I can. Garret left a five-hundred-dollar bill on my dresser
this morning. Oh Kay. You should see your face. Lighten up."

"I don't suppose you have a cigarette?"

"Have I ever let you down?" Zabeth opened her palm. Two
Marlboros nestled inside.

Coffin nails, Kay thought, long and white, with brown filters
like dried blood at the tips. She took one, lit it and sat back, expansive and sickened. "I love wasting days like this," she lied.

"Well don't get too relaxed. It's your afternoon off and you
have to go home and practice."

"For what?"

"For your concert."

"You're not coming to that thing, are you?"

"Of course I'm coming. Garret's coming too."

"On a choke chain?"

"I knew I shouldn't have told you."

They smoked in silence. Then Kay said, "I'll tell you something. I have a real crush on someone—a man who comes into the library."

"Have you slept with him yet?"

"Zabeth? It's me. Kay? I haven't even said hello to him yet. Well, I've gone that far. I know his name. Charles Lichtman. Isn't that a lovely name? He's a painter. He rides a bicycle. I've memorized his phone number, but I haven't used it yet. I have to be sure he's out so I can listen to his answering machine."

"This is pathetic," Zabeth said.

"I know it is. But he's gorgeous. And I think about him all the time. I do idiot things . . . Halloween night I took Nicky trick-or-treating to his house, and I stood under a tree, it was raining, and he came to his door and he gave Nicky a whole Cadbury bar and I've kept it."

She exhaled and crushed the cigarette out, waiting for Zabeth's hard laugh. But Zabeth was licking cheese off her fingers and studying her.

"You need something, Kay," Zabeth said. "I don't think it's a candy bar. And I'm not sure it's a job. But it may be this guy. Or it may be your own little monogrammed whip. Or it may"—she paused—"be another martini."

The third martini was as good as the first two. Better. Kay took a slow, smiling drive to the school where Nicky was waiting by the window with his jacket hood up. She kissed him on top of the hood all the way to the car. Then she drove to the grocery store, where she bought breath mints, chewing gum, a single Sherman cigarette from a stranger standing in the frozen food section, and an eight-ounce jar of aspirin. Once home, she parked Nicky in front of the television with his entire bag of Halloween candy. He looked up at her, not sure. "How many can I have?" he asked.

"Oh, honey, I don't know. As much as you want." She poured herself a glass of jug burgundy, lit the Sherman, and drifted into the chilly, unlit music room, where she sat down at the piano and pounded out the Haydn, amazed at how good it sounded, especially when she sang along, and slid through the Chopin, touched almost to tears by her own subtle shadings. It was going to be a wonderful concert. She had nothing to worry about. She probably did not even need to practice. She hummed as she cooked dinner, sipping from the glass hidden behind the juicer. Neal looked up once during the meal to praise the stir fry.

"Remember," he said, his eyes grave, "when you used to use MSG?"

"Oh the bad old days," she agreed. "Back before I knew who I was or what I wanted to do with my life." She beamed at him but he was bent over his food again. Neither she nor Nicky ate a thing, though Nicky made a nice design on his plate with the mushrooms to one side, the bean sprouts to another, and the tofu in the center, which she admired with a private toast. As she was doing the dishes, she heard Nicky scream, "I'm not going to bed and you can't make me," followed by a crash, running footsteps, a slamming door.

"Oh-oh," she said out loud, blowing bubbles off her hand. "The birth of a brat."

When Neal stormed in to take his after-dinner dose of antioxidants and purified water, she listened to his complaint that Nicky was acting hyper. "He hasn't been eating sugar or anything has he?" Neal questioned and Kay, trying to remember if the ravaged remnants of his Halloween bag had been hidden back in the cupboard or not, said, "I'll go ask."

She poured another full glass of burgundy and floated down the hall to the bedroom, where Nicky perched tense and flushed and fully dressed on top of his desk, kicking the drawers with his heels.

"Act like a human and I'll tell you a story. No. Put that di-

nosaur book down. This is going to be an old-fashioned fairy
story. Now hup-hup. Into your pajamas. Into bed." She lay down
on the side of Nicky's bed herself, the glass balanced on her
strangely drenched apron. "Once upon a time there was an unhappy queen who wanted to fly."

Nicky slid down heavily, scowled, and fell into the bed beside
her. "Why does it have to be about a queen?" he asked.

"Who knows. It's my story." Kay raised her head and took a
sip. "The king tried to talk her out of it. 'You'll kill yourself,' he
warned. But the queen didn't listen. She waved her arms and flut-
tered her legs and jumped off the top of the tower. The king
grabbed her by her cloak, yanked her back and locked her up. He
put nets everywhere, bolted the windows, carpeted the entire castle
with goosedown, and barricaded the stairs. Then he went back to
his throne and tried to rule while the queen banged and crashed
around in the bedroom. You could hear her swearing all over the
country. One day an evil troll came to the door and told the king,
'I can help with your queen problem but you have to give me your
daughter.' 'What daughter,' the king said. 'Her,' said the troll
pointing to this girl sitting in the corner spinning gold out of straw
or combing the tangles out of her hair or whatever princesses did
in those days. 'Oh her,' said the king. 'Sure. Help yourself. But
what are you going to give me?' 'These,' said the troll, and he held
up a pair of iron shoes. 'Put these on the queen and she'll never try
to fly again.' The king laughed for these were really ugly shoes.
Black as black and cold as cold. They were lined with sharp nails
on the inside, they had barbed-wire laces, and they weighed a ton.
'She'll never wear them,' he said, but he went into the bedroom,
pulled the queen down off the chandelier, said, 'Look honey,' and
to his astonishment the queen smiled for the first time in months
and put the shoes right on. 'Thank you,' she said, 'I love them.'
'They are pretty neat,' the king agreed. 'Have you any more?' 'Oh
I have a factory full,' the troll told him. 'In fact I brought an extra
pair just in case you might be interested'—and he whipped out a

pair of loafers black as manhole covers. The king sat down on his throne and put them on. 'They fit!' he said. 'What?' the queen called. She couldn't hear him from the bedroom very well because of course she couldn't walk and the king couldn't go repeat himself because he couldn't walk either. 'Hey,' said the princess, 'what have you done to my parents?' 'Oh don't worry about them,' said the troll. 'Put these on and you'll be fine.' And he held up a third pair of shoes. Black as skillets, heavy as trucks."

"Did she put them on?"

Kay drained the last drop of wine in her glass. Of course she put them on, she thought. "No," she said. "Young Prince Nicholas was riding through the forest just then on his trusty brontosaurus and when he saw what was happening he told the troll to leave the princess alone and never come back." She swung upright, dizzy, and swallowed back a hiccup. "Here's Pokey to keep you company," she said, picking his favorite stuffed animal up off the floor. "I'm sorry about the dumb story. Now sleep tight. I love you."

She guided herself down the hall by her fingertips, dropping her clothes as she moved, and fell into bed naked. She woke up hours later to the sound of Nicky screaming from a nightmare. She cradled him, listened to his rapidly recited dream—the house in flames, a skateboarder with a knife, Neal fighting wolves. At least nothing about trolls or frying pans: that was, as she'd said, *her* story. She rocked him until he finally slept. Then she eased him back down next to Pokey and tiptoed out.

She went into the kitchen, poured a glass of water in the dark, and looked out the window. Moonlight made the back yard blue. Rainwater puddled the uncut grass. The plum trees were already bare. She wondered if Charles Lichtman would stay in West Valley through the winter. His house, her glimpse of it on Halloween, had looked warm and colorful; she'd seen pillows on the floor and paintings on the wall; a homey smell of soup and baked potato and a snatch of *La Bohème* had wafted out when he'd opened the door. Nicky, in a dinosaur costume she'd sewn with green scales,

had held out a paw and piped, "Trick or treat?" Charles had seen
her hanging back under the dripping trees. "Treat," he had answered.

Treat.

She went back into the living room, switched off the television,
glanced at Neal, asleep with his earphones still on, and went back
to bed without waking him up. She checked the night table to
make sure the Cadbury bar was still there, dropped her robe, and
slid under the covers. The sheets felt sleek and cool against her
bare skin. She thought of the paintings on Charles Lichtman's
walls. She had been too far away to make them out clearly but
they looked like big clouds of soft colors. They might have been
landscapes. They might have been nudes. What would he think of
her, nude? Would he want to paint her? She lifted the sheet to
study herself in the moonlight but instead of her own familiar
mounds and hollows she saw her mother's torso: slight, white, cut
off at the knees. She bent her legs and cupped her feet with her
hands, nice rough size-eight feet with calluses and corns and
chipped blue polish on the toenails. Mine, she thought. Mine, not
hers. She pulled the sheet up to her chin and, eyes open on the ceiling, felt herself sink, deeper and deeper, into something dark and
soft and heavy that felt like sleep but wasn't, quite.

Seven

Walt Fredericks paced back and forth in the Sunday School room, luminous with nerves. Every three or four seconds he stopped, opened the door, peered into the church and counted the number of people coming in for the concert. Then he patted Lois Hayes's shoulder, punched Barry on the arm, gazed wordlessly into Zipper's calm eyes, and blew a kiss to Barbara Billings. When he came to Kay he hunched down and embraced her; she was jumpy herself and breathed in his mixed odors of garlic, mint tea, and Old Spice like a tonic. She hadn't performed in public for years. She hadn't been mauled in public for years either, she thought, edging his eager thumb down from her breast. "Lovely, lovely, lovely," Walt murmured, and she took it for what it was—cheerful lust plus an impersonal plea to the universe. "It's going to be fine," she assured him.

She knew she did not look lovely. She was wearing the last good dress she owned—a high-cut, tightly cinched, skirty black number Ida had bought for a country club dinner and given to her years ago. It was expensive, well-made, and unflattering. But it would have to do; there was no money for a new one. "I have never been this broke," Neal had said at breakfast. His voice was so frank and intimate Kay had set her coffee cup down and leaned toward him, waiting.

"Are we poor?" she'd said. "What's happening? Can I help?"

"No." Neal had taken a spoonful of bran. "You can't. For a while I was dumb enough to think your father could. But I know better now."

"You didn't ask Dad for a loan did you? Because I asked you never to ask Dad for money."

"Don't spiral, Kay. This is my problem. I got us in. I'll get us out. Just let me handle this in my own way."

Kay tugged at her skirt and walked to the door Walt had left half-open. It was odd to see so many of her parents' friends and neighbors from Manzanita Heights here. Especially since there was no sign of her parents yet. They probably wouldn't even come. Ida had felt fine when she'd called with the morning health report— her cancer was in remission, her bowels were "producing cigars" and the radiation treatments were "holy rays"—but anything could have happened since. Kay watched Pete and Peg Forrest come in and sit down in the second row. They looked happy to be here tonight but then the Forrests looked happy wherever they were. They had probably looked happy when they forked over that $300 for her abortion. She narrowed her eyes, then flushed as Peg saw her and waved. Shy, pleased, she waved back. What could she do? She liked Peg Forrest. Mrs. Holland from the library sat next to them, crocheting as she waited, her glasses slipping down her nose. She liked Mrs. Holland too. Lois Hayes's twin sister and her husband and their kids filled the next row: a nice cheering section for Lois. "Are any of your friends from the fire station coming?" she asked Barry as he joined her.

"You kidding? They've heard me practice so much they've threatened to sing along." Kay thought of Neal in his earphones and succumbed to a quick jab of envy. It wasn't just that Barry re-

ceived acceptance, it was that he accepted acceptance: that was the
hard part. All along I've been hoping no one would come, Kay realized, watching in wonder as more of her parents' friends walked
into the church. I never mailed those *Amor Musica* flyers Walt
gave me. And I never came in to check out the piano. She looked
at the chunky black piano waiting for her on the bare wooden
floor. It might be completely out of tune. Why didn't I come in to
find out?

"I feel sick," Barbara Billings said beside her.

"We'll be fine. Remember: we're geniuses." Kay turned, grin-
ning, but Barbara, holding her stomach, moved away. Geniuses,
Kay repeated to herself. She remembered a professor's assessment
of a performance she'd given: "B–." "But that's not good enough,"
she'd said, sitting in his office at the conservatory, holding her music books. He'd looked at her hands, with their torn cuticles and
nicotine stains, and then he'd looked at her, her short black skirt,
her round rouged face, the mascara smudges under her eyes, the
one gold hoop she wore to match Biff's. "No," he'd agreed. "It
isn't."

Well don't think about that old man, she ordered herself now.
Think about the music. Just the music. Nothing else.

"It's time!" Walt crowed. She followed the others onto the stage,
slid onto the scuffed piano bench, studied the keys, and settled her
skirts, listening to Walt's bubbly introductions; already the audience
was shifting, smiling, getting into the spirit of the evening. "You will
hear some whoppers and some clunkers," Walt was telling them,
"and some moments of exquisite—absolutely exquisite—exuber-
ance. We invite you to participate in our uneven adventure and we
hope you will find the trip as thrilling as we do."

Kay steadied her eyes on the plaster ceiling hung with colored
cloth banners. There was no cross in this church, no altar; even the
dull pebbled panels of stained glass were secular, worked in geo-
metric designs. She caught a glimpse of Zabeth, in a lace bodysuit
and boots, leading a plump man in a suede jacket down the aisle.

Garret? Chipmunk cheeks and a wet bunched mouth like a baby's? He must have to wear an executioner's hood over that sweet face in bed. A small hand waved from the aisle and she felt her heart expand. Good. Neal had gotten Nicky here in time after all—although where Neal was—ah, yes, sitting in a corner in back, grimly scanning the program for carcinogens. Kay curled her own hands, flexed them, and, a microsecond late, hit the first chord.

The little piano was tuned and the Haydn flew out of it with the same chirpy vigor it did on the upright at Walt's or her baby grand at home. She made the same mistakes she'd made in practice during the first movement, too, but then so did everyone else. By the second movement they had all improved. Lois was playing her viola better than Kay had ever heard, Barry was sunny and steady on the cello, Zipper flew on the flute, and Barbara was right there on the clarinet. Walt's violin soared with conviction and her own part flowed easily: we sound good, she thought, astonished. We sound like musicians. She ended with the crisp bang she had never mastered in rehearsal and rose to stand with the others as they took their bows, beaming, reluctant to meet each other's eyes and break the spell.

A shadow moved rapidly down the aisle as she sat down again and even before she smelled the L'Heure Bleue she knew Ida had arrived and had wheeled her chair as close to the stage as she could without actually rolling onto it. She looked over at the small white pointed face rising in happy expectation above its heaped collar of crushed velvet. Ida's diamond earrings flashed in the undimmed church lights and her eager smile held until it drew an answering nod back from Kay. "Darling," Ida slurred loudly. "So sorry we're late."

"Shh," someone said as Walt stepped forward to introduce the next piece. Kay looked for her father. Francis was standing in the back, talking to a tall brunette in a Chinese brocade jacket. He caught her eye and gave one of his wiggle waves, two fingers making a crocodile that bit. He was drunk too. The Junior Bentleys

and the Bernards tiptoed in, their heads ducked like children fighting giggles. Victor, sitting next to Stacy, gave her a quick look of
sympathy before dropping his eyes to the floor. Perhaps he was
praying for her.

She was going to need it. This next piece was the Chopin, her
solo. She shifted on the bench. Walt finished his introduction, nodded at her, eyes hot, and she dropped her hands to the keyboard.
She found the opening phrase, sure, spare, and so lyrical it made
her breath catch. She sank into it and moved easily into the first
trill. The second. The third. And then Ida started to cough.

It was a new cough, thick and phlegmy as a rope dragged
through seaweed, and it uncoiled forever. Kay stiffened, forcing
herself to play through it, but though she was hitting the keys correctly she couldn't balance the tempo. She slid too fast off one
note, lingered too long on another. And Ida's cough didn't stop. It
went on and on. She's going to die! Kay thought. She's going to die
in the middle of my solo. Well do it, she thought. Go ahead and do
it. She went into another trill so cold and heavy it felt like a death
stomp and under it and under the cough she heard another sound:
sobs. Ida's sobs as she tried to stop. "Oooh," in Ida's hurt and
helpless voice. "Oooh."

All right, Kay thought, defeated. You win. I can't play anymore.
I'll never play again. She took her hands off the keyboard and
turned to help her mother but at that moment Ida stopped. There
was no sound in the room at all. Ida waved to her weakly, eyes
glowing above the Kleenex pressed to her lips, and Kay, shaken,
pivoted back, steadied into the legato once more and brought the
piece to a false, showy flourish. Everyone clapped as if nothing had
happened.

During the piece which followed, Ida sat straight and attentive,
swaying only slightly. When the lights came up for intermission,
she called, "My darling!" and flung her arms out. Kay walked to
her warily. Ida gripped her and drew her down and Kay had to
steady herself, her fingers sinking into the slippery folds of Ida's

velvet coat. "I am so sorry," Ida hissed in her ear. "I don't know what happened."

"It's all right," Kay said, tired. After all, this wasn't the first time. How could she have forgotten the sixth-grade recital when Ida came in late and dropped a coin purse of change on the floor or the high school concert where she had entered escorted by a traffic cop? She straightened, rubbed her arms, and waited for Francis, who was making his way down the aisle toward them. The Bernards were right behind him, followed by the brunette. Untangling Ida's wet hand from hers, Kay asked, "Who's that?"

Ida turned to look. "That's Glo Sinclair. You know her. She sent me those gorgeous roses. Oh darling. You played like an angel."

"Very nice," Francis agreed, coming up to them. "And loud for once. We could actually hear you in back."

"Could you hear Mom?"

"Why we could indeed. And what was Mom doing?"

"I was coughing," Ida said. She hung her head.

"Doncha know better?" Francis wagged his finger at her.

Well that's that, Kay thought. She looked at Glo and held out her hand. "Hi," she said, "I'm Kay."

Glo looked at Francis. "I have never shaken a musician's hand before," she said.

"You're not shaking it now," Francis pointed out.

"I don't want to injure you," Glo said to Kay. "Aren't your hands supposed to be insured?"

"I don't even have my car insured," Kay said. Glo gasped and pulled her hand back. She was about an inch taller than Francis, with small white teeth and taut skin. Pretty, in a skull-like way.

"Kay lives on the fringe." Francis bent over Ida, who, starry-eyed and completely composed, was letting Pete and Peg Forrest each pat one of her shoulders. "Think I ought to take you home," he said.

"Oh no. Please let me stay." Tears rose at once in Ida's blue eyes. "I'll be good. I promise."

Kay waved to Nicky, who was weaving through the chairs toward her with a guarded look on his face. "Dad won't get me anything to drink," he complained. "They're selling apple juice and cookies out in front but he won't let me have any."

"Tell me I played nicely and say hi to your grandparents and I'll get you something later."

Nicky kissed Ida, who closed her eyes and pressed toward him, and shook hands with Francis, who looked down at him, laid his palm flat on the top of his head, and then lifted it, inch by inch, as if measuring.

"Yep. Just as I suspected. You're taller than you were last Sunday. Someone needs to stunt your growth and it might as well be me. Tell you what. I'll buy you an apple juice if you'll come outside and join me in a cigarette."

Glo, who had been staring at Nicky with a fixed smile, said, "Don't believe a word that man says."

"I don't," Nicky said.

"Good-o," said Francis, "let's get out of this hellhole."

"I could go for a cigarette," Ida said as they left.

Glo said nothing. Kay said nothing. Walt Fredericks bustled up, beaming. "This has to be your lady-mother! May I kiss your hand? An honor! A pleasure! You must be so proud of Kay! What exquisite shading! A Polish heart! She has one, I tell her, and now that I see her mother: ah."

Ida, dimpling, said only, "I coughed."

"But in exquisite time. Right on the beat!"

Walt talked on. Kay watched the familiar transformation, Ida beginning to lighten and lift like a plant drinking water, and Glo watched too, her long bare heel rising out of her shoe and back down again, either out of impatience or from an intense, unselfconscious interest in the phenomenon, Kay couldn't tell. Zabeth came up beside her and scratched her lightly on the arm with blunt, black-painted nails.

"Imagine coming all this way just to jinx your solo," Zabeth grinned.

"It's true dedication," Kay agreed, and then, worried, "Was it jinxed?"

"Not at all. It was totally perfect." Zabeth was too quick and Kay groaned. Dishonesty from Zabeth was not a good sign. Well: too bad. Too late to do anything about it now. People with "Polish hearts," whatever that meant, plowed on. She took Garret's moist hand as Zabeth introduced him, and tried to block the image of his plump pale body trussed and tied as she in turn introduced him to Ida. Stepping back, Kay saw that Ida was now completely encircled with admirers. She was free to slip away. She made her way back to the Sunday School room to recoup. The muscles in her hands and arms were tight with frustration.

"Hey. Piano Princess." A deep voice. Victor. Trying to be funny. She made a face and looked up. But the man standing before her was not Victor.

"Hey," she echoed, and then, to her horror, "What are you doing here?"

Charles Lichtman, up close, was so beautiful that if she weren't in shock already she would be. Caramel skin. Chocolate eyes. Sugarplum lips. He looked like a dessert to drown in. "I came to hear you play," he said. "And I was not disappointed. I enjoyed every note." He smiled. "Just say, 'Thank you, dear.'"

"Thank you, d——"

"Thank you. Break a thumb." He raised both of his in a victory gesture and walked away.

The rest of the concert passed in a dream. A Gershwin medley, less demanding than the earlier works, seemed to invite more mistakes. Lois flubbed her entrances and Barry ended too soon. Kay's part was easy, but even so she missed several notes. The audience didn't seem to mind and the clapping extended just long enough to make the performers feel good, while falling short of suggesting an encore.

"Could have been worse," Barbara said as they bowed.

"Should have," Kay agreed. She searched the crowd, saw Charles smile and wave again before he left. He had come alone. He had called her "dear." Her eyes followed him out the door, then reluctantly returned to look for Neal, who was still hunched in the back, looking miserable.

"That bad?" she asked, going up to him.

"Oh babe. I hate to see you playing with amateurs. They bring you down."

"So I was playing 'down'?"

Neal was silent. "Silent" meant "yes." "Yes" meant "divorce him." Kay smoothed a fold on her stiff black dress. "Would it kill you," she asked, "to be kind?"

"What do you or anyone in your family know about kindness?"

With surprising swiftness, Neal stood and walked outside.

Kay stared after him, then turned as Victor came up to her. "I'm going to leave him," she said.

"He'll be fine. Give him time."

"*What* a pro you are!" Stacy breathed. "That was such a groovy concert."

"You know, you really are a good pianist," Victor said. "You have a clean touch and lots of feeling. You probably could have been famous like Mom always said."

Kay, distracted, shook her head. "Mom was the one who wanted to be famous."

"Yeah but you were the one who had the opportunity and the lessons. She just had the ambition." His hand fell heavily on her shoulder. "You did great. Love to see you play in a real church sometime."

"This is a real church, Victor."

"Right." Victor turned away and Kay followed him and Stacy outside to the parking lot, then looked around for Neal. *We need to talk,* she'd say when she found him. *We need to talk for about two weeks straight.* She paused on the stairs. The Bernards and the Junior Bentleys were departing with flurries of laughter and Francis was loading Ida's wheelchair into the back of the Volvo. Ida, crumpled in the front seat, saw Kay and cried out. "Did I tell you," Ida slurred, "how sorry I am?"

Kay caught a glimpse of a silver whiskey flask in the folds of her coat and a handful of pearl-colored pills in her palm. "Yes," Kay said. "You did."

"Because I am so so sorry. For everything, darling. It's just that I have cancer."

"Mom . . ."

"You don't have cancer so you don't know how it feels. You can play another concert another place another day. You don't need me to come coughing after you all your life. But I can't. I don't have a life. I have no legs, you know, Kay. And now I have cancer. What do you think about that? Do you think that's fair? No. Don't answer. I can tell what you're thinking you little bitch don't think I can't and I don't like it. You think I deserve this, don't you. You think I've done this to myself."

"I don't think anything, Mom."

"Now look what you've gone and done." Francis's words were jocular, but Kay knew the cold tone. He slipped into the car and fastened Ida's seat belt over her mink lap robe. "Just when I'd gotten her calmed down too." He gave Kay another of the stony looks that stopped her heart in mid-beat. As if she were an enemy. Kay stood back and watched as he started the car and drove away. As she turned back to the church she was startled to see she wasn't alone. Glo was still there, watching too.

Ida bowed her head and pressed her hands together but she had scarcely begun the "Our Father" when here they came again, her husband, her daughter, naked as apes, sucking and pumping into each other as they tumbled down beside her. The bed rose and fell. It was intolerable. "I cannot stand this anymore," she said. She struggled up to see Francis peering down at her. He looked frightened. He should be. "Darling," she said, her throat thick. "There's a piece of paper by the phone with a name on it. Call him for me, will you?"

"Father Bliss?" Francis said. "The Catholic priest?"

"Father Bliss," Ida echoed. She could scarcely hear herself she felt so far away. "He's going to save us."

"Speak for yourself," Francis said. But he dialed.

Eight

Father Bliss was tall and strong and it didn't matter that he wasn't very bright; in fact, it was almost better. He went straight to the bedroom window where Ida pointed, looked out, and said in a deep thrilling voice, "Begone." He made the sign of the cross. The winter light gleamed on his thick silver hair. Then he turned to Ida, who was leaning forward on her pillows with her hands clasped. "Is that better?"

Ida laughed and nodded. The word "begone" made her shiver with pleasure. The horse and the two torturers had been gone since Christmas but there was no sense telling Father Bliss that; he'd leave too. He was a little like Kay in that regard: if you didn't give him some small task to do to make him feel useful, he'd go home. And she didn't want him to go yet. She gestured toward the empty wheelchair by the bed and shivered again as he crossed the room and sat down. He was the best-looking man she had ever seen in her life. He even smelled good: like Ivory soap and apples. "I feel safe when you're here," she said.

"You are always safe," Father Bliss reminded her. "God is always with you."

"It doesn't feel like it," Ida said, adding hastily, "Yet. Maybe it will when I get used to Him." She reached for her cigarettes, lying within reach on the bedspread, hesitated, laid her hand flat. She hadn't had a cigarette today. Hadn't wanted one. All her vices were disappearing. She herself was disappearing. "Every day in every way," she recited, trying to sound hopeful. "I do feel I'm getting closer to Him, though."

"How can you get closer," Father Bliss said, "to someone you are already part of?" He furrowed handsomely. "That's like trying to be the nose on the outside of the face when you are already the air on the inside of the lungs. It's not possible, is it?"

"No," Ida said. "I guess not." She kept her hand on the bedspread, hoping he would cover it with his own. He had done that once, during his first visit. She had told him the truth from the start—the only person she had ever told the truth to—and he knew her sins, not all the little ones, there were too many of those, but the big ones, the important ones, he knew those. He knew she had been a bad daughter, a bad wife, and a bad mother. What he didn't know, what she hadn't told him, was that she was afraid she had already become a bad Catholic.

"When I pray," she said now, "I drift off."

Father Bliss smiled, his grey eyes on the distance.

"I drift off," Ida repeated, raising her voice.

"Ah." He blinked. "And where do you go?"

"Nowhere. That's so frightening. I feel suspended in nowhere. It's better than before," she added, "when I had the horse and the demons. Then I was in hell."

"You don't need to worry about hell," Father Bliss said.

"No, I know, you told me, my soul will go to heaven, thanks to you and the beautiful, wonderful Holy Roman Catholic Church." She plucked at the spread and glanced at him, hesitant. "That frankly is one of the reasons I decided to convert."

"It doesn't matter what your reasons are. God does not care what car you drive to His garage."

"Yes, I know that in eternity I will be at peace and that's a relief. But it's now . . ." Ida continued. "Now that is so brutal."

"'Brutal' is a hard word," Father Bliss said.

"My life *is* hard." Ida opened her mouth to say more but then closed it. How could she explain to him, to anyone, how isolated she felt. How alone. Even Francis didn't know. Jim Deeds knew, but Jim Deeds was a doctor and didn't care. Kay looked sometimes as if she knew, but Ida had seen that same look of sympathetic understanding cross Kay's face when Nicky pinched his finger on the nutcracker or Stacy complained about a bad haircut. The sheer effort, will, and courage it took to lift a coffee cup, attend a conversation, or watch the evening news when all the time she felt on fire and in orbit, like a disintegrating meteorite, wanting to scream *Help me help me help me* when she knew that no one could. It didn't matter. Other people's pity was poison and always had been. I don't need it, Ida thought. I never have and I never will. "I've had to fight for everything I've ever wanted," she said.

"That's all over now," Father Bliss said. And without warning his hand, warm, strong, wonderfully human, covered hers. She almost shouted with pleasure. But nothing was simple. She had to risk what she had just been granted.

She took a deep breath. "I never told you who those demons were. They were my daughter Kay and my husband Francis. And they were fornicating."

She glanced up through her lashes.

Maybe Father Bliss didn't know what the word "fornicating" meant. He was looking calmly at the far side of the bed where Francis's pillow and ashtray and golf magazines lay. Ida turned her head and looked too. A hot flood of tears caught her by surprise, streamed down her face. She remembered how astonished Mimi Johns had been to learn that Francis still slept with her even after the amputations. But that was how Francis was, that's how he showed things. He didn't make love to her anymore, hadn't since last summer, always had an excuse, an early meeting, a late appointment. But he never acted as if she repelled him. Never acted as if she were only half a woman now. And in the middle of the night when she reached for him he was there, slight, sour, snoring. "It wasn't real, was it?" she asked.

"I don't see how," said Father Bliss.

"I'm a useless old cripple," Ida blurted. "With a sick, filthy mind."

"You are God's child," Father Bliss corrected her.

Ida softened and settled under the touch of his clean white hand. Then, eyes on her own reflection in the vanity mirror, her pale face distant as a friend left on shore, she let loose a last flash of anger and hurt. "Kay would never have the guts to do something like that anyway," she said. "Kay's afraid of her own shadow. And Francis. You know what he says about incest. 'If she's not good enough for her own family, who else would want her?' That's just a joke," she added, catching Father Bliss's mute, troubled stare. "That's Francis's sick sense of humor." And despite herself, she laughed.

Her laugh was the first thing Kay heard when she came in the next week. She banged the front door behind her, propped her umbrella in the stand, and slipped out of her boots. Outside, the January rain fell fast and cold. "You sound happy," she called. She padded toward the bedroom in her stocking feet with a dripping bouquet of garden narcissus held in front of her. She avoided her reflection in the mirrored hall. She knew what she looked like. Sweets, smokes, the daily hangover, a run of rained-out runs with Zabeth, insomnia, poverty, and Neal's silent celibacy were doing her in. Plus she had not seen Charles Lichtman since the concert two months before. His bicycle was locked up; his house was deserted. Where had he gone? Was it her fault he'd left?

Greta met her at the doorway, a tense, tiny German woman

with a stagy manner. She clapped her hands, said, "Oh how vunnerful," and grabbed the bouquet. Kay, caught off guard, instinctively pulled back. Ida laughed from the bed again and Coco barked from her cage in the kitchen.

"Let Greta do what she wants," Ida advised, stopping to cough. "You'll just be sorry if you don't."

Ida was wearing a new nightgown today, yellow silk with roses and an edge of soft lace. Her hair had been washed and brushed into a light shiny cap. Kay found her eyes skipping over the heavy silver crucifix as automatically now as they skipped over the flat space under Ida's blankets; she was stopped for a moment by the large white Bible open in Ida's hands but was relieved to see that the remote control to the television set was being used as a bookmark.

"Now your dotter is here," Greta said darkly, behind her, "we turn you."

"Can't we do it later?" Kay watched as Ida batted her eyelashes at Greta and in a baby voice added, "I haven't even had *lunch* yet."

"What can I do with her? She has the bedsores and needs to be turned. But! She is impossible." Greta flung her hands out and pivoted toward Kay. "Today at least she wants lunch. I make her such a nice lunch too. Soup."

"Not that sick soup," Ida flirted.

"Nonono." Greta wagged a finger. "This is good chicken soup. Just the way you like it. I use the bouillon, and then I add some carrot, some onion, some parsley . . ."

"No Cream of Wheat?"

"No, Ida. No Cream of Wheat. That is only for when I make you the sick soup and today is not a sick day. Your daughter is here. Your husband will be home soon. Father Bliss—oh! what a dreamboat—will be coming soon too. So today is a good day." Greta rolled her eyes, clasped her hands, and backed out.

"Wow," Kay breathed.

"Don't be mean." Ida settled back, serene, and soon Greta bustled in again with a bed tray set with a covered bowl, a plate of
cold toast, and the narcissus, clipped to an even four inches and
wedged into a baby-food jar. She put the tray over Ida's blanket
and set the jar down loudly by another enormous vase of black
roses. Kay picked up the card. Glo Sinclair must be supporting the
flower industry single-handedly.

"First your medicine," Greta fussed, and Kay looked up to see
Ida take the dime store demitasse Victor had given her for
Mother's Day when he was ten and sip something yellow. She drib-
bled, said "Damn," handed the cup back to Greta, picked up her
spoon, and bent over her soup.

"Don't watch," she said to Kay. "I slurp. Francis can't bear it."

"I'm not as delicate as Dad." Kay remembered Francis imitating
her and Victor when they were children, chewing with his mouth
open, his eyes cold with contempt. Lucky Mom, she thought, she
gets to see that side of him now. Idly she picked up the Bible and
turned as she did with most books to the back. She stopped at a
line from Revelation: ". . . and lo, there was a great earthquake;
and the sun became black as sackcloth of hair, and the moon became as blood . . ."

"It's like a cartoon, isn't it," she mused. "Exactly the sort of
thing I don't let Nicky watch on Saturday mornings. Pow. Bang.
Boom. Instant apocalypse."

"What is apocalypse, Kay?"

Kay looked up. Ida waited, soup spoon in hand. Didn't she
know? Or was the yellowish medicine affecting her? Was the cancer jangling her brain again? Wasn't she still in remission? She had
made perfect sense—almost perfect sense—since Christmas. But if
Greta called this a "good" day, there must be "bad" days, days
Kay didn't hear about. Sick days. "It means the end of the world,
Mom."

"Like that movie Francis rented last week. *Apocalypse Now.*"

"Dad rented that?" Kay dropped her eyes and read another

line. "Scary stuff," she decided, closing the book. She looked up, surprised to find Ida watching her.

"You're so funny."

"I am?"

"Yes. You're jealous of Francis and Greta and Father Bliss and now you're jealous of the Holy Bible."

"I am not. What do you mean?"

"You've always had a green streak a mile wide." Ida looked at her curiously. "You do know I love you, don't you?"

"Sure. No. I don't know. I've never known anyone loves me."

"Nonsense."

Kay shrugged, eyes down. "You didn't like me when I was a baby."

"You had colic. And you were awfully . . . I don't know . . . clingy. But I like you now. Isn't that enough? I especially like it that you have been coming up and seeing me as often as you have. It gives me enormous pleasure."

That's not the same as loving someone, Kay thought. But—"It's my pleasure," she said. It was. "Really."

"And as for poor John . . ."

"Who?"

"Young Saint John who wrote Revelation. He just got too much sun. That's what Father Bliss thinks. He was out there all alone on the rocks; there weren't any trees or shade in Ephesus so he got overexposed and probably had a minor stroke. Everything's changed now of course. The whole coastline's gone. It's not even an island anymore. Oh! Guess what! Alice died yesterday!"

Kay pulled herself back from Ephesus, wherever that was. Alice Bernard? Alice Bernard had come to the concert in November. She and Howard had tiptoed in late behind the Junior Bentleys, quaking with giggles; Alice had produced a thermos of hot spiced rum from the pocket of her fur coat during intermission. She hadn't looked sick.

"Melanoma. Howard is quite upset. But he'll be all right. He knows how to cook. And Alice used to go back East to visit her sisters every summer so he knows how to wake up alone. And he has friends. He meets with other men and they play drums. I guess you'd call them a . . . whatdoyoucallit . . ."

"Support group?"

"Yes. But Francis. I don't think Francis has a support group."

Kay shook her head. It was hard to imagine Francis in any group at all.

"I don't know what will happen to Francis," Ida said. "He doesn't have anyone."

"He has lots of people," Kay said. "Lots of friends. Plus Victor, and"—less certain—"me."

"He acts so independent but he's going to fall apart. Oh look." Ida touched her napkin to her face. "Am I sweating or what?"

Kay took the napkin and dabbed the perspiration gently off her mother's cheek and hairline.

"He's shy," Ida continued. "Cut off. He doesn't have the first idea about how to take care of himself. He'll just hole up here with his crossword puzzles and never go out. If I just had six more months . . ."

"You do!" Kay began, trying to sound firm and hide her panic, but Ida silenced her with a sad, steady look.

". . . six more months of halfway decent health, you know what I'd do? I'd put this house on the market, sell it, and make Francis buy one of those new condominiums by the golf course. He needs fresh air and exercise and upbeat jolly company. He needs a woman."

"You're a woman."

"No, Kay. I mean a woman with two legs. Maybe his old girl-friend will hunt him down again. That little architectress from New York. She was very much in love with him, you know, but I don't believe he's given her two thoughts since he came back to us. He's like that. Cold. Would you please rub my foot?"

"What architectress? You don't have a foot."

"Rub where it would be if I did."

"Here?"

"Good. Thank you. Yes, you knew he left us to have an affair, didn't you? You didn't? Well it doesn't matter. We got him back, you and I. And then Victor was born. The thing about love, Kay, you have to fight for it. You can't just wait for it to come to you. You have to reach out and grab it and then you have to hold on to it. It's a struggle, like everything else. You've had things easy. It's all been handed to you on a silver platter. Now promise me one thing? Are you listening? Promise you won't fuck your father?"

Kay started, dropping the invisible foot.

"Promise?" Ida repeated.

"Are you crazy?"

"I don't know. Am I?"

"Yeah. Yes. I'd say you are. Sick . . ."

Ida chuckled.

". . . and crazy."

Ida pushed a package of Merits across the bed. "Don't you want a cigarette, Kay?"

"Yes," Kay said. "I do." She lit one for herself and offered one to Ida, which Ida waved away. Kay's hand trembled in time to the rain that ticked on the skylight like a loud clock. How far had the cancer gone? How much of Ida was it taking? She stubbed the cigarette out. "I've never even seen Dad naked," she said at last.

"He's modest," Ida agreed.

"He wears shoes and socks to the beach."

"Yes, his skin is white as a girl's. Say, is there any stuff left in that cup?"

Kay picked up the demitasse and looked at the few yellow drops left on the bottom. "What kind of dope are you taking?"

"I don't know. Francis gets it from somewhere. He wants to give me marijuana too. Can you see that? You think I'm bad now?"

"I don't know . . . marijuana's supposed to help with pain."

"No, Kay. Nothing helps with pain. But you can't tell Francis that. He's always trying to find ways to make me feel better. Sometimes I'll see him looking at me and his look is so sweet it makes me want to cry. I'll pretend to read or be asleep because I know I don't deserve a look like that. Old cripple. He'll be better off when I'm gone." Ida's eyes circled the room, rested, at last, on the vanity mirror. "You all will. If I had any courage at all I'd . . ." She stopped talking and made a jerky slice at her stomach with the flat of her hand. "Like Duffy Sinclair. Did you know it's okay to kill yourself now? Father Bliss says suicides can go to heaven and be buried in a churchyard like everyone else. And oh darling, I hate to ask you—but Francis has to go out of town Wednesday night, his investment club is meeting up north and he has to give a presentation and can't get out of it. And Greta can't stay over and I'll need someone here. Can you baby-sit me?"

"All night?"

"Dear Kay." Ida closed her eyes against the pillow. "Tell me, does Neal still take you to the symphony? When you first told us you were going to marry him, Francis said, 'Well at least he takes her to the symphony.' Greta," she said, opening her eyes and smiling as Greta came in to clear the tray, "you cheated. You put egg in that soup."

"I just put in a little egg, missus, mixed up with some flour. No Cream of Wheat. Just flour. That is how we do it in Germany."

"It was delicious." Ida closed her eyes again. "Now why don't you turn me. I'll try not to scream."

"Why would you scream?" Kay asked.

"Because it hurts, dum-dum. Why do you think? Look, Kay, I don't want you in here. You'll just get in the way. Why don't you go play the piano."

Dismissed, Kay left the bedroom. But I don't want to play the piano, she thought. She saw the lunch Greta had set out for Francis on the dining room table—two tuna sandwiches in plastic wrap, a cup turned upside down in its saucer for coffee, a small bag of potato chips, and an orange, already peeled, drying crustily under the skylight. The afternoon paper was turned to the crossword puzzle and the gold pen lay beside it. It made an efficient and sterile composition, a picture of frugality and loneliness, and was surely more indicative of Francis's daily life than any sexy lunch he might be having with Zabeth passing bags of pot back and forth under a tippy table at the Dark Moon Grill. Oh what had Ida meant when she'd said "Don't fuck your father"? What an ugly thought. How hard it must be being Ida. How hard it was to be around her at all. Poor Dad. No wonder he had an affair. But so long ago! Before Victor was born? Before Ida tripped on the toys and took her first fall?

Maybe Dad will feel freer when she's gone, Kay thought. Maybe he will be happier, more relaxed. Friendlier. He might come to dinner and take walks with us and go on picnics on Sundays. We might even travel, he and I, the two of us, alone. We might go to Ephesus. She saw herself on a cruise ship, standing at the rail in a windblown white dress, her arm in her father's, both of them laughing . . . *Such a good daughter,* she heard other passengers saying. *Such a comfort to him.*

She shook her head and walked quickly to the piano. As she settled herself on the bench she heard a scuffling sound from the bedroom followed by a scream so uncontrolled that she trembled and hugged herself, one hand at her mouth. Brute, she thought of Greta, but she knew it wasn't Greta, Greta was doing the best she could. It was Ida, Ida's body, broken and still breaking, burnt with radiation, bursting with bedsores. She reached up and riffled through the sheets of music on top of the old piano. The scream rose again and her fingers tumbled onto the keys with a clamor.

She played for an hour, badly, passionately; she played all of Scott Joplin's rags and *Mozart Made Easy* and the "Theme from *Exodus*"—anything to block out the terrible sounds of that woman who had been in pain, in the bedroom, for almost as long as she could remember.

. . .

"When will you learn?" Neal asked. She had stopped by his shop on her way home from Ida's and sat huddled in her raincoat in his back room, morosely trying to sip the herbal tea he had made for her on his hot plate. It was green and smelled like a mouse nest. "Your mother always gets to you," Neal lectured. "It's like every time you meet her is the first time you've met her."

"That's not so bad. What's wrong with that? It sounds Zen. You don't have any whiskey do you?" Kay asked.

Neal didn't answer. His thick hair was ruffled and he had draped a crocheted shawl over his sloped shoulders. He looked like a grandmother. He had been bent over an envelope of papers when she first came in but had moved it aside; she got only a glimpse of a familiar name, Dominic Delgardo, stamped hugely on letterhead, before he shoved the papers into a drawer. "Who's that who keeps writing you?" she had asked, expecting no answer and getting none. Neal's secret life, one mystery after another. Still, the touch of his hand on her wrist was welcome, even though he had found and was rubbing a new bruise, and his eyes, as he regarded her, were quiet, ready to receive what she had to give. Which wasn't much. The usual muddle. Neal, pressing down a final time on her bruise, rose and began to busy himself at the worktable. The rain continued. His favorite radio talk show droned on. What was the subject today? She tried to catch a word. "Potassium." The subject today was "potassium." If you ate a banana a day instead of an apple a day you would live longer. Well: good. Living longer was good. Wasn't it?

"I saw Father Bliss today," she said after a while. "He was driving up the hill as I was coming down. Big, tan, white-haired guy in a Cadillac. He looked confused, as if he couldn't remember the address. Mom says he's able to cast out demons."

Neal looked up from the photograph he was matting. "Who's Father Bliss, hon?"

"Oh Neal." She slid off the table, walked to the sink, and poured her tea down the drain. "What should I do?"

"About what?"

"Us. Them. Me."

She came up behind him and put her arms around his waist. His body felt slight, bent, soft. She looked at the blown-up photograph he was matting. "What's this?"

"West Valley in 1926. This is what the stables looked like then. Here's where the shop is now. And the old theater. And Moriarty's Emporium. And look at the railroad station. People came for miles to shop here. This place was a hub. And it could be again."

Kay followed his finger across the brown and white paper, taking in the boxy wooden buildings, the wide main street, the woman with the parasol, the boy in knickers. That could have been her and Nicky years ago. "So," she said, trying to understand. "You want to re-create the past?"

"I'd like to salvage some of the good things from it, yes."

"Like us?" She met his blank look. "Remember when I used to come in here and meet you? You'd lock the front door, turn the CLOSED sign to the street, take the phone off the hook?"

"Lost a lot of business," Neal conceded.

"You didn't use to care about business." Kay walked to a stack of prints and began leafing through them. The same old rock stars—Janis, Stevie, Grace—mixed in with the same old romantic stuff—Pre-Raphaelite nymphs with red hair and curled lips. Neal's idealized women didn't have much to do with the moody matron in a stained raincoat she had somehow turned into. She paused, eyes narrowed on a Chagall bride and bridegroom. She had just had an idea. "Want to go away? Take off for a few days? Nicky could spend the night at a friend's house and you and I could drive up the coast, like we used to, just the two of us, have dinner at a little inn, spend the night."

"What for?" Neal said.

"I don't know—conversation. Food. Romance." She paused. "Sex."

Neal shook his head. "I don't think so . . . Now what are you suddenly so mad about? Where are you going?"

"I'm leaving you. I meant to do it last November after the concert. Why didn't I? What happened? I can't believe we ever got married and had a son."

"Stop. You're doing it, hon. You're spiraling."

"Don't tell me what I'm doing. Look at what you're doing. You're the one who is making me spiral."

"I can't keep up with you," Neal said. "You just asked if we could go away next weekend and I said I didn't think so because I had too much work to do."

"Is that what you said?"

"Yes."

"Is that what you think happened?"

"Yes."

"No. Neal. No. What happened is that I propositioned you and you rejected me. Like you always do. So what is the point of being married to someone who always rejects you? What am I doing being married to you at all?"

"If you'd calm down—"

"I can't calm down. If I calmed down I'd be like you. I'd be dead. Oh, listen. There's the doorbell. Can you believe it? You actually have a customer. Now maybe you *will* have too much to do." She spun on her heel, slipped, caught herself, and strode shakily toward the front door. At the threshold of the workroom she stopped. "You don't even take me to the symphony anymore."

Neal lifted his palms. "What is that supposed to mean?"

She gulped back a surge of tears and gripped her shoulder bag to stop it from slamming against her hip as she hurried out. Even so she brushed against the man who had just come in. She tugged at the front door and his hand fell on hers.

"It's a little stuck," he said. She looked up. Chocolate-drop eyes. A gap between the two front teeth. Sunburn on the rosy cheeks. It must have been sunny in Mexico. Or Tahiti. Or wherever he'd been.

"That de Koonig book came in," she said.

He lifted his eyebrows, said nothing.

"The one you ordered last summer."

"Oh. De Kooning."

"Is that how you pronounce it? Well. It's on the Reserve Shelf. So whenever you want to come pick it up."

"How about Thursday?"

"Thursday's fine."

"At four?"

"Four?"

"It's a date."

And she was out on the street in the rain again with tears in her eyes and a grin on her face and her mother's scream in her ears and Neal's puzzled face in her mind and the heat of Charles Lichtman's brown hand on hers. It was no wonder, overloaded as she was, that she dropped her keys into a puddle by the side of the car and had to kneel in the street to retrieve them; the wonder was, as a truck driver shouted down, that she wasn't run over and killed on the spot.

Nine

"**Want** to come?" she asked Nicky Wednesday night. "I could use the company."

"No way." Nicky lay on the floor pedaling Pokey up and down with the soles of his feet. "I don't like the wind at Grandmère's," he explained. "And it's always cold."

And you're afraid of the dog, Kay thought. And the people. And you ought to be. As soon as it stops raining, she promised herself, I will take Nicky on a long holiday. We'll go to Disneyland or a dinosaur park, someplace simple and sunny. We'll eat watermelon and ride roller coasters. Charles Lichtman might come with us. "What do you think?" She held up her too-tight red sweater and her too-low black sweater for her son's inspection. They were the sexiest tops she owned and she was determined to dazzle Charles Lichtman with one of them when he came in for his art book Thursday.

"Neither," growled Nicky. "*I like this one.*" He pulled her brown sweater with the hood out of the drawer and handed it to her.

"Oh yick," she said, "that makes me look like Friar Tuck," but she packed it, along with the other two. Neal passed by the door, a stooped shadow. He had forgotten she was going to spend the night with her mother and when she'd reminded him he'd blinked and said, "Why? You've got your own family." "Do I?" she'd snapped, not sure what she meant exactly, only feeling, wildly: I don't have anything of my own. Neal had retreated, and the look he shot her now was hangdog with hurt.

"Would you please just tell me what's bothering you?" Kay asked, her voice harsh and impatient.

"Nothing."

He did not say goodbye, and frankly, Kay thought, as she kissed Nicky and slipped out through the rain with her backpack, I don't care. He can go to hell. I'm going to marry Charles Lichtman and he and I and Nicky are going to talk and laugh so much we're going to need throat lozenges before breakfast.

"I don't like pain," Francis said. "All it does is hurt you." He opened the refrigerator and showed Kay a plastic beaker of yellowish fluid. "So when she starts to feel bad I give her this. We call it the Stuff. It's something this fellow Garret cooks up. Probably illegal. I don't ask. It does the trick, so don't you ask either. She guzzles it like gin."

"What's it made out of?"

"God knows. Eye of newt and bat blood. Now these," he continued, shaking out a handful of pink, blue, and white pills and arranging them around the saucer of a rosebud demitasse, "are just your ordinary opiates. Tonight she gets extra because of her arm."

"What arm?"

"Her broken arm."

"How did she break her arm?"

"The usual." Francis set a shot glass of Scotch in the corner of the tray, picked it up, and carried it into the bedroom. "Here's your junk, junkie," he said to Ida.

Ida opened her eyes, smiled, and closed them again. "They get heroines in English," she said.

"No one knows what you're talking about." Francis set the tray down, his voice even.

"She means," Kay translated, "that junkies in England get heroin."

"Lucky stiffs," Ida corroborated.

"Glad you two understand each other," Francis said. "Because you're both too clever for me. I'm out of here. I'll be back tomorrow afternoon. Kay will stay with you all night, dear, and Greta will be here bright and early. So you're not to fear. *Comprenez-vous?*"

"Wee, wee." Ida smiled, eyes closed.

"Good." Francis bent and kissed her forehead. He wiggled his fingers goodbye at Kay and stepped swiftly out of the bedroom. His light steps paused at the dog's cage. "Don't let anyone bite you," Kay heard him tell Coco. Then he was out the kitchen door and into the Porsche and out of the driveway.

She was alone for the night with her mother.

Ida looked awful. Something had happened these last few days. Maybe it was only that she was not wearing her diamond earrings or bright red lipstick—but Kay knew it was more than that. The face on the pillow was small and damp and swollen as a lump of clay. Ida's smile shrank the minute Francis left and she let out a quick exhalation, as if she'd been holding her breath. Putting on a show for Dad still, Kay realized. And he still doesn't know it. She looked for a place to sit, found none, and perched on the edge of the wheelchair. Always the fear that if she relaxed into the chair, she would never get out. That she'd have to stay there forever. She pulled the cuticle she was gnawing out of her mouth and wiped it hastily on her jeans.

"Dad said you broke your arm."

"Oh. Is it broken? They didn't tell me that. Could I have some pills now, darling?"

"What color?"

"One of each, please."

Ida opened her mouth and Kay placed the pills on her tongue. She waved the Scotch away but took the water Kay offered in tiny sips.

Kay watched her, concerned. "Is it hard for you to swallow?"

"Everything's hard." Ida lay quiet, collecting herself. Then, "Did Francis tell you what Jim Deeds thinks is wrong with me? He thinks I'm immature." She opened her pale lips to smile and her white teeth gleamed. "He thinks I'm the most immature nineteen-year-old he's ever treated."

"He likes you," Kay said.

"Oh yes. I think so. So tell me. How's your marriage?"

"My marriage? You've never asked about my marriage before."

"I'm asking now."

"My marriage is terrible. I'm going to leave Neal and file for divorce."

"Is there someone else?"

"No. Sort of. A man I don't even know."

"It's our fault," Ida said. "We should have paid more attention to you." She seemed to sleep for a moment, then in the same quiet voice, said, "Don't get a divorce. Give old Stick-in-the-Mud another chance. Try that marriage encounter Victor talks about."

Kay tried to unwring her hands, which had flown into automatic prayer position at the word "marriage." "Neal isn't into encounters."

"Then you ought to go."

"Alone?"

"I did such a stupid thing," Ida murmured. "I thought I could walk." Then she was silent again. She seemed to be truly asleep this time.

Kay, shaken, looked around the bedroom. A lamp was on by the window, throwing a yellow glow against the dark glass. Blankets and sheets and sheepskin pads were folded in piles on the

floor. The vanity and the nightstand were cluttered with medicine
bottles, cosmetics, jewelry, more roses from Glo, and books. So
many books—junk novels, classics, biographies, how-to books,
mysteries, *Beginning French*, the Bible, volumes of poetry. No
wonder I work in a library, Kay thought. I grew up in one. She
rose and walked around, trying to be quiet. For a long time she
studied the familiar photographs on the dresser: Francis and Ida at
their wedding, sleek and elegant, both holding cigarettes; Victor in
his Boy Scout uniform; herself at age seven seated at a white Stein-
way for her first recital; the paired pictures of Nicky as a baby and
Coco as a puppy in matched silver frames. No photos of Stacy.
None of Neal. She turned as Ida stirred and opened her eyes.

"Know any good jokes?" Ida's face was still pale, but mischievous now, expectant.

Kay, caught off guard, said, "No. Only one bad one: What did
the Buddhist say to the hot dog vendor?"

"I give up."

"'Make me one with everything.'"

"Explain it, darling."

"It's . . . Buddhist. I'm going to pour this Scotch back into the
bottle. Do you want anything from the kitchen?"

"Yes. Another twenty years please."

"Oh Mom."

"And check the barometer, would you?"

"What barometer? You don't have a barometer."

"Yes we do, dum-dum. In the hall."

But the big brass barometer Francis had won at a golf club raf-
fle thirty years ago was not in the mirrored hall. Kay, as always
avoiding her own reflection, *Red-Eyed Woman with Tea Tray*,
tried to remember when she had seen the clunky instrument last.
Perhaps in the hall of two houses before this. Like the battered
chrome toaster and the checked gingham potholders, it had been
abandoned long before the move to the Heights. "Rain," she said,
obediently reading the blank wall. "Lots more rain." That's all it's

done for months, she reasoned, that's all it's ever going to do again.

"Liar," Ida called.

"Don't talk to me like that," Kay whispered. She braced, waiting for Ida's "I will if I want to" to come winging back to her, but Ida was quiet and for once must not have heard her. She swallowed the Scotch. It tasted great, strong and sharp. She went into the kitchen, rinsed the glass out in the sink, and opened the refrigerator. There wasn't much there besides the beaker of Stuff. She brought it to her nose and sniffed; it smelled like mimeograph fluid. She set it back, poured herself a glass of white wine from an open bottle, and cut off a small hunk of cheese, paring the mold off at the sink. Looking down, she saw Coco bright-eyed and abject in her cage, head on paws. She bent and unlatched the wire door, prepared for the scrape of thick claws down her thighs, the sharp bark in her face, but Coco surprised her by creeping out and meekly slinking into the bedroom, where she circled the carpet on Francis's side twice and went to sleep.

Ida's eyes had closed again when Kay returned, but she was alert. "What are you eating?" she asked.

"Cheese."

"We don't have anything but cheese."

"That's what I'm eating."

"I haven't eaten since the fall."

"When did you fall?"

"I don't know. What day is today?"

"Wednesday."

"It must have been Monday."

"I talked to you Monday. You were fine."

"No I wasn't 'fine,' Kay." Ida opened her eyes then and even across the room they were so scary Kay gasped: huge blue fire balls, the twin demon moons of her childhood nightmares. "I haven't been 'fine' since you were born if you want to know the truth."

"Not me, no ma'am, I don't want to know nuthin'."

"What?"

"I said, 'Nothing.'"

"You've always mumbled. Scared of your own shadow. That's one thing you and Buffy had in common."

"Who's Buffy?"

"That criminal you ran off from school with."

"Biff. He wasn't a criminal. He was a twenty-year-old boy."

"I never could understand one word he said. I sat him right down and told him he wasn't good enough for you and he got mad and stammered at me for five solid minutes. He did take the check though. Oh God, what am I going to do? I've been such a bad person. Aren't people supposed to change on their whatever this is? Deathbed?"

"You're not on your deathbed," Kay corrected automatically. She pulled her cuticle out of her mouth. "Did you buy Biff off?" She remembered the last thing Biff had said to her, before he roared off on his motorcycle with the waitress: "Go back to your parents. That's where you belong." She had always heard him clearly. And she had taken those words as he had intended her to, as a curse.

"He was all wrong for you. You've never had taste. Who's this new one?"

Kay hesitated. Then: "Charles Lichtman." His name sparked the air as she spoke, evoking first his curls, then his eyes, then his smile, until all of him was there in the room with her, in his honey-eyed pinks and browns. Tomorrow, she thought. He'll come into the library tomorrow; I'll see him; we'll start. Whatever it is we are going to start will start tomorrow and whatever has to end with the life I am living now will end tomorrow too. She waited, wanting something. It took her a second to recognize it herself. She wanted Ida's blessing.

But Ida turned her head away on the pillow. "Lichtman," she said. She wrinkled her nose. "Jewish? Say: I really am hungry.

Would you cut me a piece of that cheese you were having and we'll
eat like little rats together? Nibble-nibble."

Kay went back into the kitchen and scowled at the Bleeding
Heart, which had somehow been rescued from the deck and was
flourishing on the sill above the sink. She took a fresh pack from
the carton of Kent Lights Francis had stashed on top of the dryer,
tore it open, and smoked in spurts as she assembled a small supper
for her mother. Cheese sticks stacked like faggots laid for a miniature bonfire. Applesauce sprinkled with brown sugar and cinna-
mon, strawberry yogurt three days past its shelf date. She arranged
it all on a glass plate, stubbed out her cigarette, and went back
into the bedroom. Ida was wide awake and had managed to pull
herself up on the pillows. Her broken arm hung from a sling tied
around her neck. "Let's watch a video while we eat," she called.
Her smile was wide and incandescent. What was in those pills?
Vampire plasma? Kay set the plate down and looked through the
huge stack of tapes by the television set. She paused at *The Taming
of Tami.*

"Some of these are X-rated," she said doubtfully.

"We're grown-ups."

"Speak for yourself." Kay pulled *My Fair Lady* out of the pile
with relief.

"Wasn't that funny," Ida said, "when Neal was trying to set our
new VCR up?"

Kay shook her head. "I was at work," she reminded Ida as she
inserted the tape.

"Oh it was funny. Neal spent hours installing it, he was so slow
and careful, and he finally called us in from the swimming pool for
the grand christening. But Francis had taken the remote control
and was hiding it behind his back. So every time Neal turned the
set on, Francis turned it off and Neal couldn't figure out what the
problem was. Mimi Johns and I were laughing so hard we thought
we were going to pee in our pants."

Kay frowned. She could see Neal working on this VCR—trying

to please, screwdriver tucked behind his ear, instruction booklets strewn over the carpet, doing everything he could to be a good son-in-law. Failing. They had never given him a chance.

"Why do you want me to stay married?" she asked. "You don't like Neal."

"Who said that?" Ida looked genuinely amazed. "Francis and I are very fond of Neal. Now what's on that plate you brought me? I'm too hungry to eat, if that makes sense. Starving. But you'll have to help me. I can't move my arm."

Kay began to feed her. At first it felt awkward, lifting the spoonfuls, but she soon fell into known maternal rhythms, leaning toward this wrinkled old lady–baby of hers with sweet pleasure, parting her own lips to prompt Ida to part hers. "Open up," she sang. "Open wide. Now close. I love you," she added. The words fell out of her mouth, easy and apt.

"I love you too," Ida said.

They smiled.

I should have fed her all her life, Kay thought.

My Fair Lady was a slow go; Ida kept falling asleep and waking up and Kay also drifted off, slumped in the wheelchair. She woke to the sound of her mother singing along to "I Could Have Danced All Night."

"If I'd had your ability to play the piano," Ida said in a strong conversational voice as Kay, disoriented, opened her eyes, "I never would have asked for one thing more."

"You did other things," Kay yawned. The bedroom shimmered around her, hot and crowded, mirrors everywhere, loud with the television and Ida's voice. "You danced all night."

"I was doomed as a dancer," Ida said. "I was no good at all. My muscles were too short. Isn't that the craziest thing? It didn't matter how hard I worked or how long I practiced. I could not do extensions. It ruined my life."

"Mom. Ruined? Isn't that a little drama———"

"It ruined my life."

"Okay. Sorry. I never knew you cared that much."

"That's because you don't care at all. You have talent and look what you do with it. Nothing. You don't study. You don't practice. You could have been a concert pianist."

"No," Kay said wearily. "I couldn't. I wasn't good enough. That was your fantasy, not mine."

"Don't blame me. You should have had your own fantasies. Oh look." She turned the sound up on the movie. "This is my favorite part. Where she tells 'enry 'iggins to go to 'ell. Isn't it time for my Stuff now?"

"Dad said whenever you want it."

"I want it now."

"How much do you take?"

"Three bags full."

"Let's settle for a tablespoon." Kay rose to go to the kitchen.

"You're a good daughter," Ida said as Kay returned with the beaker. "I have been meaning to tell you that. A very good daughter. Except for your temper. And your sarcasm. And your sulks. Oh don't look like that. I'm kidding. We've done some terrible kidding in this family, haven't we. Listen. Is that the wind?"

"More storms," Kay said. "Just like the barometer said."

"Is that ugly old brass barometer still here? I thought we left it in the house before last. I'll be damned. No. Oops. I won't. Ha-ha. Not anymore, thanks to the blessed Father Bliss. You ought to get yourself baptized, Kay. And Nicky too. Before it's too late. Oh I wonder what they're feeding Francis at that dinner meeting tonight. He always brings me his dessert. Baked Alaska the next day is not a pretty sight. But Coco likes it, don't you, Coco? Kay? That Stuff? Give me a spoonful? Now? This is the damndest thing," she said, her face falling into soft ripples Kay had never seen before, her forehead beading with sudden sweat. "It's like labor, darling. Remember that, when your time comes. Just like labor. Only . . . different."

Kay hurried to pour a second spoonful, but by the time she

had it filled Ida was already gripped in some deep private sleep, her arm in its sling propped sideways on the blanket, her hand palm up.

She was still asleep when Francis came home at midnight. He tiptoed in, his finger to his lips, saying "Shhh" as Coco struggled to her feet and skittered toward him. Kay looked up from the piano bench, where she had been picking out the melody of a love song. She stood up quickly, her heart racing, guilty, caught. She tugged the big brown sweater down over the tee shirt she used as a nightgown, picked up the stuffed animal Nicky had slipped into her backpack as a comfort and surprise, hid it behind her back so Francis would not know she had been singing to it as if it were Charles Lichtman, and said, "What happened, Dad? What are you doing home?"

"I live here," Francis said. He looked flushed and jocular. "How was our little im-patient?"

"Fine. We watched a movie. And she ate some dinner."

"Well wunnerful. I see you've been drinking tea. Afraid I have not been drinking tea. Can I get you a nightcap before you go home?"

"I'm not going home, Dad. I thought you were going to be gone all night, remember? So I made arrangements to sleep over."

"If you want to do that, that's fine too. Might as well, actually, it's storming out there. Brandy all right?"

"I'd love a brandy. Thanks."

"Fellow sat next to me at the banquet has a great rental space out there in the new shopping center," Francis said as he returned with the bottle and two snifters. "You ought to tell Neal about it."

"Why? Neal likes the stables in downtown West Valley. He's happy there."

"Downtowns are dead." Francis settled into his leather chair, pulled off his shoes, unhooked his bow tie, and lit a cigarette. Kay sat across from him, hands folded on the couch. "Can't bring back the past. Neal's living in some dream of dime stores and soda fountains." He yawned. "Got to live in the present," he said. "Even though it'll kill you."

Kay nodded. "Sometimes the past feels like it will kill you too," she agreed. She thought about asking Francis about Biff—or the woman in New York—or his reasons for ending that affair and coming back to Ida. She opened her mouth, closed it, bounced Pokey on her knee like a child. No nerve. She had been rebuffed by Francis so often when she tried to ask about the past that she had given up. Don't be like Neal, she scolded herself. Make an effort. "Dad?" she ventured. "All our photos are of Mom's family. You never talk about your own parents, or your brothers and sisters or how you grew up. You've never told me anything about your childhood."

"Nothing to tell," Francis said. "I survived it. That's all that's asked of us."

"Francis?" Ida's voice from the bedroom.

"Coming dear."

That's not all that's asked of us, Kay thought, watching him rise and head off to her mother. Survival is only step one. She finished her brandy, shivered, and stood. Then she went in to say goodnight. She saw Ida sitting up, pale but smiling, Francis bent over her with the rosebud cup, the dog curled at his feet. She felt like an intruder as she blew a kiss and backed out. "I'll see you both in the morning," she said. "Sleep tight."

"Oh, Kay?" She turned, saw Ida leaning toward her, beaming, nightgown slipping coquettishly off her shoulder sling. She looked slight and luminous. "Buddhists don't *eat* meat." She beamed, triumphant, then paled. "What's that thing you're holding?"

Kay looked down at Pokey in her hand. "An old toy of Nicky's. He snuck it in my backpack so I wouldn't feel lonely."

"It's not a horse, is it?"

"It could be a horse. It could be a hippo. But I think it's a dinosaur. Actually," Kay remembered, "it's something you gave to him. Years ago, when he was a baby."

"I want it out of my house," Ida said.

"What?"

"Put it outside the house. Throw it in the garbage can."

Francis clucked his tongue and said, "Now now, Old Crazy," but Ida's eyes blazed and Kay shrugged and said, "Okay." She opened the front door and took a deep whiff of the clean black air, then placed Pokey carefully in the crook of a jade tree under the overhang, where he could stay dry and guard the house all night.

Ten

Rain. And more rain. Fine. Let it. Wind? Wonderful. Cold? Great. Even if the power goes out, the house will hold. Built of glass, stone, steel. I designed this house for light, Francis thought, because I know enough about dark to know I don't like it. He pinched the bridge of his nose, opened his eyes, and stared up at the pattern of branches blowing across the bedroom skylight. Not one leak this wet winter. He'd had to watch that roofer who came out last summer: What was his name? George? All Greeks are named George. Strange when you think about it. Which I don't intend to do, Francis reminded himself. He shifted his weight on the mattress. I don't intend to think about anything but getting back to sleep.

The wind pounded the windows down the length of the bedroom and Coco whinnied from the floor. Francis checked his parts: clear brain, headache centered toward the front and fitting over his eyes like a cat burglar's mask, sore throat, the usual wet weight in his lungs, the twinge in his sacrum that meant he'd have to get the back brace out of the closet and start wearing it again, cement in his bowels, half-hearted erection, burning itch in the rectum. Nothing new there. But something had awakened him. Not guilt. He had no use for guilt, never had, and anyway, nothing had happened last night. He'd meant to leave town. Meant to spend the night out, free and alone, in a quiet motel. Give himself a quick vacation before the final siege. But he missed her. Old Ida the Spida. Worried about her. Coco whinnied again and he reached down and patted her kinky head. "Shaddup," he said gently. Ida's breath sounded rough. And that frown on her forehead, that was new. Maybe Kay gave it to her. Maybe Kay and Ida spent the night boohoohooing in each other's arms, like they liked to. That whole mother-daughter thing. Started years ago, between them, when he was in New York. "Take care of your mother," he'd said as he left, a simple thing to say, any father would say it, but Kay, only three, the serious way she'd answered, like a marriage vow, "I will."

Odd about George the Greek, though. He'd thought Kay was the wife. Saw her out by the swimming pool and winked, man to man. Thought Nicky was the son. Flattering me, making me feel young so I'd give him the job. Must have thought Ida was my mother. She can't help looking old, after all she's been through, but still—hard to see her crumpled now, happened so fast, hard to be lying beside someone who looks like your mother. Happened to Oedipus—another dumb Greek.

He settled back, hands folded one upon the other under his chin. But still he felt restless. He raised his watch, looked at the glow. Almost five. Ida usually had to be lifted onto the commode at least once before now. What if she's died? he thought. A clamor of relief and grief together made him sit up. He reached across to her side of the bed, heard her moan as he touched the strap of her sling. If she could feel enough to feel bad she was all right. She was clutching her crucifix, he saw, and her night-light was still on; even after the official baptism she didn't like to sleep with it off. Jim Deeds said let her, if it helps with the delusions. That was something Jim hadn't warned him about. The goddamn delusions. Most

of them were drivel, but the other day she'd said, in a perfectly
reasonable voice, "Francis? I'm going on a journey. I have a suit-
case, and it's all packed, and I'm ready to leave," which was an elegant metaphor, really, and for a short while it had eased his worry
about her, but then she had thrown herself out of the wheelchair in
a jealous fit when he was talking to Glo Sinclair on the phone, and
last night when he asked her how the packing was coming along
she had burst into tears. "You want me to die," she'd said. No.
No. Never wanted anyone to die. Wouldn't mind if they left him
alone, however. He'd just calmed her down when Kay wandered in
with her backpack, looking lost as always, as if she'd come to the
wrong house.

A feeling he knew. He'd lived in the wrong house himself for
years. "Tell me about your childhood," Kay had said. What
childhood? He hadn't had Kay's luck. No one had ever given him
music lessons or sent him to summer camp. No one had encour-
aged him to succeed; no one had paid his bills. His father had
been a bully and a fool; lost every cent in the Depression and
never recovered, padded around the stuffy flat in his bedroom
slippers making bad deals on the telephone. His mother lived at
church. His sisters and brothers were noisy and nasty as a nest of
rats. He'd made a space for himself behind a cardboard screen in
one corner of the flat, a spare space by the only washed window
where he could do his math. When he was old enough to leave,
he took the scholarship, caught the train. Never went back. No
point. Life was what you made it. The opportunities were there.
You just had to see them.

He lit a cigarette and looked over at Ida. He remembered the
first time he'd seen her, walking down a city street in the sun, head
up, back straight, legs moving to some quick dance beat only she
could hear. And then that smile. A stunner. She'd taken his hand,
light, weightless, a sure touch that touched him still. He bent down
and kissed her cheek. When you're ready to go on that journey, he
thought, you let me know. Because you're going in comfort. You're

going first-class. Her breathing suddenly stopped and her whole body went still. He sat back, alert. Now?

He got up, creaking, stepped over the dog, and walked around to Ida's side of the bed. There, as he'd been doing for weeks, he opened her nightstand, picked the silver mirror out of the drawer, held it to her lips, and examined it under the lamp. He heard her breath start up again and then he saw it, the white cloud of her life slowly lifting off his own pale reflection. He watched his face emerge, unadorned and all alone, then he slipped the mirror back into the drawer and padded into the bathroom.

Either rain or someone crying, Ida thought. Who would cry for me?

I would.

Oh no. Not you again. I thought Father Bliss—

You did? Really? I mean he's a sweet man and good-looking in a simple way, Ida, but he's not very effectual. You put your weight on a weak reed with that one.

Francis then. Francis!

Another hero. You know how Francis loves it when you halluci-nate. How helpful he is. How warm. How sympathetic.

Kay then. Kay could get rid of you.

Kay couldn't get rid of a snowball in hell.

Victor?

I hate to see you scraping the bottom of the barrel like this, Ida, I really do.

This is so unfair, to be stuck with you after all I've been through. Damn it anyway! I wish—

If wishes were horses—

They wouldn't look like you! Big blue ugly thing. I can't stand your peepee hanging down like that. Couldn't you—whatever you're supposed to do—sheathe it? And your breath! Your breath smells like . . .

—beggars would ride.

Death. It smells exactly like death. And I'd like to ride, yes. If beggars were choosers, which you were undoubtedly going to say next, you bet I'd like to ride. I'd like to dig some spurs into you, buster, and take off like the wind.

Good. That's what I'm here for.

Really? I thought you were here to torture me.

Oh no. You've had enough torture.

That's true. I have. I surely have.

So let's go.

To Blue Horse Land?

Ida.

Why can't I stay here? I like it here. Francis keeps talking about some "journey" I'm supposed to take. I don't want to take any journey. All I want is to stop feeling so rotten and get my old life back again. Is that asking so much?

What do you think?

I think it's a perfectly reasonable request. Clear and simple: just give me my life back.

Too late.

I'll do everything better. I'll hold my temper. I'll bite my tongue. I won't try to walk! You'll see. I'll be good.

Too late.

I haven't learned French yet. I've never been to Crete.

Too—

Oh do shut up.

—late.

Well hell then. The hell with it. The absolute lousy hell with it. I give up. Tell me what to do.

Just reach up, here, put your arm around my neck and swing your legs over my back.

My arm is broken in case you've forgotten and I don't have any legs.

That doesn't matter anymore.

Maybe not to you. You've got four damn legs. What do you care? Oh listen, I'm tired. And the rain's still coming down. I used to pretend it was applause, you know. For me. I was supposed to be a star.

You're a star.

Right.

You are a star. You shine.

A three-dollar flashlight shines.

Not like you. You shine with beauty, you shine with heart, you shine with spirit.

I do?

You do. And everyone knows it. Everyone follows your light, and honors it, and envies it, and loves you for it. You shine with courage, Ida. You shine true. Now stop sulking and reach for me.

I can't.

Of course you can. You've done it a hundred times. Every time things have been rough in your life you've reached for me, and every time I come you act like you've never seen me before. As if I weren't part of you. Maybe not the best part, granted. Maybe Father Bliss got the best part. But I'm here now. I'm what you've got. So reach once more and let's go.

It's hard.

You like things to be hard.

I do not.

Reach, Ida. Are you reaching?

Dum-dum, Ida said. Can't you even tell?

Kay woke to the sound of rain and the smell of coffee. Francis had made one cup for himself and was sitting at the dining room table working the crossword puzzle. "Your mother won't wake up," he said. He stubbed his cigarette out into an overflowing ashtray and lit another without looking up from the paper. He was dressed for the office and his raincoat was folded neatly over his lap. "She won't go to sleep and she won't wake up."

"Oh-oh." Kay slipped two aspirins between her lips, went into the kitchen, and swallowed them down with water from the tap. A few drops spattered on the front of her sweater, the black one with the scooped neck, the one she'd chosen to wear for Charles Lichtman today. She brushed at the spots, feeling the material catch and pull against her shaking hands. "Do you think she's in a coma?"

"Something," Francis said. "Go take a look."

Kay tiptoed into the bedroom. Ida was even tinier today than she had been last night, a white infant bundle topped with gold curls propped up on the pillows. Her breathing was loud and rapid and two raised veins crossed back and forth in her forehead like two swords in a duel. One is good, Kay thought childishly. One is bad. If the good one wins Mom will get through this and recover. If the bad one wins she won't. She bent over, clasped Ida's hand and brought it to her lips. Ida moaned. Oh God, Kay thought, is that the broken arm? She dropped the hand quickly. "I'm sorry," she whispered. She backed out of the room.

"Did you call the doctor?"

Francis put down his pen and stared straight ahead. "Jim Deeds is in Barbados."

Kay followed his gaze to the garden outside the window. The rain was pelting the crocuses pushing up in the planter tubs. The dwarf orange trees had blown over. The outside lights were on for some reason and the swimming pool rippled in swift burnished wavelets.

"We've got to have a doctor up here. I'm sure he left someone on call."

Francis nodded, stood, and moved toward the phone.

"And Victor should know," Kay added. "And Father Bliss."

Francis lifted the receiver and dialed the hospital. Kay heard his light relaxed rumble, the graceful false laugh. Looking down, she saw the crossword puzzle open on the table. British composer, she read, blank blank *L* blank *U S*. "Delius," she wrote. Francis's gold pen was warm and solid in her hand. She put it down. "Are you hungry? Shall I make you some breakfast?"

"I don't know," Francis said. "Just had some yesterday."

Same old jokes. Kay rose to go into the kitchen when a sudden spitting noise came from Ida's room. She caught her breath and glanced at Francis. He looked pale, his face alert as a boy's above his striped oxford shirt and bow tie. Something about his expression struck her as she hurried in to Ida's side but she forgot it when she saw her mother. Ida's head had fallen to one side and a thick grey putty was pouring out of her mouth. Moving quickly, Kay staunched it with Kleenex from the box by the bed so Ida could breathe. When the flow slowed she pressed another tissue to her mother's lips, wiping them clean. Then she laid her cheek to the cross pulsing in and out on Ida's forehead. It kicked with stubborn life. Good. The phone rang from the nightstand and Francis, behind her, picked it up.

"Neal," he said. "We're having a hell of a time up here. Kay can tell you about it."

"I'll take it in the kitchen." Don't let her die while I'm gone, Kay prayed, handing the Kleenex to Francis and hurrying to the other phone. "Neal," she said, sinking against the kitchen wall. "I'm glad you called. Mother's bad. This might be the day." There was silence on the line.

"You knew this was going to happen," Neal said.

"But that doesn't help when it does happen." She straightened, easing her shoulders. Strange, she thought. I can almost feel my hackles rise. Whatever hackles are, I have them with Neal. "Do you have any sympathy or help to offer? Or are you just going to be an ass?"

"Do you have to call me names?"

"What's going on with us?"

"I don't know. What is? You tell me."

"Okay. I'll tell you. We're fighting but we don't have time to pay attention to it. This is what I need you to do right now: Give

Nicky a lunch and a dollar for the field trip. His class is supposed to go on a whale watch today unless they're rained out. Then I want you to call Mrs. Holland and tell her I can't come to work. Tell her someone's coming in for an art book and it's under my desk in the left-hand shelf; she'll find it."

"Is that all?"

"No. Yes. Tell me you love me."

"Oh babe."

"Joke. Listen. My mother's dying. There's stuff coming out of her mouth and the thing is, she was fine last night. We watched *My Fair Lady*, she sang, she made sense, she even ate a little when I fed her."

"What did you feed her?"

"Applesauce and strawberry yo——— No. Neal. I'm sure it was not the yogurt. You're not going to tell me the yogurt put her in a coma."

"It's a known fact, Kay, that dairy——"

"Is Nicky there?"

"I'm just telling you."

"I'd really like to talk to Nicky now."

"Hi, Mom." Nicky's clear enunciation, so welcome. "I'm sorry about Grandmère. Daddy says she's sick. Are you all right? It's really storming down here! We might have a flood. Daddy's got candles and the flashlight on the table in case our electricity goes out. He says if the creek gets really high we can fish in the living room!"

"Your dad said that?" So he could be kind and playful. He could make a joke. Just not with her. She set the phone down and returned to the bedroom. Francis was hunched in the wheelchair staring into Ida's face.

"I don't like this frown," he said. "She's struggling too hard. Tell you what. We're going to give her a little help-me-out. Why don't you go get the Stuff."

"Did the doctor——?" Kay began, but Francis waved his finger at her.

"The doctors have done enough damage."

She stared at him a second, then went into the kitchen. She found the beaker of medication on the refrigerator shelf, brought it back, and watched as Francis poured the drug into the demitasse and picked up a silver spoon left on the nightstand.

"You might want to close the door," he said.

"Why?"

He looked at her and Kay edged the bedroom door shut. He was right. Someone might come in. Someone might see them. But see them doing what? Coco looked up from the floor, eyes black and bright. Kay's head throbbed, her face felt hot. She watched Francis, hoping he would say something to her, explain what they were doing. What were they doing? She was doing what she was told—she was obeying her father. It felt good to obey him, to stand beside him like this, to be his assistant. She fixed her eyes on his hands as he filled the silver spoon to the brim, bent over Ida, and tried to insert it between her lips. Ida's lips would not part. Kay leaned closer and touched Ida's ear with her breath. "Open," she said, in the singsong nursery voice she had used the night before when she fed her. "Open wide. That's good. Now close."

A single large clear tear pooled at the corner of Ida's eye but her lips relaxed and Francis slipped the spoon in.

"Now swallow," Kay said. "Swallow it down."

The tear jelled and trembled. Ida's throat contracted and some of the medication went down. Francis pulled the spoon out, re-filled it from the cup. "Oh no," Kay said. "That's too much." Francis looked at her, stony. "Open," Kay stammered. "Now close. Now swallow."

When the cup was empty Francis handed it to her, and Kay took it with the beaker and spoon back to the kitchen. Her pulse was beating as fast as the rain on the flagstones outside. The grains of undissolved aspirin still burned in her throat and she felt a dizzy, distanced panic, as if she had stepped on a moving raft without asking first where it was going. We just gave her a help-me-out, she thought, something extra to ease the pain. If it's too much she'll throw it up. She put the beaker back in the refrigerator, washed the cup and spoon, dried them, and put them away. She heard Coco's sharp bark and looked out the kitchen window to see Victor's car pull into the driveway a length before Father Bliss's white Cadillac. If only she hadn't cried, Kay thought. She pressed her fists to her own eyes but they were wide open and dry.

Ida's tears formed and reformed all morning. Not even Father Bliss could stop them. He stayed with Ida in the closed bedroom while Victor and Stacy prayed at the dining room table and Francis worked on his crossword. Kay stood at the window looking out at the rain and smoking until she could stand her uselessness no longer, then she opened the refrigerator door, blinked blindly past the beaker, and pulled out two blackened bananas and an egg. In the cupboard she found flour, bran, oil. She began to stir a muffin batter together.

Coco followed her as she moved around the kitchen, her cold nose bumping into the back of her knees. "Go bark at someone," Kay suggested, and Coco promptly began barking at her, the yips so insistent that Kay finally had to stop and scratch her hard frizzy head until she calmed down. When Father Bliss came out of Ida's room he asked for a glass of water and Kay watched him sip it, wondering what he would say if she told him her sins, if she confessed then and there that she had overdosed her mother.

Silent, she poured the muffin batter into a tin. Father Bliss patted his lips. "Nuts?" he asked.

"I looked," Kay answered, "but all I could find were cocktail peanuts."

"Those wouldn't work," Father Bliss agreed and Kay, comforted, said, "No." The priest left, pausing to talk to Francis outside under the overhang; Francis was standing there watching the rain, drinking Scotch. The two men laughed. Then Father Bliss walked out to his car and Francis came back in, poured himself another Scotch, picked up a book, and settled down in the recliner.

Kay put the muffins into the oven and slipped back into Ida's room. She hoped Ida would open her eyes and ask for something, anything, Kay would get her anything. But Ida was still unconscious and the tears were still coming. A hospice nurse arrived, read from a chart, and gave her some morphine. A technician drove up with an oxygen tank that was somehow defective and left to get another one. Howard Bernard dropped off a casserole he'd made himself, the Forrests phoned, a florist delivered a huge bunch of white roses from Glo, a young Indian doctor in a turban appeared in the driveway in the pouring rain on foot, stayed a minute, and disappeared again.

And still Ida cried. Her tears were like nothing Kay had ever seen before, they were like tears from a fairy tale, mermaid eggs, each one perfectly oval, clear, gelatinous, and as she knelt by her mother's bed dabbing each one up with a tissue, another one formed. I could stay here forever, Kay thought. This could be my job. This could be the one job I am meant to do and can do well. She bent her head praying she could continue to do this job well forever. I still haven't said what I wanted to say, she thought. I still haven't said, *Thank you.* I still haven't said, *I love you, really love you. Oh Mother! I really love you!* But before she could lean close and frame the words out loud Ida gave a loud gasp and her mouth hissed open like a fighting cat's, pale lips tight over small sharp teeth. The technician stopped fiddling with the new oxygen machine and he and the nurse hurried to the bed.

"Get everyone in here," they said.

They all stood at the far end of Ida's bed. Stacy swayed, humming to herself, holding one of Victor's hands and one of Kay's. Neal was somehow there—when had he arrived?—holding the other. Neal's touch was warm and solid, and Kay was glad for its human weight, but when she glanced up and saw Neal's eyes still averted she frowned and fought the pull to sink against his shoulder. She looked at Francis. He was standing apart, his hands folded, his eyes on Ida. We could not, Kay told herself, have given

Mom too much; we would never do such a thing; we gave her just enough to help with the pain; not enough to even do that, for look at her: still crying, still in pain. Ida's breathing was terrible, loud and harsh as a stalled car. "Brain stem breathing," the hospice nurse explained. "It should end soon."

But it didn't. Breath after breath: it hurt to hear it. Mom's still fighting this, Kay thought. Mom's still suffering, and we're still standing around, like we always have, doing nothing. She is dying right in front of us and we're letting her, and she's dragging it out. Milking the moment. Everyone wants to get this over with, Kay thought, but her.

She dropped her eyes, paralyzed with love and pity and a stone-hard intense irritation. Let go, she thought. Give up. Just die. She swallowed hard, the smell of scorched sugar suddenly making her eyes sting. The muffins! She released Neal's and Stacy's hands and backed on tiptoe out of the bedroom. The kitchen swirled with char-coal-colored fumes and as she pulled the blackened tin out with a tea towel, burning her wrist, the smoke alarm over the door went off and Coco began to howl. Before Kay could climb up on the foot-stool to dismantle the alarm she heard the nurse call her name from the bedroom and, clutching the screwdriver, she hurried back in.

Ida lay on the pillows, white and quiet, eyes open, one last tear pearled under her lid. Neal turned to Kay. "Oh babe," he said. "You missed it."

And she wanted to cry then but something moved, something cheerful and restless and pushy and free, urging her swiftly toward the closed windows. "Smoke," she explained, as the siren contin-ued to scream from the kitchen. "Smoke," she repeated, as the fresh morning wind blew into the room, pushing the sheer white curtains inward, lifting the sheets up over Ida's broken white arm, cuffing Francis against his wrists as he bent over the bed with the silver mirror in his hands, but it wasn't the word "smoke" she wanted to say, it was "soul." My mother's soul, Kay wanted to say, wants out.

She tugged at the door to the garden, stepped into the fresh air, and walked toward the pool. The rain had just stopped and the sky was settling like a wash of winter rags, eggshell and pewter, with a core of pure silver in the center that opened as she watched. That's where Ida's soul longed to go: straight up. She heard something small rush by her ears and felt its quick delight as it shot through the air, tumbling like an invisible sky otter in playful release, gay and graceful and glad to be out of its crippled body at last. Oh, I'll miss you, Kay thought. Go and God bless.

Eleven

"Sit," Peg Forrest ordered as Kay moved past with a tray of sandwiches. "You're working too hard. Can't you sit down and visit?"

Kay paused before her mother's old friend but she was reluctant to sit. The tablecloth had a large stain she hadn't noticed before. Ida would hate to know her "going away party"—as everyone insisted on calling it—was being hosted in a hastily cleaned house with supermarket food laid out on soiled lace. She set the sandwiches over the spot, repositioned the crystal bowls of nuts and mints, relit one of the candles, and perched next to Peg on the couch. Peg looked into her face with a frank concern that made Kay want to cry. Everything made her want to cry, perhaps because she hadn't yet. No time, she told herself. Too much to do.

"I'm sorry there's nothing to drink," she apologized. "Victor won't let me serve the champagne until Father Bliss gets here."

"No one needs a drink," Peg assured her.

Kay nodded, not so sure. Nancy Carpezio had already asked twice. Other guests had glanced longingly at the empty glasses set on the table as they moved around the living room, chatting in small groups, subdued and pleasant. The women were wearing wool dresses and knit suits in pastel shades; the men were uniformed in grey and navy blazers. Francis wandered from group to group like an affable stray. He had changed into the dark suit Kay had laid out for him, but his cowlick stuck straight up and for some reason he had put on white socks. He held a glass of unwatered Scotch that Victor had not been able to get him to put down and Kay watched, worried, as he used it to gesture toward the swimming pool when a guest asked him where the bathroom was.

"Poor man," Peg said. "He's exhausted. This has been a terrible time for all of you." Kay pulled her eyes away from Francis and nodded. Peg's shoulder felt warm and solid and the hand covering hers was wrinkled but strong. Peg would never know that Francis called her "Pig" because of her blond eyelashes and red cheeks or that Ida used to push her nostrils up with her middle finger and mouth *Oink* whenever Peg phoned.

The couch sank lightly as Glo Sinclair settled beside them. Kay caught a whiff of sharp perfume and heard the scratch of manicured nails as Glo adjusted her skirt. She had arrived half an hour ago with a huge jar of Russian caviar to contribute to "Ida's party" but she had not, Kay saw, taken her jacket off yet. "I was wondering," Glo said in her harsh voice, "what your father's plans are now."

"I don't think he has any." Kay tried to keep her voice light. Why didn't she like this woman? Everyone else did. Victor treated her with the reverence he accorded anyone with money, and even Neal brightened when he was around her. "It's only been three days."

"He needs to get away," Glo said.

From us? Kay thought. Some of us might want him here. She released Peg's hand with a squeeze and rose to get back to work. She still had the turkey to slice and the coffee to measure out into the percolator. Greta had left for Cabo San Lucas two days ago with a tearful wringing of hands, singing out that she hoped they would understand, but she loved Ida too much to ever come back to work in her house again. Neal had silently helped with the vacuuming and dusting, but now he was nowhere to be seen; he had slipped into the television room an hour ago and had not emerged since. Nicky and Stacy had disappeared too, taking Coco on a walk up the mountain. Victor, blond hair blow-dried, cheeks healthy red, was working the living room, stopping to tell everyone that he found it "just a little odd" that Father Bliss had not shown up yet. "My pastor," Kay heard him say, "would have been here an hour ago."

Just then the doorbell chimed and Kay looked up but it was Zabeth; she was wearing a minidress and fishnet hose and carrying a silver tray of small black lamb tongues floating in mustard sauce, an offering so peculiar Kay could only take it and stare. "It's delicious," Zabeth said. "Trust me."

"Okay." Kay inhaled Zabeth's familiar odors of sweat and tobacco interlaced with something light and springlike as celery. "I'm sure glad to see you."

"I wanted to be here for you." Zabeth pressed Kay's elbow with her fingernails and knifed into the living room. Kay saw her walk straight toward the group where Francis stood and kiss him on the cheek, leaving an imprint of blackberry lipstick. Francis touched his cheek, pleased. There was something different about his hand, Kay noticed. It looked bigger somehow. Barer. Oh-oh. She turned to Victor.

"Dad took his wedding ring off."

"Speak of the devil." Victor, not hearing, pushed past her to greet Father Bliss, who had just come through the door. Kay introduced them, then carried the priest's cashmere coat into the bedroom. She stopped in the doorway, taking in the bare polished surfaces of the vanity and nightstand, the empty space where the wheelchair had been, the stiff new bedspread heaped with the coats of Ida's friends. She felt the weariness she had been fighting buffet her again as she laid the coat next to Hazel Kent's Persian lamb and Peg Forrest's hand-knit cardigan. She had been working steadily since Ida's death. Francis had wanted all of Ida's things cleared out of this room. Kay had filled thirteen plastic garbage bags with silk dresses and underwear to give to thrift shops. She had thrown a wheelbarrow of pills away. She had repapered the emptied drawers, vacuumed the emptied closets. She had bought new sheets, new towels. Had it made any difference? She looked at the fresh pillows piled on Ida's side of the bed and again she saw the small golden head, the tears. She swallowed, turned, and walked to the window. What if she had misinterpreted that wild rush of wind? What if it didn't mean Ida was released, at rest? What if it meant Ida wanted revenge for her murder? Had she been murdered? Kay rested her tired forehead against the cool glass.

She heard footsteps and saw Francis wandering outside alone, looking rumpled and lost, headed toward the swimming pool, a cigarette in one hand, the freshly filled glass of Scotch in the other. She pushed the window open. "Hey, Dad," she called. "Come on back. The priest is here. We have to pray now."

Francis turned and looked at her in the polite, mildly attentive way he had been looking at her, listening to her, for the past three days. "Well," he said, "if we have to." He ground his cigarette out on the flagstones. "Got to do what my kids tell me," he explained to Glo Sinclair, who was outside too, Kay saw, picking her way toward him across the puddles and fallen tree branches left by the storm. "If I don't, they'll get mad at me. Now Victor, that's no problem. Victor can't stay mad. But Kay? Mad? Not a pretty sight."

What are you talking about? Kay grumbled to herself as she closed the window and headed into the living room. When have I ever been mad at you? I've done everything you wanted and then some. And when have you ever thought I was a pretty sight? Never. Glo Sinclair is your idea of a pretty sight. Zabeth is your idea of a pretty sight. Leave me out of it.

Nicky came up out of nowhere and took her hand, an act so welcome it made her knees buckle. She looked down into his toothy heart-shaped face. He was like a present she had forgotten to open. "Come on," he said. "It's time to say goodbye to Grand-mère."

"It's what Ida would have wanted"—that's what everyone said. After prayers came champagne and the party tumbled on through the long afternoon. Ida would have wanted Mimi Johns and Wes Jasper to embrace out by the pool; she would have wanted Wes's wife to find them and throw their wineglasses in the water; she would have been glad those were the plastic glasses and not the good crystal. She would have approved of Ansel Lipscott announcing that he had "declared himself" to her once and been rebuffed. Even though everyone had heard this story a thousand times from Ida herself, it was good to get it "straight from the ass's mouth," as Francis whispered, none too softly, to Nancy Carpezio. "What did a beautiful woman like Ida ever see in Francis?" Ansel asked, raising his hands in a mournful show of mystification, and everyone looked at Francis, who said "I never could figure that out," while Glo Sinclair clicked the gold clasp of her purse like a referee with a stop watch. Ida would have been glad for the late winter sun falling on Father Bliss's silver head as he pocketed Victor's business card, and she would have been glad for the Chinese vase of white tulips slowly opening on the dining room table, blooming in the heat of old friends' voices before falling petal by petal onto the lace cloth with its hidden stain.

Kay fetched and carried, served and smiled. She had been to parties like this all her life and she had seen these handsome, cheerful, well-to-do people age as she aged—although none of them, she marveled, watching Hazel Bentley flirtatiously punch Howard Bernard on the shoulder, had ever quite grown up. Maybe the Forrests, who sat hand in hand, looking genuinely sad, as if they had really come to mourn Ida, had grown up. Or maybe they were preoccupied with problems she knew nothing about. She remembered Ida saying that Pete Forrest had been having prostate trouble. Looking around, she remembered other things Ida had told her: Nancy Carpezio was going through a difficult divorce. Pepper Mills had had a mastectomy. The DeWitts' oldest son had recently changed his name from Robert to Barbie and one of the Morrissey twins had tried to kill herself, leaving a note blaming them. Everyone here had suffered. Everyone here had been hurt. Ida had been one of the first to die, but then Ida had always been a leader.

"You're the musical daughter?"

Kay paused with the teapot in her hand and looked into the pretty face of a woman about her age. The woman had cropped red hair and was wearing a leotard and a colorful shawl wrapped around her slim hips like a skirt. Her brown eyes held Kay's with open curiosity. "I knew Ida from my painting class," the woman explained. "She was one of my students. She was . . ."

Kay waited, the musical-daughter-smile dead on her face while the art teacher searched for the right word.

". . . formidable."

Kay exhaled, surprised and relieved.

"Her determination to succeed. And the way she lashed out when she didn't. I'll never forget the day she cut her canvas up. We were all afraid she was going to slash her wrists with the palette knife next. Or cut my nose off. I was the one who said her colors were muddy." The art teacher ruffled her short hair and chuckled. "But she was wonderful, wasn't she? Dynamic. And she was so proud of you. I meant to get to your concert last fall but the P.S. on her invitation put me off: 'Come say hello to my daughter and goodbye to me,' it said. 'I have a terminal illness.'"

Kay pressed the teapot to her chest, trying to feel the heat through her clothes. "My mother sent out invitations to my concert? That announced her own death?"

"Yeah, it was a little like getting—I don't know—cow poop in the mail. Hey, you look shook up. I'm sorry if I said anything I shouldn't."

The woman grinned, showing perfect white teeth and two deep dimples. She probably says things she shouldn't all the time, Kay thought, and gets away with it. She suddenly remembered Ida talking about this art teacher. She had called her The Braless Wonder.

"My friend Charles says I talk the way I paint," the woman continued. "I blurt."

"Charles Lichtman?"

"You know Charles?"

"No. I mean I've seen him. Are you his . . . girlfriend?"

"No way. But he does owe me lunch, the ho. Oops. There I go again." The woman covered her lips and rolled her eyes. I like hos, Kay told herself. She put down the teapot and offered the woman a lamb tongue, which she accepted at once and cut into with quick satisfaction.

"We've got to go, dear." Peg Forrest touched her shoulder. "We'll see you when Francis gets back from his trip."

"What trip?"

"He's decided to drive up the coast and rest for a week or two. He told us you're in charge until he gets back."

"In charge of what?"

"Hey, Kay," Ansel boomed, "your dad says he can't play golf with me again unless you say it's all right."

"Well he never could play golf——" Kay began.

"You tell 'em," Francis said. "She's the boss now, Ansel, gotta do what she says."

"No I am not," Kay said.

But the thought pleased her. And the sight of her slight, pale father pleased her too. He looked rumpled and rowdy. The cigarette trembled in his hand; his belt was too big and flopped out of its loops; someone had tucked a tulip into his buttonhole. If I were his "boss," Kay thought, I would put him to bed for a week and not let him go anywhere.

"Wake up." In one of her hot fits of kindness, Zabeth was at Kay's elbow, slipping a Sherman cigarette into her palm as a goodbye gift. She smiled, her small red eyes as merry inside their spiked lashes as coals burning in a grate.

"Don't go." Kay pulled Zabeth aside. "I need to ask you something. What was in that medication Garret whipped up for Mother?"

"Who knows. Did it work?"

"I think it killed her."

"Be real."

"No. I think . . ." Kay amended, "*I* killed her. I gave her too much."

"Look Kay, could I tell you something? No one—but no one—do you understand me?—could kill your mother. Ida was tough. If you gave her too much whateveritwas, it was because she was in a lot of pain and wanted you to. You always did what she wanted you to."

"No, I did not—" Kay began, but Zabeth stopped her.

"You still think she wanted you to be this famous pianist person? Sit on a stage and get all the attention? No, no. Think again. Ida wanted you to be just who you are." Zabeth's voice softened. "Your own sweet self. Look. I feel bad. I'll be a better friend. I'll do more things with you. I know I've spent too much time with Garret. I'm like that when I'm in love. But I'll be better, I promise. In the future."

"The future. I keep forgetting I've got one."

"A great one." Zabeth looked into Kay's eyes. "Listen to this." And in a stoned, smoky voice she leaned close and sang "Ding-Dong! The Witch Is Dead" into Kay's ear.

The party was still going strong in the living room. No one needed her there. She drifted down the hall toward the bathroom. On the way she heard voices from the studio so she walked up the ramp, pushed open the door, and looked inside. She hadn't cleaned up in here yet and Ida's old projects stood shrouded, more mournful than the real mourners downstairs. But Stacy and Nicky had found the radio, turned it on to a rock station, and were sitting on the floor, surrounded by pillows, playing Sorry.

"May I come in?" Kay asked. "Or don't you want company?"

"You don't have to ask," Stacy said. "We always want you here."

"Always," Nicky echoed, his eyes on the board, intent, ready to score. "But you have to apologize." He raised Pokey up with one hand. "You left him out in the bushes."

"Ouch. Sorry, Nicky."

Nicky nodded, shouted "I'm 'Sorry' too!" to Stacy and swooped his hand down to remove one of her men.

Stacy pressed her tongue against her teeth. "You are sooooo good at this game."

Kay kicked off her shoes, curled up on the daybed, and watched. "What did you think of Father Bliss?" she asked. "His eulogy?"

"I liked it," said Stacy.

"I liked it too," Kay admitted. It had been a quirky talk, hard to follow, something about God being the hurt and jilted host at an enormous dinner party no one came to, but somewhere in the middle she had thought: What if there is a God? and what if He does love us? and what if Mom is with Him? sitting at the end of His dinner table holding forth on her bowel movements? and these thoughts had pulled her lips up for a second and eased her sore heart. "Except he kept calling her Ada." She yawned and wiggled her toes. It felt good to lie down. "You're going to get sick if you don't slow down," Neal had warned her that morning. She had seen his worried look. But it hadn't stopped her from snapping something stupid back. "I don't want to 'slow down,'" she'd said. "I might turn into you." "Better than turning into your mother," he'd said.

"What do you think makes a person get sick?" she asked now.

"Lack of forgiveness," Stacy said promptly.

"But Mother didn't have anyone to forgive."

"She had to forgive herself," Nicky said.

"I won't let you watch daytime TV anymore if you talk like that, honey."

Nicky lowered his head and said, "It's true."

"You're so wise. So tell me. What do you think she had to forgive herself for?"

"For hitting me that time with her fake leg."

Kay nodded, propped herself on her elbow, and studied her son. No visible scars. But the nightmares continued, worse all the time. And that tremor down his backbone as once again he shouted, "Sorry!"—that was new, the nervous twitch. She had not protected him well enough from herself, her marriage, or her mother. What sort of childhood had he had? She remembered yanking the artificial leg out of Ida's hand last Easter, sticking it on a top shelf of the coat closet where the old drunk in her wheelchair couldn't get it. Oh God, she thought. The leg is still up there. "Did you forgive her?" she asked.

Nicky didn't answer at first. Then: "She sent me twenty dollars the next day."

Twenty dollars and a beautifully written, heartbreaking note: yes. But all the rest, Kay thought. All that "lashing out" the art teacher had mentioned. The red lips stretched in anger: *You did this to me.* The stump still trying to kick. *You made me a cripple.* "I'm not sure I've ever forgiven her," Kay said.

"You had more to forgive than the rest of us," Stacy said.

Kay looked up. It was easy to see why Victor loved Stacy. As to why Stacy loved Victor, well—what was life without mystery. Stacy smiled toward the door and said, "Howdy, cowboy" to Victor, who had come up the ramp and was peering into the room. "Your genius nephew is wiping me out."

Kay made room for Victor on the edge of the bed and he sank heavily beside her. "Look." He opened his palm and showed Kay a key. "Dad gave me Mom's Volvo."

Kay felt a twinge, just a twinge, she told herself, of envy. She and Neal could have used that car; the Lincoln had been dying for years and Neal's van needed new brakes. "You just got a new car," she permitted herself. "What are you going to do with another one? Sell it?"

"That's the trouble." Victor's face flushed and twisted. "I promised my pastor I'd tithe the commission of the next automobile I sold to the church."

Stacy looked up from her place on the floor but did not say a word.

"So don't sell it," Kay offered. "Keep it and let Stacy drive it."

"Stacy's doing fine with the bus. The thing is, if I sell it, I'd have a lot of money. Volvos have fantastic resale value."

"Sell a new BMW to Father Bliss next week and tithe that commission to the church," Kay said.

Victor looked at the floor.

"Or will that be a big commission too?"

"Better pray," Stacy advised. She turned back to Nicky. "And 'Sorry' to you, tiger," she added as she swept up his men.

"Ah-ha," said Francis, peering in from the doorway. He ducked and stepped inside, swaying slightly. "The children's room. Here, children." He threw a small silk pouch into Stacy's lap and tossed another, larger, pouch at Kay. It struck her on the shoulder and glanced off the bed. Victor picked it up and handed it to her with a long steady look. "Mom's jewels," he said.

"I don't want them." That wasn't true, but Kay made the gesture and pushed the bag back. Stacy, more honest than she, pressed her tongue fatly to her upper lip and began to open her pouch with poised fingers.

"Oh Daddy Francis," Stacy cooed, her voice hushed. "The little gold watch! Are you sure? Oh I always loved this little gold watch. And the rubies! Victor! Look! He gave me the rubies!"

"Open yours," Francis said to Kay. He rocked, smiling, his hands in his pockets. Kay could not tell how drunk he was.

"Are you sure you want us to have these?" she asked.

"I'm not sure of anything," Francis said. "But that shouldn't affect you."

"Everything affects me," Kay said.

Francis, still smiling, shrugged. Kay opened the pouch and spilled the contents into her lap. Out fell a jumble of gems and junk. Gold chains and real pearls were tangled in with the plastic lanyard Victor had made for Ida one summer in day camp and a string of seashells Kay had bought her years ago in Carmel. She picked out the diamond teardrop earrings and centered them uneasily in her palm. Then she picked up the sapphire ring. It had been on Ida's hand the morning she died.

"Come sit here." Stacy patted the stool in front of Ida's easel and drew Francis into the room. "Tell us the story of some of these things."

"Not much to tell." Francis sat down, pulled out his cigarettes, and crossed his legs. "You all know about the sapphire. Ida's reengagement ring."

"Reengagement?" Kay turned it in her fingers. "I thought this was the original ring."

"No, no. Ida's first engagement ring is in there somewhere, one of the smaller diamonds. This sapphire was the one she really wanted. She saw it in a window downtown. I borrowed the money and bought it for her a few years after we married, to cheer her up."

Kay stared at the ring, trying to repiece the past. "Was this after you came back from New York? After she tripped on my toys and fell down the stairs?"

"Correct-o."

"The first time she was in the hospital?"

"No, Kay. The first time she was in the hospital," Francis said, lighting a cigarette with a snap of his lighter, "was when she quote unquote almost died giving birth to you. Now these rubies that Stacy likes so much are what I bought off an Algerian in the flea market in Paris. One thing you're not supposed to do, y'know, is buy off the street. But Ida liked them. Cost me forty dollars each. Turns out when we get home they're worth four thousand! Al down at Straub and Levy's made them up into earrings but he was mad; said I had too much luck; said the only thing he ever got in Paris was the clap."

"What's that?" Nicky asked.

"Don't you know anything?" Francis said.

"It's like a cold." Kay held her breath and slipped the sapphire on her finger. It was too small for her ring finger; she had to wear it on her pinky. It perched on her freckled skin uneasily, the dark blue mocking her gnawed cuticles and reddened knuckles. Still, though it didn't look good, it felt good, like having a solid piece of Ida to keep, a chunk of her courage and will to use as a charm. "I love it," she lied. "I'll never take it off."

"Wear it, sell it, do what you want with it." Francis stubbed his cigarette out into Ida's old palette and rose. "It doesn't matter to your mother anymore. And it never did matter to me."

"Thank you so much," Stacy breathed. She reached up her arms and hugged Francis's knees. He looked down, looked up, made a face, droll.

"Thank you," Kay echoed. She was about to rise and try to hug him too but Francis stepped nimbly away and down the ramp and was gone. They heard Nancy Carpezio call, "We wondered where you were," then they sat in silence for a while. Finally Victor said, "Four thousand apiece or four thousand for the set?" and Kay reached down and wove his shoelaces together with the lanyard. She watched the ring glint as her hands moved.

"I'll look like Jerry Lee Lewis when I play the piano," she said, sitting up. "I hate it," she added.

"But it's a beaut——" Stacy began. Seeing Kay's face, she stopped, and, oddly gentle, added, "Don't worry."

. . .

Don't worry about anything. If your life feels bleak, and blank, and wrong, somehow wrong, if your eyes are dry, your heart empty, your breath shaky—don't worry. If Neal goes home without saying good-bye, Nicky looking back over his shoulder to say, "But what about Mom?"—don't worry. If that art teacher dimples as she bounces bralessly off, probably for a late date with Charles Lichtman—don't worry. Shake hands with the guests. Look into Father Bliss's blank eyes and thank him again. Find rides for those too drunk to drive. Accept Victor's "wish" that he could help clean up and his offer to do more "next time." Do not say, "You mean after the next funeral?" Don't say anything at all. Just do what you've always done and clean up the mess yourself. If you can clean up the mess outside then maybe the mess inside will straighten out too. Do not think you killed your mother. You did not kill your mother.

Kay stood at her parents' sink in an apron and Greta's tight yellow rubber gloves, loading the dishwasher. It wasn't late—a little after eight. Neal would be asleep on the couch by the time she got back to the cottage but Nicky would be waiting up for her; she'd have time to tuck him in. It seemed like ages since she had done anything as normal as tuck her son in. She looked up as Francis padded into the kitchen in his white socks. He smiled at her and, surprised, she smiled back.

"I was thinking about the times you sang Victor and me to sleep," she said, to say something. "When Mom had one of her headaches."

"Ah yes." Francis closed his eyes and in the true sweet tenor Kay remembered sang: "'With 'er 'ead tucked underneath 'er arm, she walks the bloody tower.'"

"That song scared Victor."

"Everything scares Victor. That's why he's so reliant on God Almighty." Francis's voice was still amiable, matter-of-fact, but there was an edge to it and Kay retreated.

"I've finished up so I'll go on home now," she said.

"What? This isn't home? You've been here so long I thought you'd moved in. Not," he continued, getting the Scotch bottle she had just put away back down from the shelf and pouring more into his glass, "that this place has ever seemed like home."

"I thought you liked this house. You designed it."

"We don't always like what we create, you know. No. Your mother liked it. She had a thing for castles. I never cared for it much myself."

"So where," Kay asked, "would you like to live?" We're having a conversation, she told herself. Don't get excited—but this is a real conversation. The second or third in the last few days. Nothing big. Nothing important. But words. Back and forth. Like a regular daughter and a regular father. Amazing. Maybe he will tell me something about his childhood. Or his time in the Army, or college, or New York, or his first job, or his work now. Maybe he will tell me what he thinks and feels and wants from the world.

"I'd like a room in a hotel," Francis said.

Kay, attentive, worked with this, and came up with a penthouse suite in the city. "Like the Mark Hopkins?"

"No. Like the Traveller's Inn near the bus station in Rancho Valdez. A downtown dump where I could smoke cigars and read the paper all day in peace." Francis took a swallow of his drink and pointed at the counter. "Don't forget your loot."

Kay saw the sapphire glowering there, abandoned. She flushed as Francis picked it up, blew it off, and slipped it onto her outheld hand.

"They had to cut it off her, y'know," Francis said. "Henry Service, down at the morgue, called me, said, Francis, it's stuck, what do I do? I told him, take the damn finger. What's one more amputation."

"Oh don't tell me that," Kay winced. "That makes me sick."

"I didn't know what else to do." Francis set his glass down too close to the edge of the counter, caught it before it fell, laughed softly. He's as lost as I am, Kay thought.

"I just feel . . ." she started. Stopped. Took a deep breath. "That everything I've ever done has hurt her. Even at the end, when we were giving her extra medication. I don't think we helped her. I think we killed her."

"What extra medication?" Francis's eyes were clear, and, drunk as he was, swaying, still smiling, they were surprisingly steady.

"When we overdosed her."

"I don't know what you're talking about," Francis said. "But I know I don't like the sound of it. This Stuff," he finished, opening the refrigerator door and pointing to the beaker, "isn't medication, exactly. It's happy water." He lifted the beaker out and held it to the light. The liquid sloshed, homely and harmless-looking as pickle juice. "Hate to see it go to waste. Want some?" He reached for a goblet.

"You mean . . . drink it?"

"That's the idea, sweetie."

"I don't know." Kay shifted, uneasy. She had not had anything to drink today aside from black coffee. Zabeth's Sherman was still untouched in her purse. She'd been good. She planned to stay good, stop drinking, stop smoking. Change. But he's my father, she thought. And he just called me sweetie.

"All right," she said.

"Good-o." Francis reached for another goblet and poured. There was only enough for an inch apiece. One inch couldn't hurt her. "Good girl," he said. He raised his glass to hers and they clicked. "You won't regret it."

But she did. When she woke up it was dark and she had nothing on. At first that felt fine. She had one hand over one breast and the other tucked between her thighs. Then she realized where she was. In her parents' bed. On her father's side. She sat up. A siren began to buzz in her head and her heart began to swell and flare like a house collapsing in fire. She looked at the clock. One A.M. She leapt out of the bed. She found her shoes in the living room, lying in front of the leather recliner. Her nylons and underwear were in the back bathroom. Her dress was on the floor of the studio. The pouch of jewels was still in the pocket of the discarded apron and the sapphire ring was somehow in the pouch. She pulled her clothes on and slipped from room to room but there was no sign of Francis. He was not in the basement, not in the guest room. When she ran out to the garage she saw the Porsche was gone. The night was dark and cold and amazingly empty and her brain was dark and cold and empty too. She could not summon an image, a word, a single sensation from the last four hours.

She opened Coco's cage, dragged her, alert and resistant, out to the Lincoln and shoved her into the back seat, then threw the car into gear and headed down the hill. Halfway down she braked, pulled into a stranger's driveway, and threw up out the window. This is it, she thought. This is the worst thing that's ever happened to me. And I don't even know what it is.

Twelve

Francis saw the sun rise and smiled. He'd outraced the storm. The Porsche had been missing and sparking all night, but now, after cresting the Sierras, it didn't matter if the engine gave out or not; he was out of the mountains, back on the flatlands, safe. He rolled down his window and turned off the windshield wipers. "We made it," he said and put his hand out to touch Ida's shoulder, realizing even as he spoke that it was not Ida beside him at all, but a brown paper bag of groceries he must have shopped for at some point. So that's how the Stuff worked.

He glanced down to see what other jokes had been played and was relieved to see he was dressed, if not well. He was wearing suit pants with a polo shirt, loafers with no socks. He pressed his pocket. His wallet was there; credit cards, license; he had a vague memory of stopping for gas somewhere and telling the attendant he was going to Mendocino, then thinking—Why would anyone in their right mind want to go to Mendocino?—and heading east instead.

Toward the sun. Toward the light. Toward some wide open

spaces where he could take some wide open breaths. He peered through the windshield, which was a sheet of silver in the freezing dawn, and snapped the radio on, but it was still too early for news and he was in no mood for the country music, Christian quackery, and drugged human voices whispering about sextraterrestrials on the talk shows he picked up. Maybe the paper bag held some surprises. He reached in and pulled out a bottle of Cutty Sark, a pack of Benson & Hedges, two oranges, and a box of the chocolate-covered raisins he'd devoured in secret as a boy. A whole box, he thought, all to myself. Pleased, he took a long draught of the Scotch, and automatically—it would take time, that was all—held the bottle out to Ida before remembering, again, she was gone. It had been years since she had been able to get into the Porsche anyway; no room for the wheelchair. But when he'd first bought this car there had been good times, good trips for the two of them, he in his tweed cap from Harrods, she in the big sunglasses that made her look like a bee, the wind blowing her skirt up over two perfect thighs, the silver thermos of martinis pinched between her two perfect knees.

Long ago, long ago. He leaned forward and stretched out over the wheel. If he could remember the oh-so-distant past it was only a matter of time before he would remember the not-so-distant present. It was clear he was running from something that had happened last night, and it was equally clear he'd find out soon enough. His blackouts had never lasted long. Better enjoy this one while I can, he decided. Amnesia, like everything good, passes.

He tried to focus on the scenery but that was the trouble with Nevada: you couldn't, really; it was a state to get through as fast as you could, and with these identical new design-by-number construction sites standing out in the cold it almost hurt the eyes to look. An image of Kay's hurt eyes floated forward as if summoned and he let it, taking another sip of Scotch. Kay's eyes were bunny eyes—you couldn't say anything that wouldn't set them scurrying. Her rapid helpless blink when you raised your hand, say, to scratch your nose or push back your glasses, the blink of a victim who'd been abused all her life—but who had ever beaten Kay? He'd never hit her; he'd barely disciplined her. He never really even lectured her about her lying. Victor stole, Kay lied, they both ate like peasants, threw their clothes around, lost things, broke things, spent money like water, what else. Normal kids. Normal childhoods. No sign they ever knew how lucky they were. He paid their bills. Took care of their teeth. Gave them both cars. Almost left once. Almost stayed in New York. But didn't. So why the hurt in Kay's eyes all this time? What had gone wrong? She'd been such a quick little thing, bright and chatty and so intuitive that both he and Ida had almost felt frightened of her, of her ability to read their minds and parrot back what she saw.

"She still does it," Ida had complained last Christmas, "and I still can't stand it." But Ida meant because of the pity; Ida never could take pity and Kay never could hide it. So was it pity he had seen last night? Contempt? Accusation? Let's have it, Francis thought. What did I do this time?

The trouble with total recall was that it worked like a charm once it got going. Francis tapped an unlit cigarette and clicked his tongue against the dry roof of his mouth as the first scene from the night before began to play out, followed, a little more nimbly, by the next, then the next, until the whole evening was spread before him like a bad hand of cards.

It had started with a toast. To Morpheus, God of Sleep. He and Kay had stood in the kitchen, clicked goblets, and drained their glasses. Then they had a cigarette together. Last time, Kay had said. She was quitting. As well she should. Then they said good night, her breath on his cheek, his hand patting her shoulder, one-two, one-two, and then she remembered some toy of Nicky's she'd left in Ida's studio so she went in to get it. And didn't come back. Passed out on the cot in there, he'd decided, which was probably a good place for her, safer than driving home. He'd had a few more cigarettes and gone to bed himself.

And then?

"Daddy?" The soft, wounded, curious voice. The hand on the back of his head as he hunched in the dark by the side of the bed. "Daddy, are you all right? What's the matter? What's wrong? Daddy, are you crying?"

Crying? No. Francis lit the cigarette at last and inhaled. He had not been crying. Kay should have stayed in the studio. She had no business sneaking into his bedroom and catching him off guard, doubled over himself. She thought he was grieving. He had not been grieving. He had been having some sad, rigorous drug-induced sex with himself and it was no business of anyone's, certainly not of his grown daughter's, if he did it stone drunk fallen off the side of the bed whimpering like a wounded wolf. He did not need her sympathy. He did not need her understanding. The only thing he needed was his privacy. Whatever happened to his privacy? He shuddered, remembering the heavy surge of her body against him as she tried to raise him from the floor, her intense, stricken whispers. "Daddy, poor Daddy," she'd said. "Don't feel bad, I'm here, don't worry, we'll make it, we're going to be all right." Her tears, tangled hair, warm breath on his bare skin as she tried to lift him onto the bed. He'd had to contort like a yogi to conceal his erection and he still wasn't sure what she'd seen and what she had not. It would serve her right to see her old dad buck naked and coming on himself but it was not the way he would choose to be remembered. He had always been so careful.

So he'd pushed her.

He shouldn't have.

But he'd always pushed people who pushed him. You had to fight for your space in this world. You had to fight for your life. Ida knew that. Why didn't Kay?

He'd said, "For God's sake, get away," and he'd pushed her, hard, and she'd flown back, no resistance, and crashed into the vanity. She hit her head on the edge, her shoulder on a drawer. He'd had to haul her up and lay her flat, passed out on the bed.

He'd checked her eyes for reflexes, felt her pulse. And, yes, he'd looked at her. The raincoat she'd been wearing as a bathrobe had fallen open and her woman's body, with its full white breasts and its pelt of dark curls, lay open like a question mark. Not the baby he'd diapered when Ida forgot. Not Ida herself. Someone new. He'd started to cover her, and then damn if her arms didn't come up and if she didn't octopus around him and drag him down, off balance, on top of her. "Daddy," she'd said. "Oh Daddy."

And he couldn't breathe, couldn't do anything but lie there, stirred, stricken, and suffocating, not moving until he was sure she was talking in her sleep. And then he'd jumped back like a man on fire. Grabbed some clothes. Grabbed some keys. Left.

So what had he done?

Nothing.

Nothing at all.

Francis watched as light filled the car, limning his knuckles. The frost had crushed to a thin diamond jam along the sides of the windshield. He could feel the heat of the winter sun on his face, its bright bite on his tired eyes. He pulled into a motel somewhere near Vegas, fell into bed, and slept without dreaming for eleven hours. When he woke, he showered, went out to breakfast, found a shopping mall, bought some jeans, a sweater, a jacket and six pairs of wool socks, and went into a casino to try his luck. After he'd won the first thousand dollars he remembered the dog and went to a pay phone to ask Kay to feed her. If she wants me to say I'm sorry for pushing her, he thought, I will. I should not have pushed her. As for the rest of it—she should not have pushed me.

"Hey," he said when she picked up the phone. "Kay."

"Dad?" That hesitant voice. "Are you all right? Where are you? We've been worried."

"About me? Waste of time. It's the dog I'm worried about. When I left she was still at the house."

"Coco's here, with me. I brought her home. Dad . . . ?"

"Well good. Guess there's no problem then. You know how to feed her."

"Yes. Dad . . . did something happen last night?"

"Wunnerful, wunnerful. See you when I get back then. Whenever that is. Toodle."

That was easy, he thought, returning to the casino. Winning the next thousand was going to be the challenge.

The dog followed Kay everywhere, nervous, cringing, and it was the dog, Kay explained, who needed therapy. "Much more than me," she said. "I."

Dr. Tamar straightened her skirt and crossed her legs. "Why do you need therapy?" Dr. Tamar asked.

"I told you." Kay was wringing her hands again but it was all right here, she reasoned, this was a place where many people must weep and tear their hair. Dr. Tamar's office was a small dim cubicle in a large medical complex; it was painted in solid beiges and tans, with a leather couch Kay wouldn't go near and a butternut-colored chair with armrests she would not lower her arms onto. A crazy person had sat here an hour before she came in and another would be sitting here an hour after she left and it was possible that they all left crazy germs which could be contagious. She untwisted her hands, floated her palms a careful half-inch above her lap, and stared at a calendar on the wall that showed a desert scene, endless sand dunes with a camel trudging across it. She noticed the date. Ten days ago, Ida had still been alive.

"Tell me again."

"I killed my mother. And I slept with my father."

"Are you sure?"

"No."

"So what's the problem? That you did these things or that you don't know what you did?"

Kay shifted in the chair. Dr. Tamar didn't like her. That was all right, she didn't like Dr. Tamar. How could Zabeth have recommended her? She was a plain, brainy-looking middle-aged woman in a pin-striped business suit. Her sharp manner made her seem more like a criminal lawyer than a confidante. This is how I was raised, Kay thought, some adult mocking me in a snotty voice. Transference should be no problem here.

"Have you ever been in therapy before?"

"No. I've never been well enough to see a therapist."

"Humor?"

"But I've always wanted to see a therapist."

"Why?"

Kay shrugged. The word "why," as always, worked as an instant eraser, leaving her mind smudged and clouded but essentially empty. Dr. Tamar leaned forward. "Let's go back and review what you've already told me. First: Do you have any physical evidence to support your verdict against yourself? Did the doctor say your mother died of an overdose?"

"No."

"And as for what you think may have happened with your father. You say you blacked out. Did you perceive signs of penile penetration when you came to? Any soreness or signs of lubrication? Any semen? On your clothes, on your skin, in your vagina?"

"No." Kay bit back tears and looked down at her hand, automatically moving to twist the sapphire. But the ring was not there. She'd left it at home, convinced that if she wore it to Dr. Tamar's it would relay the interview straight to Ida in the heavens like some surreal transmitter. "But my mother had this hallucination this would happen."

"You think you enacted your mother's fantasy."

Kay could see how crazy the words were when the psychiatrist said them, but they were true, weren't they? Ida had known she and Francis could kill and then copulate. She had called them demons.

"What about your fantasies," Dr. Tamar pursued. "Is having

sex with your father on your mother's deathbed one of them?"

"Oh no. That's not what I want."

"What do you want?"

"I don't know. The usual. Love."

"You want your father to love you."

"Yes."

"But not like a lover?"

"No!"

"Not like a husband?"

"No, no, no. Although, actually, my husband isn't much of a lover either." She stopped. She had not come here to talk about Neal. She did not know how to talk about him. He had been subdued and tender ever since she had driven home in a stunned panic from her father's house at three in the morning. He had rubbed the back of her neck as she bent over the toilet, throwing up the last of the Stuff. He had held her as she'd shivered all night. He had accepted her excuse—flu—with the same easy incuriosity he probably wished she'd show him.

"You know the easiest way to find out what happened," Dr. Tamar said, "is just to ask your father."

"He's not that easy to talk to."

"No. He doesn't sound like it." Dr. Tamar made a note. Kay sank further into the nut-colored chair, brought a thumb to her lips, bit down on the cuticle, and closed her eyes. For the thousandth time she tried to remember what happened that night, and for the thousandth time, she failed. "I'm really in bad shape," she said, "if it's all in my head."

"Oh I don't think it's all in your head. What interests me is the way you appropriated what was in your mother's head—her worst nightmare—and botched it. This overdose certainly sounds botched. Your mother was already in a coma and yet she lived another ten hours after you and your father administered the 'extra Stuff,' as you called it, so it doesn't sound as if it had anything to do with her actual death. It didn't seem to hurt her or help her. As

for the incest: that doesn't make sense either. Your father and you
seem to have a lot of issues but lust isn't one of them. For now,
what I'd like you to do is stop drinking."

Kay nodded. Okay. That was easy enough. She'd been meaning
to anyway, and except for that half-bottle of Chablis last night,
practically had. "Anything else?"

"That's all. Just quit drinking. And go to an AA meeting
tonight. I'll see you next week."

"Next week? You think I should come back?"

"Of course. Don't you think you're worth it?"

"If I thought I was worth it I wouldn't be here," Kay said.

Dr. Tamar tapped a pencil against her lips. "Do you know who
you remind me of? Someone from mythology. He killed one par-
ent, married another, and blinded himself. Do you know who I
mean?"

Kay nodded. "A cat I used to have. Eddy Puss."

"Humor again?" Dr. Tamar handed Kay an appointment slip
and the next minute Kay was out on the street, buttoning her coat
as she hurried head-down through the rain toward the Lincoln.
She coaxed Coco out from behind the steering wheel where she
had curled shivering and pushed her into the passenger seat. She
turned the key and looked up to see a blond woman in a wheelchair motoring into another medical office, her proud head and
the set of her hands over the controls so like Ida's she almost drove
after her.

"I like you just the way you are." That's what Mister Rogers was
saying as she walked in the front door. Nicky looked up from the
television set with the pleasant masked expression that meant he
was hiding something—he'd probably been watching war robot
cartoons until he heard her drive up. She paid the sitter, then carried the groceries into the kitchen, Coco close to her heels. It was
not until she set the bags down that she noticed the letter from

Francis among the other pieces of mail on the table. She recognized the small square print at once. Oh-oh, she thought. He
couldn't tell me what happened on the phone. But he's going to tell
me now. She reached for the last bottle of red wine in the cupboard, remembered her promise to Dr. Tamar, and poured herself
a glass of water instead. She was trembling as she opened the
freezer and groped through the mysterious agars Neal kept in
there, looking for a cigarette, but there weren't any. No help for
it—she would have to take her father's letter straight.

She pulled a chair to the kitchen table and sat down. She tried
to think if she had ever received a letter from Francis before. At
any of the fat camps she had been sent to in the summers? No. At
Tanglewood, after she won that music scholarship in high school?
No. At the conservatory, that brief year? No. Never with Biff or in
the years since. Ida used to track her down wherever she went—a
phone call to every safe house she fled to in her twenties, a letter in
every mailbox. *Come home, I'm sick again, I need you.* But Francis? Never. This is a first, Kay thought. She reached for the envelope and drew it toward her. It was date-stamped four days ago,
mailed from Nevada—what was he doing in Nevada? Just open it,
she thought.

She did. A check for $10,000 fell out.

And nothing else.

Without taking her eyes off the check she reached for the phone
and dialed her brother.

"Isn't it incredible?" Victor's voice was warm and young and
happy. "Stacy just brought mine in from the mailbox."

"But what is it?"

"It's Mom's inheritance, Kay. I can't believe it's so much and he
got it to us so fast. This is a miracle. It solves all my problems."

That was what Neal said too, when he walked in, heels dragging, lunch box in his hand like a schoolboy's. "Oh babe!" His
face broke into the old lines of radiance she remembered from
their courtship. "We're saved!"

"From what?"

"For a while, anyway. Man oh man. And to think this came from Francis. I never thought . . . I take back everything I ever thought about your dad. This is a lifesaver, Kay, believe me."

Kay watched him, pleased but wary.

"We need to celebrate," Neal said. "Where's that French champagne?"

"Still in the refrigerator where it's been for the last six years."

"This is the time to open it if ever there was."

"I'll join you in a toast. But I can't drink. I have to go to an AA meeting tonight. I saw a psychiatrist today and——"

"You don't need a psychiatrist." Neal drew her to him, and suddenly she found herself once again back in the warm bony hollow of his chest, that old sanctuary. "You just need me to stop being such a prick."

"Hey," Kay breathed. "Yeah." She jabbed him lightly in the ribs. "I do."

"Well I'm going to change, babe, I promise. This money helps so much. I can't tell you. I was afraid we were going to have to sell your mother's ring."

"We?" Kay lifted her head, alert. The money—well, that was all right—she'd already decided Neal could have the money. But the ring was hers. And she'd never sell it. Again her finger curled to her pinky, found it bare, and again she reminded herself: the ring is on the bathroom counter.

But it wasn't. She looked for it after dinner, on her way to the AA meeting. There was nothing on the counter but their toothbrushes, and nothing on the dresser but a handful of change and Neal's comb, which she absently ran through her hair and dropped into her purse. I probably put the ring in with the rest of Mom's jewels, she thought. Which meant that they were either tucked into her piano bench or lodged behind the space in the window seat or hidden inside a Tupperware container of turtle beans.

I'll check when I come back, she told herself, for already, despite her hurry, she was late for the AA meeting. It was hard to leave Neal, who was still glowing, sitting in the living room with the television off and Francis's check propped before him, working out figures in a notebook with a smile on his face, and it was hard to leave Nicky, who was having a dinosaur war in the bath. It was even hard to leave Coco, who had scrambled to her toes at the sight of the car keys and had to be locked, yowling, inside. "I really don't want to go to this meeting," Kay confessed.

"Then don't," Nicky called in his clear and reasonable voice.

"What meeting?" Neal said, not looking up.

She went.

The meeting was held in the same church where her concert had been held last November. Kay slipped into a seat near the door. Tonight was an all-woman's session, and she recognized another mother from Nicky's school and a checker from the supermarket. This is where I first met Zabeth, she thought, and she looked around, hopeful, as a few more latecomers came in, but no one tonight had Zabeth's style; these were just normal, tired, after-work women: alcoholics—all of them. What am I doing here? Kay thought. She felt the same spasm of revulsion she had felt earlier in Dr. Tamar's office, staring at the depressing calendar. This is no place for me. Bad as I am, I'm too good for this. She glimpsed a cap of silky blond hair in the front row and caught her breath, but the woman who turned in profile was older than Ida. And anyway, Ida wouldn't be caught dead at an AA meeting.

Kay got up and left.

She half-expected someone to stop her, to yell "Halt! Seize her!" but no one did. Two women smoking in the parking lot kept talking as she passed. She sat in the car listening to Bach until her heart slowed down. I did the right thing, she told herself. I can quit drinking without any smug, sanctimonious, twelve-step program full of strangers telling me how sick I am. And I don't need therapy either. I already know how sick I am. She started home but halfway there she veered and turned off toward Charles Lichtman's house. She parked and watched the lights in his studio for an hour. You never knew. He could come out, cross the street directly to her, open the door and say, *Come here, dear Kay. Come in. Come home.*

Neal was asleep on the couch when she walked in the door an hour later, same as always, though there was a faint smile on his face and he did not groan when she woke him and sent him shuffling off to the bedroom. Nicky was asleep too, but with a piece of bread and peanut butter in his hand, and as she bent to kiss him she got a whiff of his unbrushed teeth. She let the dog out of the music room—hadn't anyone heard her whimpering?—and cleaned up the kitchen before starting to look for the ring.

It wasn't in the piano bench or in the Tupperware container or the window seat or in the sewing basket with the other jewels. It wasn't in any of her drawers; it wasn't in any of her pockets. Still, it had to be somewhere. She could see it so clearly, sparkling as Francis slipped it on her finger that night. It could not be lost.

Thirteen

It was a big world, without Ida. Big and flat and not all that interesting. There was beauty—you could not look up without seeing beauty, all those black and white clouds colliding across that fierce blue Colorado sky—and there was history and art and culture, of sorts, but Francis had never cared much for sightseeing; what Francis liked to do was drive. He drove fast and expertly, with an open bottle of Scotch between his legs, a cigarette in his mouth, and the cheap pair of sunglasses he'd bought in Vegas propped over his bifocals. He only stopped twice: once in Grand Junction to see his brother Harry, and once in Aspen to see the town his great-grandfather had sold for $20.

The visit with Harry was predictable. He found the hardware store on the strip mall and saw Harry, now hairless, grinding keys for a customer. "Hullo, Fancy," Harry said. "What's it been? Forty years?" Still fat with a fool's wet mouth, still a toucher, his hand so heavy on Francis's jacket it felt as if he wanted to tug it down, take it, tear it to shreds. For the rest of the afternoon, Francis sat in a darkened bar and listened to the Tale of Woe—the ex-wife with

MS, the present wife with kidney failure, the grandkid in the cult, the stepkid in detox. At the end of the Tale, Francis peeled off five $500 bills and gave them to Harry with the wrong address, a made-up telephone number. "You know what happened to Mick?" Harry took the money as he took everything, without protest. "I can guess," Francis said, and what he guessed was close: dead, thirty years ago, shot robbing a gas station in Phoenix. "And Kip?" Dead eleven years ago, no one knew how, alone in a motel room, might have been drugs, might have been heart failure. Arlene?—still in the mental hospital. Joanie, God, last seen, she lived in a trailer park with another woman, weighed three hundred pounds. "So what about you," Harry asked. "Did you make it with the music?" Francis wiped his lips, pushed back his chair. "Your singing," Harry persisted. "You ever make an album?" Francis rose. Harry followed him out to the vast brilliant street. "I remember those solos at mass, Ma crying, Pa trying to get you auditioned on the radio . . ." he trailed off. As they parted, he moved to embrace him but Francis stepped back. "Some things don't change," Harry said, his eyes flickering, and that was true, Francis thought, and that was why families, seeing families, being with families, having families, was not such a good idea. You might, if you weren't careful, end up not changing.

He drove off worried Harry might have written his license number down.

By the time he reached Aspen, it was almost midnight, pitch black and freezing, but he got out anyway and walked around. Great-grandfather McLeod had owned this place back in the 1800s. They'd all have grown up differently, he, Harry, Mick, Joanie, Arlene, and Kip, if the old mining engineer had kept it. Or maybe not. "Nothing up there but snow." Francis could hear his own father's voice, the astonished drawl of one bad businessman miming the words of another. He looked down a block still bright with bars and restaurants, still lined with the expensive new cars of skiers and tourists, turned a corner, felt the wind burn his face, and turned back. His ancestor idiot, first in a long line that included him too. That had to be faced. Included him too.

For he'd made his share of dumb deals. Been tricked, been trapped, had tricked and trapped others. His marriage probably the worst deal of all, but who could have predicted that Ida would get so sick, so soon, and stay there. It wasn't money, with him, he was smart with money, it was people. He didn't understand people. How could Ida have changed from the light-stepping dancer with the laughing eyes to the old lurcher in the wheelchair? And why was it the lurcher he missed? All the next day, driving blind through white snowfields, green canyons, and high red plateaus, he thought about it. No one to work for anymore. No one to please. For the last twenty years he had waited on Ida hand and foot, and the secret was—he had liked it. Without Ida to serve he felt lost. Unanchored. Unreal. He descended into high desert, watched a tumbleweed blow across the highway, fought the urge to follow it, tightened his grip on the wheel.

By the time he got to Santa Fe he was lonelier than he had ever been in his life. His head was full of dead voices, none of them saying a damn thing worth hearing, and his body was breaking down on him too: his back hurt, his right leg spasmed from the strain of accelerating all day, his left eye had developed a twitch like Popeye's, his cough was gooey and his breath came hard. He was an ill, idle old man with nothing to do. It didn't matter if he went forward or back, kept going or stopped where he was. So he stopped where he was. The little painted adobe church at Chimayo, the church Ida had always wanted to go to, the one, she said, that "was better than Lourdes" for miracles, stood before him. He parked the hot and spitting Porsche under the shade of a pepper tree, walked past the tables of souvenirs and artifacts, and paused in the entry, appalled by the crutches and crucifixes hung on the walls by the pious. Then he ducked into the tiny alcove with a few other tourists. The dirt below the altar was supposed to be holy. He poked it with his finger. Didn't look holy. Looked like dirt. A dab of this, and then what? No need to pray for Ida: she was gone. Victor and Kay were grown, on their own. So—for himself? What did he want? Little Fancy Francis McLeod, the altar boy who sang like an angel, the scholarship kid who hid behind boxes, the architect with the false address . . . ? He didn't want anything. Make me a miracle, he said to the dirt. Make me want something.

He dusted his hands off, stepped into the sunlight, and saw a tall brunette in new turquoise cowboy boots slide out of a Ford pickup and walk toward him, her shadow angling into an uncertain arrow. He felt a delirious leap of relief, suppressed it, frowned and tipped an imaginary hat. "Howdy, podner," he said. "What are you doing out here?"

"Stalking you." Glo Sinclair stopped in front of him and swallowed. Nervous as a debutante. "Do you mind?"

"Don't know yet. It's flattering. But it's probably a waste of your time. And," his voice softened, "no offense, my dear, but it's crazy."

"I am crazy," Glo Sinclair said. She picked up his hand, kissed it, pressed it shakily to her side. He felt her craziness, recognized it as part of her quick, hot, generous sexuality, smelled her money, a palpable stink of silver and leather, and saw, reflected in her deep-set, dark, boldly terrified eyes, a zigzag chink of light, a startling staircase to an airy haven that had been reserved, he realized, for years, for him. "I can make you happy," Glo said. Her tuneless voice was oddly restful, her touch was cool and strong. Her large lips, dabbed with miracle dirt, parted over large white tomboy teeth. Her tongue flicked through, bright red.

Francis smiled and shook his head.

"I know you're a cynic," Glo said, "but I believe in happy. I believe it can be done. I've *been* happy. You never have. All your life you've served other people."

Francis considered this. It sounded true—but it wasn't true. It was like Ida saying, *You're too good for me.* Like Kay saying, *We killed her.*

"I want to serve *you*," Glo said. Her eyes on his face didn't budge and again he saw it, that sudden opening to safety, that lightning slash exposing sun behind storm clouds. She'll never understand me, he realized. And that will be fine. I will have privacy with her and freedom and space. I might even get some real work done. "Come see the ranch I just bought." She led him toward her truck. He shrugged, followed. He didn't have anything better to do.

Kay didn't see Francis again for weeks. She called his office, his answering machine, drove up to the house, let herself in, paced around the vast glassy rooms frowning, looking for signs of life, finding, now that all traces of Ida had been removed, none. His chair, his table, his desk—one bare polished surface after another. Where was he? Why did he leave so few clues? What was he thinking? He appeared in her dreams, an old man in a snowfield, alone in the Arctic, breath faint and frosty, but surely he would not have gone to the North Pole. Francis took good care of himself. Still— was he all right? Mrs. Holland told her about a widower who refused to eat and willed his heart to stop. Was Francis barricaded in some lonely hotel room, face to the wall? Zabeth told her about an ex-lover who took cyanide after his wife died. "It wasn't until after she died that he even felt guilty about cheating on her," Zabeth said brightly. Maybe Francis was feeling guilty now too, maybe he was feeling the weight of ugly confusion that Kay herself was staggering under, alone and unaided. What had happened that night? What had they done? Help, she thought. Help.

She was in the mall, shopping for Valentine cards, when she heard Nicky say "Hi, Grampa." She looked up to see her father, slight, straight, hands in pockets, whistling to himself as he strolled by. He was dressed for work in a grey suit, bow tie, polished shoes. He looked as dapper and self-satisfied as ever. She didn't know whether to hit him or hug him, realized neither would be possible, ever, and froze, feeling as she always had around him: on tiptoe with pleasure and at the same time scared to death.

"Dad," she blurted, "what are you doing here?"

"Same as you." Francis Dutch-rubbed Nicky's head. "Spending money I don't have."

"We have lots of money," Nicky said.

"We do." Kay, forgetting, took a half-step toward Francis; Francis took a half-step back. "We have ten thousand dollars. I can't thank you enough. It's made all the difference in Neal's mood, outlook, everything."

"Neal?" Francis raised his eyebrows. "That check was for you."

"What would I do with ten thousand dollars?"

"I don't know. Get a haircut. Go back to school. Aren't they offering geriatric studies these days?"

Kay stood her ground. "No, but they should be. I've been having a lot of problems with my memory," she added. She looked at him. "Have you?"

"Can't remember if I have or haven't," Francis said. "So it must not be important. Don't you want to ask me how my trip was?"

No. I want to ask you what happened the night after Mother's memorial, Kay thought, but Francis was already talking. "I had a very nice trip," he said. "Thank you. Saw a lot of the country. Especially liked New Mexico." He made a pincher with his finger, caught Nicky's nose and shook it lightly back and forth. "You ought to go there."

"I'll put it on the list," Kay said. "So when shall we bring your dog back?"

"Coco? That miserable beast? I don't want her back."

"Dad."

"Isn't she happy at your house? Big yard to dig up? Dark corners to throw up in? Little boy to terrorize?"

"I like her," Nicky said, the first time he'd said it. "She doesn't try to bite me anymore."

"I like her too," Kay admitted. "But she's not happy with us."

"She's not happy anywhere. Look, Kay, the thing is, I'm probably going back to New Mexico a couple of times this spring, so tell me the truth: is Cuckoo too much for you to keep for a while? Because if she is, I can put her in a kennel until I know what my plans are."

"No. Not really. I can keep her until you know."

"So we've settled that. That's good. Toodleoo."

"Tood— Dad? Would you like to come to dinner next Sunday?"

"I would," Francis said. "Except I'm not free next Sunday."

"The Sunday after?"

"I'll have to check my extensive social calendar and get back to you on that one, Kay. Oh. What's the name of that restaurant you and Neal used to like so much?"

"Le Petit Jardin. In Rancho Valdez."

"Right." He pulled his gold pen and a notebook out of his pocket and wrote the name down. "Thanks. And thanks for taking on the damn dog too. I 'preciate it. Happy shopping."

Kay watched him walk away, whistling, his head bobbing as he gazed at the windows lining both sides of the mall. He paused outside a candy store, studying the display of chocolate hearts, then he held the door open for a stooped old lady, said something that made her smile, and stepped inside. Kay turned away. It's not fair, she thought. It's not fair I have to figure this out all on my own. Why doesn't he help me? Why doesn't he just say, Look, this happened forty years ago and then that happened thirty-five years ago and then that happened six weeks ago and that's why I don't love you?

"So how was Valentine's for you? Get anything from a secret admirer?" Zabeth tied a long chiffon scarf around her head and stretched first one tiger-striped leg then another against the trunk of a flowering plum tree. Kay, bending over her baggy sweat pants in a rag doll bounce, watched petals fall onto the jogging path. It had rained last night and the rich smell of the wet earth startled her—the smell of an open grave, she thought. She straightened, already winded, refused the thermos of hot coffee and brandy Zabeth held out, and said, "Neal gave me a single ticket to the ballet. *Romeo and Juliet,* if you can believe it. How about you?"

Zabeth held out her hand. A heart-shaped diamond in a heart-shaped setting sparkled on a finger darkened with a henna tattoo.

"Garret asked you to marry him?"

"He went down on his knees. You can be my matron of honor if you want."

Kay glanced up to see if Zabeth was being serious. By the soft gentle look Zabeth threw her, she saw that she was. "I'm honored," Kay said honestly. "I'd love to. But—what about the bar? Aren't you going to finish law school?"

"Sure. I want it all. You don't have to give up one thing to have another."

"You don't? Are you sure?" Kay fell into step beside her and started to jog.

"Ha-ha," Zabeth said. That was all. A short soft ha-ha that sounded happy. Kay glanced at her in wonder. Zabeth's style hadn't changed, but Zabeth had. Once again Kay was glad she'd never told her about whatever shameful thing it was that had happened to her with Francis that night. She'd opened her mouth to try a dozen times but had always pulled back, afraid Zabeth would not only assume the worst—that she and Francis had had actual sex—but would enthusiastically endorse it. *Fucked your father? Ha-ha-ha. I always fucked mine when I lived back East.* But now, Kay suspected, any confession about that dark lost night would only shock her. "I wish you every joy," Kay said. "I do."

They ran in silence for a while. A woman with a short cap of blond hair ran past them on the trail but Kay's heart stayed steady; she was almost used to it now, Ida's emissaries popping up to remind her. As if she needed reminding. As if she didn't miss and mourn her mother constantly. *Perhaps if we'd said a proper good-*

bye, Kay thought. Perhaps if we'd ended it right. If I'd told her out loud, and clear, that I loved her. But as it was, unfinished, inconclusive, she could neither step forward nor back. Loss had affected her body like a chronic hangover, and even after weeks of not drinking or smoking, her legs didn't work right, her lungs didn't expand; she could barely keep up. She fixed her eyes on the silver pom-poms bobbing on the back of Zabeth's socks, pushed wet hair off her already hot face, and concentrated on making it to the edge of the madrone grove. Suddenly she heard "Watch out," and looked up to see Charles Lichtman bent over his handlebars racing straight toward her down the path. His cheeks were flushed, his dark hair blew in curls around his face, his eyes were happy slits against the cold. She lost her footing at once, slipped on a root, and sat down hard in the mud by the side of the trail. Charles Lichtman flew past, braked, and stopped a few yards beyond her.

"Honey lamb," he called, "are you okay?"

"I'm so sorry! Yes! I just. I don't know. Fell."

"Let me see." He swung off his bike and walked toward her. Why wasn't he wearing a shirt? It was February! This was like having Tarzan come toward her, male muscles pumping under bare brown skin. She struggled up to her feet before he could extend a hand. Her ankle throbbed and she was shaking with lust and horror and misery. Zabeth's eyes, when she met them, were wide, staring as if she'd never seen her before in her life.

"I'm all right," Kay chattered. "I just fell."

"No. Turn around."

Kay, trembling, turned while Charles Lichtman examined the seat of her sweats.

"You think she broke her butt?" Zabeth marveled.

"She hit hard." Charles Lichtman touched the small of Kay's back, turned her toward him. "You all right?"

"Yes. Thank you. Fine. Just embarrassed. I should have looked where I was going."

"No, I should have."

"There's only one solution. You," Zabeth said, pointing to Charles Lichtman, "have to ask her," pointing to Kay, "out for a drink."

"Why?" said Kay.

"When?" said Charles Lichtman.

"Tomorrow," said Zabeth.

"Can't tomorrow," Kay and Charles Lichtman said together. "But I can the Monday after," he added.

"Good." Zabeth tapped her watch. "The White Oak at five-thirty a week from tomorrow."

"You sure have a bossy friend," said Charles Lichtman.

"She's a recovering dominatrix," Kay explained.

He gave her his beautiful smile, got on his bike, and rode off into the morning.

"That was great," said Zabeth. "You did that like a pro."

"Did he really call me 'honey lamb'?" Kay crouched down and clutched her swelling ankle.

"Of course you watched a pro for years," Zabeth continued. "I just never thought it rubbed off. I guess I thought you were too pure or something."

"What are you talking about?"

"Your mother. This is the way your mother operated. She always crippled herself."

Kay stood up. "I have not crippled myself," she said indignantly.

"It's okay," Zabeth mused. "It's a great old gimmick. All you have to be is helpless."

"I am not helpless."

"Remind me: how did you meet Neal?"

Kay started to hop down the path.

"You locked yourself out of your car, right? And had to go into Neal's shop to ask for a hanger so you could jimmy it open? And that guy Biff. Didn't you seduce him by literally falling out of your chair because you were clapping so hard at his recital?"

"You are going to make a great lawyer, Zabeth. You have a real calling. And anyway—you're the one who engineered this whole thing, not me."

"So what do you say?"

"Thank you."

"Welcome."

Kay paused mid-hop. There had been something in the encounter that puzzled her. Some ease. Despite the body heat and the golden hairs on the bare brown skin there had been too much ease, in a way. When she had finally brought herself to meet Charles Lichtman's eyes it had been . . . a little . . . like meeting anyone's eyes, and his touch on her back had been like anyone's touch. I am thrilled, she lectured herself. I am in love. I am about to commit adultery and live a real life at last. She hobbled back to the car with Zabeth's laughter ringing in her ears but it wasn't until she was almost home that she felt an answering laugh rise inside her.

Her happiness lasted all week. It was a strange and fragile happiness, an eerie rainbow-colored bubble that hovered around her heart, always ready to disappear or drift away, but in the meantime doing neither, simply hanging there, alive and demanding. This odd elation made her hands tremble as she measured protein powder into Neal's fruit shakes and walked Coco through obedience school. It swelled and spilled as she watched Nicky at karate class. She was happy at work, missorting cartloads of books, and she was happy in her car, driving to the market, her wallet forgotten on the table at home. But she was happiest at the piano, playing alone when the house was empty. She tried to bring the image of Charles Lichtman, bare-chested, into the music room, but time after time it was Ida who came, quiet in the corner, her presence close and dear and somehow more welcome than it had ever been in life.

Only thoughts of Francis could bring her down, and when a

week had passed and she still hadn't heard from him she dialed with such difficulty she got the wrong number twice. His voice, when she did reach him early one morning, was so warm, a playful rising "Hello?", that she thought she'd misdialed again.

"Dad? This is your daughter? Kay? Wanting to know if you'd checked your calendar and would like to come over this Sunday."

"Can't think why not. What time?"

"Around six?" Here Kay heard a scuffling sound and a growl and—she couldn't be sure—a laugh. Francis's laugh. "Dad?"

"Just talking to the dog."

"I have the dog."

"This is a different dog."

"You have a new dog?" Kay looked out the kitchen window to the pen Neal had built in back. Coco shivered and bit at herself in its open doorway.

"It's a temp. Leaving right now as a matter of fact."

"Does it have an owner?"

"Whoa." Francis's voice was merry and distant, and then he gave that sound again, that laugh, and then he hung up the phone. She stared at it before setting it down. Why did every encounter with Francis make her feel as if she'd stepped into a box full of bees? He didn't have to love her if he didn't want to. He didn't have to open up or talk. She'd settle for politeness. Simple politeness. At least one thing was clear, she thought, as she turned from the phone. They had not had sex. She and her father were not intimate enough for incest. You had to be related for that and they weren't.

She spent the next few days cleaning the cottage, studying recipe books at the library, and weeding and replanting the front walkway with primroses. Nicky helped her, his eyes on the ground, trained to look for anything blue and shiny that might be a sapphire. By Sunday afternoon the floors were polished, the windows were shining, she and Nicky were showered, the dog was fed and calm. There were fresh flowers everywhere, a butterflied rack of lamb in the oven, an asparagus salad in the refrigerator, a cherry pie cooling on the counter. Francis would see nothing here to complain about. Except of course the still missing ring.

"I just know he's going to ask." She sat on the edge of the bed and watched Neal take a shirt from the closet, pull it on. How slow his movements were. "I don't know what to tell him."

"Don't tell him anything."

Kay stood up and rebuttoned Neal's shirt. She handed him his belt and he slipped it on, loop by loop, missing the one in back as he always did. He'd been putting on weight and his chin doubled as he bent his head to buckle. His eyes, when he looked up, had that mild, clouded, inward expression she hadn't seen since they'd received the inheritance.

"What's the matter?" she asked, alarmed. "You're not worried about money again, are you?"

"My worries are my worries. I'll deal with them. You," Neal added, as the doorbell rang, "have enough of your own, babe."

Francis was scraping loose paint off a shingle with his fingernail as she opened the door. "I know," she said immediately, seeing, through his eyes, how shabby the front porch looked, even after she and Nicky had both swept it. "I've got to paint it. I will. But come on in. Let me get you a drink. I bought a bottle of Scotch especially for you."

"I don't drink Scotch," Francis said. "And I won't come in until you've all come out and seen my new car." He pivoted and started to walk back down the path. Kay, frowning, called to Neal and Nicky and hurried after him. A sports car, bright red and built like a bullet, was parked at the front gate.

"Fire and Ice," Kay murmured. "Same shade as Mom's lipstick."

"That right? Look at this." Francis's voice was expansive and pedantic as he opened the door and explained the dials on the dash to Neal and Nicky. Kay reached out and touched the hood. "Careful," Francis called. "Don't scratch the paint."

"I wasn't." Kay glared and turned away. She heard him tell Nicky about the time she'd hit the baseball into the windshield of a Thunderbird when she was ten, the time she'd accidentally slammed a Mercedes door on Ida's finger when she was twelve. "Six hours in emergency for that one," Francis finished. "Kay the Klutz." She made a face and continued to walk around the new car. It was bigger than the old Porsche and probably went faster, but what was the point? Maybe buying it was one of the ways her father was helping himself through. Everyone grieves in different ways, she reminded herself. Not all ways are visible.

"Think it will be safe out here on your street?" Francis gave the car a final glance as they turned back toward the cottage. Kay rolled her eyes and took another deep breath. This was going to be a hell of a night.

But oddly enough it wasn't. Francis drank only wine and did not smoke. He ate everything on his plate. He was expansive with Neal, jocular with Nicky. He seemed to enjoy being in the cottage, with the three of them, and although his eyes sometimes lingered a little too long on the tattered plaid wallpaper, he said nothing unkind until coffee. And then, setting his cup down, he said, "You're not wearing the sapphire, I see. Did you take it in to have it sized?"

Neal was out of the room, getting an old photograph of the West Valley stables Francis had asked to see. Nicky was still at the table, bent over a piece of butcher paper with a crayon in his hand, drawing. "Sized?" Kay repeated. "Yes. I did. I took it in to have it sized."

"Must need a good cleaning too."

"That's what the jeweler said."

"Al?"

"I don't know his name."

"Bald with a belly. You didn't go to Ned down in Rancho Valdez did you? Because Ned is a crook. So what did Al say?"

"Just that he'd fix it. But not right away. He's got a real backlog."

"She lost it," Nicky said. "We've torn the whole house apart but we haven't found it yet. I get ten dollars if I find it first." Neal, coming toward the table, said, almost simultaneously, "Here's that blown-up photo, Francis. I think you'll see what I mean," and it was to Neal that Francis turned, with a final, easy, "Al's the man you ought to talk to if you ever need to get your watch fixed," over his shoulder to Kay. Kay let her breath out. He hadn't heard. Hadn't been paying attention. She glared at Nicky, who lifted heavy-lidded traitor's eyes and said, "What?" and she blew a kiss toward Neal, who, startled, actually glanced over his shoulder as if it was intended for someone behind him.

"Well, she's a good businesswoman," Francis said to Neal. "I'll say that about her. Knows what she wants and goes for it."

"Who's that?" Kay asked, clearing the table. She paused, blinked. "Me?"

"No. Oh no. Glo."

Kay laughed. "The hara-kiri queen?"

"That's not appropriate, Kay," Francis said.

"No," Neal chimed in. "It's really not."

Kay stared at them. They looked alike, she realized. Zabeth had pointed that out long ago but she'd never really seen it before. Neal had always seemed so soft and slumped, Francis so quick and straight. But now, as they stood shoulder-to-shoulder, she saw the resemblance: different coloring, different builds, but the same cold eyes, cold lips. Ice men. "I'm sure she's a very nice woman," she said.

Francis nodded. "Any more of that good coffee?"

He stayed another hour, helped Nicky draw a dinosaur's dream cave, talked to Neal about some unrelated Sorensens he and Ida had met in Norway years ago and asked Kay, with no irony, if the jeans she was wearing were "the new style now." He stood at last, creakily hamming his own aches and pains, and said, "Well if I'm going to log in my usual twelve hours a night, I better get going."

Kay rose too. "You're sleeping a lot?"

"Can't stay awake."

"Me either. No energy."

"Tonight's the first meal I've been able to eat."

"Tonight's the first meal I've been able to cook."

"What's it been? Two months?"

"Fifty-seven days."

"Then I'd say we're doing all right. Considering."

"Considering," Kay agreed. She did not attempt a hug but gave a shy wave goodbye and watched from the porch as he walked away, her elegant father, picking his way between primroses toward his toy car. I'll ask him to come back next week, she thought. And the week after. I'll take care of him. I'll help him, Mama. Don't worry. You're not forgotten.

Fourteen

S h e was dreaming of Ida the next morning, an odd, unsettling dream of Ida turning to strike her with a silver mirror. When she woke up, arms thrown over her face, Neal was nuzzling her. They had not made love since Christmas. Why was he aroused now, the day she was finally supposed to meet Charles Lichtman? She struggled with about ten different emotions, then gave up. Maybe he loved her after all. Maybe it was as simple as that. "Hey," she said.

"Hey," he said back, his voice sweet and deep.

"Hey," she conceded. She brought his hand around to her breast, settled it on top like a baby's cap, and cuddled back into his embrace as he water-witched around, looking for entrance. She shivered with welcome as he finally slipped inside. What a sweet connection. Surely she had never done anything this warm—this friendly—this human—with her father. Again she realized that whatever had happened that night with Francis, it hadn't been sex. Sex was too innocent and too easy and too much fun. She let herself relax and open in a soft rush.

"Whoa," Neal cautioned. "Slow down." His low, excited breathing filled her ear; married music. Drenched and dreamy, she gazed out through half-opened eyes into a charcoal grey room. The curtains glimmered, the alarm clock glowed. Somewhere down the valley a rooster crowed. What a good feeling it was to be alive after all—fresh-throated, headache-free—no wine last night, she remembered, no cigarettes either. Neal, inside her, felt young and strong, a little slow. Slower. Very slow. Stopped.

"What is it?" she whispered. "Are we waking Nicky up?"

"Garbage."

She heard it too, the high whine of the garbage truck down at the corner. And that was another good thing: the world was in fine working order this morning, all those strong men running up and down the streets of town, hauling everyone's rubbish away. "Umm," she said, reaching back to cradle Neal's small velvety balls, like tomcat balls, she'd always thought, high and firm and that plush pretty pink.

"I didn't carry the can out last night," Neal said.

"It doesn't—"

She was about to say "matter" when Neal slid out of her, pulled on his robe, kicked into his slippers, and slammed out the front door. She lay still for a second in shock, feeling the cold air pass over her body. Then she went to the window, parted the curtains, and watched him hurrying down the driveway with the big green can of trash in his arms. She heard him call out to the garbage men, heard them call back, heard a word or two of cheerful morning exchange, a rumble of laughter.

She went back to bed and sat straight, hugging her knees, staring blearily at Mrs. Sorensen's framed photo on Neal's side of the dresser. She touched her ankle, which still ached from her fall in the woods, and rubbed her shoulder, which still ached from her fall at her father's. "Why did you do that?" she asked when Neal returned.

"Do what?"

"Choose the garbage over me."

"Don't go into one of your spirals please." He hung up his bathrobe, slipped back into bed, and reached for her. But his skin felt clammy, his erection was gone, and his fingers smelled like compost. She pulled away. "You're making a big deal out of nothing," he warned.

"Am I? Sometimes I feel like I'm trying to make a whole life out of nothing."

Neal raised his hands in the air and clapped. She stared at him as he sat up, threw his covers back, and began to get dressed. What a remarkably unattractive person he was. That double chin. That big mole like a greasy salmon egg right between his eyes. "The way you behaved last night . . ." Neal said.

"What do you mean?"

"That crack about Glo Sinclair was totally unnecessary."

"Glo Sinclair is unnecessary."

"You owe her some thanks."

"For what?" Kay turned on the pillow, waiting.

"Big thanks. She got us out of debt."

"What debt?"

Neal didn't answer.

"What debt?"

He left the room. Kay pulled on a long sweatshirt and followed him. The house seemed foreign to her in the early morning dusk; someone else's, always had been. A dim ugly place she was visiting. She stepped on a loose nail in the flooring and swore, her anger sparking around her like an electric outline. I can go to Charles Lichtman tonight with a clear conscience, she thought. There is nothing to stop me. She stumbled into the kitchen where she switched on the light and stared at her bent husband. "What debt?"

"All right," Neal said after a minute. "Sit down. We'll talk. I should have told you about this before." He plucked at a corner of the place mat as he sipped from a glass of wheat juice. "You know I bought the stables."

"No, I didn't know." Kay sat. "When?"

"Last October. I was going to surprise you on our anniversary, but you had a lot on your mind, with your mother—"

"You always blame my mother." Kay rose and looked in the refrigerator. Maybe there was an overlooked Marlboro in there after all. No. Just the remains of last night's dinner; nothing else. She closed the door and sat down. "How did you get the money?" She leaned forward. "You didn't ask my dad, did you? I have asked you and asked you never to borrow from my family."

"Calm down. Yes, I did, but he said no. So I borrowed from a loan shark."

"I hate you, Neal. What's a loan shark?"

"A so-called broker who charges thirty percent interest." Neal's voice rose for the first time and he sounded aggrieved. Righteous. As if he had a point to make. As if he had a case. As if he had not betrayed her trust and in some essential way her honor. He held her eyes, willing her to sympathize. Slowly she remembered the junk mail she'd seen him reading all year, the "literature" he'd been "studying."

"Oh Neal. Not that Dominic DelGotcha person."

"Delgardo. And yes okay, you're right, the guy's a crook. But it could have worked. Only I had to put the business up for collateral. And the house."

"This house?"

Neal was silent.

"Your mother's house? You know I will say one thing about not drinking. I don't have a hangover. Do you? I just feel worse than I've ever felt before in my life. But clear. Pretty clear. So go on."

"Well. I paid the first installment on time . . ."

"How."

"We had. Oh babe. You know. Your mother's money."

"That ten thousand? It's gone?"

"You'll get it back. Triple, I promise. So then the second installment came due. And I hadn't landed the other investors I'd been trying to get. So I didn't have the money." He took a last sip of juice. "And then Glo Sinclair dropped by the shop." Kay, impatient, clicked her tongue; Neal ignored her. "So we started talking, and I told her what I wanted to do with the stables and it turns out she had some capital gains tax she needed to invest so it made perfect sense that she invest in me." His voice rose. "Thanks to her, I'm going to make it, I'm going to make a minimall. It's going to have shops. Restaurants. A health food store. You know how you've always said there's no good music store around here? I thought you could open your own music store, stock it yourself, run it yourself."

"You want me to run a music store?"

"Why not? What's wrong with that?"

Nicky came to the kitchen doorway, Coco clattering at his heels, took a look at both of them, and said, "I'm going back to bed."

"Good idea," Neal and Kay said together.

"Everything's 'wrong,'" Kay said at last. "With all of it." She thought of all the nights Neal had dragged home and she had met him at the door, taken his jacket, handed him a towel and a cup of steaming miso, all the times she had pattered after him like a trained dog, barking the same old questions: *How was your day, dear? See anyone? Talk to anyone? Anything interesting happen? Have any thoughts, dreams, desires, plans, fears, feelings?* "I can't believe you never said a word to me."

"I know. I should have. I tried to once. You'd been . . . I don't know . . . you were drinking. You made some crack about . . . you seemed to think I was going to convert the stables into feed stalls and give pony rides and sell alfalfa, I don't know, so I"—he raised his head—"kept the rest of my plans to myself. I wanted to be sure before I told you."

"I don't remember making jokes about it, Neal."

"You have a sharp tongue. I'm sorry. But you do."

"So it's my fault you don't talk to me."

Neal met her eyes. "Sometimes," he said. "Yes. It is."

Kay took this in. It wasn't bad. Like throwing a few lit fire-crackers into a clothes dryer already loaded with ball bearings. "There's a lot I haven't told you either," she said at last. "You're not the only one sitting on secrets. I've been going through a lot too." She waited. If she could talk to Neal about her last night with Ida, her last night with Francis, there would be no need to go to Charles Lichtman.

But Neal said, "You don't know what worries are," drained his glass, spun it wearily between his palms, and added, more to him-self than to her, "I know I screwed up. But it's all over now. And it's worked out fine."

"I don't see how." Kay let her breath out. "We're still in debt. Only now we're in debt to Glo Sinclair."

"Yes, but now," Neal explained, "we have time."

Kay shook her head. "I don't think so."

"What are you talking about?"

"Us. You and me. We just ran out of time. Our marriage just ended."

"Don't do this, babe. I know I screwed up, but—"

"It's not just you. It's everything. You know what I think it is? I think it's the garbage."

"I have my priorities, all right?"

"No. Not all right. We're married. Married people have each other as priorities. Married people talk about major investments that affect both of them. They make plans together. They make love together. They share what they're going through."

"The way your parents shared their cigarettes and booze?"

"We can't hold a candle to my parents, Neal. We're amateurs. We're nothings."

Neal opened his mouth, but closed it. He knows I'm right, Kay thought. He knows we're through.

"So you think we should separate?" he asked cautiously.

"We are separated. How could we get any more separated? This is it."

"Look. I know you're mad right now but things are going to work out. I'm going to pull this whole stables thing together for you."

"It has nothing to do with me, Neal."

"It has everything to do with you. Everything I've done I've done for you." Neal pushed his glass away and stood up. "I'll stay at the shop for a while," he said, "until you cool down. Tell Nicky I'll call him."

"Tell him yourself, he's standing right there."

But Nicky was gone by the time they both turned, the front door slamming as he ran down the street.

"You look like two ties twisted," Mrs. Holland said.

Kay paused, her arms full of books. "I had a rough morning," she admitted. She thought about telling Mrs. Holland that Neal had moved out and that she'd spent the last half-hour coaxing Nicky back into her car, but decided against it. "I still can't find that ring," she said as something to offer.

"I lost a diamond once," Mrs. Holland said. "It fell out of its setting when I was walking in the city. The minute I saw it was missing I turned right around and retraced my steps. You know how shiny those sidewalks are. They put mica in the pavement. It looked like the whole block was paved with little diamonds. I thought I'd never find it."

Kay waited. "But you did," she prompted.

"It was lying right by the curb next to a fireplug."

Kay nodded and stacked the books onto the cart. She was about to wheel the cart away when she saw the college catalogue Mrs. Holland had placed there with a red arrow pointing to the Library Science section. She picked it up, turned to the page that gave admissions information, and jotted the phone number down. One day at a time, she reminded herself. One day at a time until five-thirty tonight.

. . .

But five-thirty still seemed far away as she dragged up the path
that afternoon at three.

"You ought to paint this porch." She looked up to see Victor
perched on a piece of newspaper on the top stair. Oh-oh. Victor
never just dropped by. She smiled cautiously but he did not smile
back. He continued to scrape at the stair with a pocketknife. "You
could probably get Stacy's brother's friend Ed, he's in the trades, to
give you an estimate," he said. "God, look at it. It flakes right
off."

Kay settled beside him, kicked one shoe off, and rubbed her
aching ankle. "You said 'God.'"

"What?"

"You took the Lord's name in vain."

"Yeah, well it's an old habit. A bad habit. I've been working on
it. Thank you for pointing it out to me."

Victor cracked his knuckles, snapped his knife shut, and shifted
on the step. He rolled the closed knife back and forth between his
hands the same way he used to roll his marijuana cigarettes. Kay
closed her tired eyes. "Do you miss Mom?" she asked.

"I don't think about her much," Victor admitted. "She was
closer to you." He pinched a dead leaf off a begonia and threw it
away. "So what's happening with you and Neal? I dropped by the
frame shop and Neal said he was sleeping there tonight."

"And tomorrow night and the night after that."

"But it's just temporary, right? A temporary misunderstand-
ing?"

"No. I don't think so, Victor. I think our marriage is over."

"Because?"

"Because I was a bad wife and he was a bad husband."

"What? He hit you? Beat you?"

"No. He withheld emotionally, as they say. He kept secrets. He
lost money."

Victor smiled and shook his head. "If it's just money . . ."

"'Just money' are two words I never thought I'd hear from you. You take money more seriously than anyone I know."

"Well, sure, but I don't let it come between Stacy and I. Money doesn't have anything to do with love, you know. And sometimes, you got to consider this, love doesn't have anything to do with marriage. Marriage is holy. A holy contract you have to honor no matter what. So what is it besides money? Is it sex? Because sex, you know, that's not important either. You already have a child."

Kay shivered and pulled her sweater tighter across her shoulders. It was March but still felt like winter. For a minute she wondered what the summer would be like, if she would be sitting here rocking and fanning and growing old behind the fence by herself. No, she thought fiercely. I'll be in Iceland or Jamaica or sailing the South China Sea with Charles Lichtman.

"I just need some time," she said.

"That's what I told him. I told him you're the type who takes things hard. But after you sort it out you come back."

"I do? That's how you see me?"

"Course it might speed things up if you both came in and talked to my pastor. Okay, okay, don't have a cow, just a suggestion. But Stacy and I hate to see you guys so unhappy. It's not good for Nicky. And Dad's got enough to deal with."

"Dad doesn't care." Kay bit her cuticle. "Did Neal tell you Glo Sinclair loaned him a lot of money? Why would she do that? Is she trying to snag Dad?"

"Snag him? No, Kay. She's just a nice woman."

"She doesn't strike me as nice."

"She just bought a pickup from me a few weeks ago. I think she's nice."

"A truck? Glo Sinclair in a truck?"

"I wouldn't worry about her. She's too skinny for Dad. Besides"—Victor looked, for a moment, as puzzled as Kay felt—"Mom just died."

Kay hugged her knees. "Mom and Dad were happy, weren't they? They had a good marriage. Remember how he used to whistle when he came home from work, and she would whistle back? I loved that. It made me feel safe. I always wished Neal would whistle."

"Teach him," Victor said.

"I can't. I don't know how myself."

They were silent for a while, then Victor said, "I never felt safe. Dad was always gone and Mom was always mad about something. Or sick." He rubbed his forehead. "You did all the cooking, didn't you? You made my lunch. What were those coconut cookies you used to make? Macaroons? I liked them. And I liked those stories you used to tell me at night."

"What stories?"

"About the brave brother and sister who escaped from the witch and lived on the moon."

Witch? Again Kay heard the tune Zabeth had sung in her ear the afternoon of Ida's memorial—and again she tried to suppress it. The Munchkins' singsong had insinuated itself into some mental repertoire and she found herself humming it when she was driving or working at the library, always stopping with a frown, hand pressed to her lips, guilty. Caught.

"I always felt bad about my own escape," she said now, adding, as Victor looked at her blankly, "about leaving you alone with them, when I dropped out of school to be with Biff."

"Were you gone long? I don't remember. You came right back, didn't you?"

"Yes. Oh yes. When Mom had her hysterectomy. But I should have taken you with me. And then we both should have stayed away."

"Why? Was it that bad? I just remember being cold. Every new house we moved to got colder and colder. The truth is," he continued, "I don't remember much about Mom or Dad or our childhood. None of it matters anyway. My real life didn't start until I found Jesus."

Kay glanced at his handsome face set against her in profile. She remembered enough for both of them—Victor wiping Ida's red lipstick off his mouth, Victor squirming as Francis flicked his report card aside, Victor sitting under the piano counting the coins in his piggy bank while Kay banged through Bartok. "At least you found your real life," she said. They sat in silence for a while and then Victor looked down at his watch and stood.

"I gotta go. But hey. I'll pray for you. And Neal. And your marriage."

"Do you think prayer will help?"

"God, Kay! Are you kidding? Of course it will help."

"There you go. You said 'God' again."

"Your trouble," Victor said, shaking his trouser crease straight, "is that you're a joker. You can't take anything seriously. You're always looking for ways to make fun of people."

Kay opened her mouth to say, *I don't have to look very far,* but closed it and waved as Nicky kicked through the gate.

"Daddy home?" Nicky asked as he trudged toward them, his sweatshirt hood pulled up over his head.

"No, honey, he's not."

Nicky went into the house and slammed the door.

Kay looked down at the porch floor after Victor left and noticed he had scraped a bare spot on the stairs that almost matched the bare spot Francis had picked off the shingle. Between the two of them, she wouldn't have to do any prep work before she painted the porch for repossession. She rose to go in and prep herself for Charles Lichtman, then remembered something. The garbage. She went down the driveway and lugged the empty can back in from the street.

Fifteen

Francis woke up in the leather chair with an open book in his lap and looked at his watch. Still early. So why did he feel as tired as if he'd been working all day and all night? Those nights are over, he reminded himself. The strain of pushing Ida's wheelchair up the driveway so she could watch the moon rise over the mountain, the 2 A.M. crying jags, the ritual of lifting her on and off the commode, the backache from shampooing her hair in the sink while she cursed him—he didn't need to do these anymore. Yet for weeks he'd been unable to do anything else. He'd been telling the truth when he told Kay he slept all the time. He did. He put the yoga tape Mimi Johns had given him in the VCR, lay down on the exercise mat, and fell asleep. He went to the therapist Howard liked so much—some grim female named Tanya Tamar—and fell asleep. He slept in the movies with the Junior Bentleys and he slept in the car waiting for Father Bliss to show up for their golf game. Sunny-at-the-Office knew to tell clients he was busy so he could sleep at his desk.

The only person he woke up for was Glo. Ever since they'd re-

turned from the Southwest, Glo came at dawn. She let herself in
the back door, went into the kitchen, brewed decaf so dark it almost fooled him at first, poured fresh-squeezed orange juice from
one of her own trees into a frosty goblet and unwrapped a low-fat
croissant from the new French bakery down the hill. She put these
on a tray along with a dozen different vitamins and Chinese herbs,
slipped into his room, set the tray on the nightstand with a rose,
walked back to the door, said, "Wake up, Francis," and left him
alone. When he had stretched and sipped himself into conscious-
ness she returned, silent as a geisha, and knelt to tie his walking
shoes. Then, still without a word, she led him out of the house, up
the driveway where she unleashed Pal, her fat golden puppy, and
the three of them walked on the mountain, Pal dancing in a comi-
cal celebration of life, Glo moving easily at his own slow pace, the
sun gilding the day as the year moved into spring. She had taken
him to a hypnotist to cure him of smoking, she had bought him
tickets to the Open next month, and she had given him the red
Alfa to drive until his Porsche got rebuilt. This morning, hesitant,
he had put his hand on her hip for the first time and left it there,
feeling her smooth muscles flex and flow as they walked.

"I'm sorry I can't do more right now," he'd said. She'd looked
at him as if he'd been speaking Siamese and said, "We have time."

He wasn't sure. He'd felt stirrings he didn't like, silent breakages occurring along the heart lines, in his lungs. He was almost
seventy years old. When he looked in the mirror he saw his
brother Harry's face, hangdog, accepting bad news as if he de-
served it. Well Harry might, but I don't, Francis thought. He
looked at the book on his lap, a gift from Peg Forrest called *Clo-
sure; Saying Goodbye to a Loved One*. Blah blah and more blah.
But one thing Peg had underlined might work. Make a ceremony.
Create a ritual. He got up and began to pad around the house
gathering some of Ida's things together—things that for some reason he hadn't wanted the kids to take—the silver mirror. A hand-
blown champagne glass from Venice. A red silk negligee. A

photograph of Ida as a six-year-old, all curls and dimples, another photo of her just a few years ago, naked in the swimming pool, tanned arms reaching up to him. Her white Bible. The rosebud demitasse. He put these items in a shoe box and drove the old highway out to the coast. It took an hour to get there and it was almost sunset when he arrived. He and Ida used to drive out here and neck to get away from Kay and Victor. He parked and threw the box off a cliff into the sea.

When he let himself back in the house the phone was ringing. "Did you read the book?" Peg asked. "Did you do what it said?" Her earnest, warm, relentlessly sympathetic voice made his stomach churn.

"I made a dump run," he admitted.

"And did it make you feel better?"

"Didn't make me feel worse." He rotated his arm, still sore from the throw, and again heard the box burst open on the rocks, the explosion it made, like a woman's laugh. Not Ida's. Glo's? He had never heard Glo laugh. That was one of her charms. "Felt a lot like littering."

"Oh you," Peg said indulgently. "You make a joke about everything."

"Not about everything." He remembered an old quip of Kay's. "Just about the things that matter." He told Peg he was sorry, but he was too tired to come to dinner or lunch; he never went out for breakfast; he'd get back to her soon. "And now if you'll excuse me, Peg, I really do have to take another nap."

It was dark inside the White Oak but not dark enough. Kay adjusted her sunglasses as she scanned the stools along the length of the bar, taking in the mismatched tables and chairs jumbled across the wooden floor, the alcove with the dart board. Charles Lichtman wasn't here. She rubbed her damp palms against her thighs and moved to a table in the corner. She would give him five min-

utes. That was fair. Then she would go home and curl up under
the piano like a dust clot.

"Can I get you something?" the bartender asked.

"Oh no," she said brightly. She sat down and looked up as if
fascinated by the moose antlers, paper leis, and copper wash boil-
ers suspended from the ceiling.

"Hi there." One of Nicky's teachers waved to her across the
room. A grey-haired couple looked up over their beers and nodded; they had been at the library that morning, checking out books
on Bali. Wishing she'd brought a book herself, Kay reached in her
purse and pulled out an AA pamphlet, shoved in there months
ago.

"Just for today," she read, "I will have a program. I may not follow it exactly, but I will have it. I will save myself from two pests:
hurry and indecision." She took a breath and looked up, calmed.
This was good. This was like reading a recipe for a complicated but
delicious dish she would never make. She read it again. Then she
folded it back and looked at her watch. Two more minutes.

"I said," the bartender repeated, "what can I get you?"

"Oh! Nothing. I don't drink."

"This isn't a bus station."

"No. Of course not." What did that mean? "A Coke?"

"Pepsi all right?"

"Yes."

"Come and get it."

I hate Pepsi, Kay thought. She rose and walked to the bar. She
had dressed as sexily as she dared, in jeans, black ballet flats, and
the red sweater, which she had tried to depill with an emery board
and strips of Scotch tape. Her push-up bra pinched and she was
wearing so much mascara it took effort to blink. She was still in
the act of raising her lids when the bartender plunked one, two,
three maraschino cherries into her drink. She opened her mouth to
protest, but instead heard herself say, too softly, "Thanks." The
bartender smirked.

She gave him two dollars, waited for change, realized there wouldn't be any and that she probably owed a tip as well, dug a quarter out of her coin purse, placed it on the bar, and walked back to her table. She tried to stop trembling by propping her chin on her hand. I could balance my checkbook, she thought. I could play Patsy Cline's "Crazy" on the jukebox and dedicate it to myself. I could buy a whole pack of cigarettes. I could get drunk. The heave of true longing at that thought made her quiver. She smoothed the AA pamphlet out and read it again.

At five-forty she rose to go. Stood up was stood up. The phone rang at the bar and she paused, dum-dum, but the bartender cradled it close to his lips as he talked and bent over the mouthpiece, shielding it. She turned to walk out just as Charles Lichtman walked in.

"Thanks for waiting." His dark curls bounced, his eyes shone, his full lips shimmered. "I was afraid you'd leave. I hoped you wouldn't. Sorry I'm late. I was painting."

Kay swayed, fingering her purse strap. "What were you painting?"

"Blurs. I'm doing blurs. You know. The landscape as seen from a bicycle. Let's sit down. May I buy you a drink?"

She shook her head and sat back down. Charles Lichtman went to the bar, and returned with a beer, still smiling at her over the top of the foam as he sipped.

"Cool sunglasses," he said.

"My disguise." She took them off, blinked. She hoped she didn't look too homely with her poor face exposed. Charles Lichtman looked appealing as ever, fresh and lightly sheened from a day in his studio doing work he loved. "You always look so healthy," she said. It came out sounding like a complaint. "Your cheeks are always so pink."

He grinned. "It's overcompensation."

"For what?"

"For being HIV-positive."

Kay opened her purse, closed it. "It's only blurred when you're going downhill, right?"

"Right. So. You okay with that? I thought I should be frank from the start. So you'd know who I am. So we could be friends."

"Friends."

"My lover died of AIDS last year. His name was Jimmy."

Kay looked up. "I'm sorry!"

"I know. That's why I like you. You are sorry. You even mean it. Well let me tell you, honey lamb, you're rare. Most people don't give a shit."

I don't give a shit, Kay thought. I didn't know Jimmy! Don't think I'm nicer than I am! Blushing so hard she could feel her pulse, she looked away. Her eyes focused on his beer. It looked good. She'd love to have one. What was one beer? Nothing! It would give her just the little push she needed to float offshore from her life, calm, amused, detached. The man she'd dreamed about and devoted her fantasy life to was gay? So what? Ha-ha-ha, as Zabeth said. It was just another cosmic lesson. In something. Heartbreak. She tore her eyes away from his beer, ducked her head, and reached for her Pepsi instead.

"The first time I saw you," Charles continued, "you were pushing your mother in her wheelchair through downtown Rancho Valdez with one hand and tugging this skinny poodle along on a leash with the other. Your mother was holding an armful of packages and complaining about something and you were listening with this sort of sweet and sour expression on your face and then you said something to her that made her light up. She literally lit up. I remember thinking: now there's a trick. To make someone smile like that." He sipped his beer. "And what a beauty."

Kay nodded, glum. Even dead, Ida outshone her. She saw Ida's sudden, wide, lipsticky smile, nested in dimples. Ida would have known how to talk to Charles; she would have flirted and teased and made him fall in love with her anyway. "Yes," she agreed, "she was."

"Not her. You."

"Right."

Charles laughed. "Don't you look at yourself? Lush 'n' creamy." He leaned forward and lowered his voice. "Totally toothsome."

"Would you mind writing those words down? Just so I can remember them later?" She flushed, trying not to smile. "Now tell me about Jimmy. Was he an artist, like you?" She paused. "Was he a beauty?"

"Not at the end." He was silent for a second. "I'm not good around sick people. Illness scares me. You were there for your mother. You helped her. Every time I asked for you at the library that lady you work with told me you were gone, taking care of your mom. And I always thought how amazing that was, not to be scared."

"I was afraid all the time," Kay said. "And, to tell the truth, I did a terrible job."

His brown eyes waited.

"I bungled things. I couldn't turn her in the bed or support her on the commode without feeling I was hurting her. I read the wrong books to her, played the wrong music, cooked things she couldn't eat, made fun of her priest."

"Still. When she called, you came."

"Late," Kay agreed.

"I couldn't do that for Jimmy. I couldn't be around him. He died in Seattle surrounded by strangers. Want to play pool?"

Kay glanced toward the pool table and shook her head. "You really asked for me at the library?"

"Lots of times. I always knew we'd be friends."

"You're smarter than I am. I always hoped we'd be lovers."

"But you're married." He sounded so shocked Kay smiled. We're both prudes, she thought. We have that in common.

"Separated," she explained. "As of this morning."

"From that nice old sleepy guy at the frame shop?"

"Don't tell me he sleeps in front of his customers!"

"No, no. That's just how I see him, you know, nice guy, no visible fire, but who knows. People who don't talk can fool me." He looked at her closely. "He doesn't feed you, does he. Doesn't feed the little Kay animal within."

Kay sniffed, repelled. What sort of therapy was Charles into? SPCA? She rapped her chewed nails on the table then relaxed. Charles was right. There *was* something alive and wild inside that was starving. Some wimpy little ferret. "No," she said. "He doesn't."

"Well he ought to." Charles leaned over and kissed her cheek. His breath was warm and beery. For months she had been in an erotic hum about this man, breasts and belly abuzz, but this, she saw, would have to do. Bravely she left her cheek against his lips and kept her napkin down. She would not wipe off his spit, at least not where he could see her. She would read everything she could about AIDS at the library tomorrow; she would learn. She looked across the room at the pool table again. "Do you have any friends who don't know how to play pool?"

"Sure don't, honey lamb. Come on. I'll teach you."

She was good at pool, not great, but good. The same lucky hand-and-eye coordination that got her through difficult passages in music served her well at the White Oak, and Charles cheered every time she hit a ball, any ball, into any pocket.

"Remember, always take the easy shot," he said.

"That goes against everything I was raised to believe in," Kay marveled. She bent, centered, aimed. What a good clean sound that click-click-click was. High on Pepsis, happy, she finally said good night to Charles and headed home. He was going to show her his paintings next week; she was going to play Beethoven for him; they were going to be supportive and nurturing and intimate and honest and maybe, someday, who knew, he might look at her the way a man looks at a woman and she could—no—I am not going to be like that, she lectured herself. I'm not going to think I can change people. I am going to let go of all those romantic idiot fantasies and accept everyone as they are. Still, strange things did happen. And he had called her lush. Not a lush. Just "lush." Wow. The last compliment she had received from Neal was on her radio skills. "No one can tune a station in like you," he had said, and she had glowed for days.

It was still early, but downtown West Valley was deserted and she could see a small light in the back of the stables as she drove by. At once she felt her good mood falter. Neal would be alone back there, spooning up some malt and molasses concoction, his shoulders slumped, his long grey hair loose on his shoulders, watching a show about the nesting habits of the blue-footed booby on his miniature TV. She slowed. Neal was her husband and she was still, through no fault of her own, his faithful wife. She should go to him and press his unhappy head to her push-up bra and comfort him until he felt healed and whole and better. She could do it. She knew how.

But I don't want to, she thought. She raised her chin. He screwed me. They all screwed me. Except Charles. Who screwed me by not screwing me. The little animal inside of me is sick of canned food and kibble. Even if that's all there is, I want more. I want a hot human heart. She touched the gas and headed home.

The house was empty when she entered. Nicky was spending the night with a friend and Coco was at the vet's with an ear infection. On an impulse, she called Francis. She would be a better daughter. More open and honest. She would tell him about her separation from Neal, ask his advice. She would let him know that Neal was inattentive, absentminded, careless, cold, remote, and timid, and Francis would say, *Then of course you ought to leave him*. She would tell him that Neal wouldn't make love, that he wore a dust mask and earphones in the house, that he slept on the couch and sat in his van for half an hour in the driveway every night before coming in after work, that he lied about money, borrowed without telling her, and made business plans on his own, and Francis would say, *Good for you, sweetie. You did the right thing. I'm proud of you.* She dialed his number, listened to the busy signal, dialed again, and finally, slowly, hung up. She really did live in dreamland. Victor hadn't understood any of her problems with Neal. Why would Francis? He did the same things Neal did. They were all alike. We marry our fathers, Zabeth had said. But marriage to Francis hadn't been that bad; Ida had liked it. They'd traveled, laughed, danced; they'd had fun. Maybe now, with Ida gone—and Neal gone—Francis could have fun with her. The cruise boat beckoned, her white dress billowed at the helm. She dialed once more and this time Francis answered. "Dad," she said, "it's Kay. I was hoping we could get together next week."

"Next week? Didn't I just see you yesterday?"

"Yes. But I have something I need to talk to you about."

"Next week's booked," Francis said.

"The whole week?"

She heard him click his gold pen. "Tell you what. I'll get back to you."

Get back *at* me is more like it, she thought as he hung up. She went in to play the piano, loud, so the notes could crash through and cleanse her. When she came out of the music room a few hours later she saw the light blinking on her answering machine. But it was only Walt Fredericks. He missed the rehearsals, he said. He missed the exquisite pleasure of seeing her play. "Darling girl," he said. And then again. "Darling, darling girl." She set the phone down, raised her head, and heard something scamper through the roof beams overhead. Rats? Probably. Tears, for the first time since Ida's death, ran down her face.

"It's not fair," she explained to Zabeth later that week, "the way everyone reaches out for everyone else, and misses."

"Not everyone misses." Zabeth stirred her daiquiri with a bone pulled out of her hair and licked the bone. "Most people don't reach out at all, for starters, and those that do usually know what they're reaching for. It sounds to me like your Dr. Fredericks has checked you out, knows you're separated, and has a pretty good idea he can have you."

"Well he can't." Kay heard Walt's hot liquid voice and saw his eager eyes fixed on her as if she belonged to him. She had always succumbed to people who claimed her. But she didn't have to. It wasn't a rule. "I don't want *him*," she added.

"So that's a start."

Kay nodded. Who else had used those words? Dr. Tamar, the first and only time she'd seen her? Or had she heard them at AA, the second and last time she'd gone? She looked around the Dark Moon Grill. What was she doing, still sitting in here? Shouldn't she have moved on by now? Shouldn't she be someplace else?

"Of course there's another option," Zabeth continued. "The old gent could be calling for the same reason he says he's calling, that is, to talk you into performing again. He could actually think you're talented and want to see you succeed. Not that you'll ever believe that." She paused, thought. "Maybe if you heard it from your father. Or he heard it from you."

"What do you mean?"

"Have you ever told Francis what a great architect he is?"

"But I don't like his houses."

"So why should he like what you do?" Zabeth pointed her bone. "It's ridiculous, the way you two treat each other."

"He started it. The day I was born, he brought his boss to see me in the hospital but I was too scrawny and red-faced and homely to claim so he pointed to another baby. Some rosy cherub in another crib. He said she was his daughter."

Zabeth winced, and Kay balanced the tippy table with her knees. She had at some level always thought that was sort of a funny story. "So we got off on the wrong foot," she continued. "And we've stayed there ever since. I sure wish I knew what he was doing these days though. His car's never there. He's on leave from work. Won't answer my phone calls."

"Well, give it a rest. He's just living his life. You've got to grab a life of your own."

"I have a life," Kay said. "I've quit drinking, I've quit smoking, I've quit Neal. What more can I do?"

Zabeth shrugged. "How should I know?"

She's tired of me, Kay realized. Tired of my endless questions, my need for support and demands for direction. I don't blame her. I'm tired of myself. "Have you and Garret found a house yet?" she asked, and for the rest of the lunch hour she feigned interest in Zabeth's detailed descriptions of easements, slate roofs, and mortgage rates. I will have to feign everything for a while, she thought. I will have to practice until I can pass as a normal person again, if I ever could.

Practice began that afternoon and continued through the week. She walked Coco through one obedience training exercise after another until Coco, confused, began to heel. She insisted Nicky eat dinner with her instead of alone in front of the television set. She met with Neal in the back of his shop, listened to his plans for the stables without interrupting or wisecracking, offered to help and did not throw boiling ginseng tea in his face when he said, "No, what could you do?" She bought rat traps and baited them. She told Walt Fredericks she missed their rehearsals too but was not ready to perform again and she could not, sorry, see him alone for a drink. She played hymns at Victor's church when Stacy phoned to say their organist was ill. She played pool with Charles at the White Oak and firmly said "no" to the bartender when he tried to drop cherries into her ginger ale. One afternoon she sat at the piano, felt the spring sunshine come in the music room window at last, decided to lift the lid of the piano to air it now that the rains had finally stopped, and saw something round and bright glittering beneath the golden wires. The ring. She must have taken it off during one of her nights of drunken chord crashing and knocked it off the music rack. She fished it out, rubbed it clean on the tee shirt over her heart, and held it up to the light. Ida's eye, implacable and proud. "Hi, Mom," she said. "Welcome back."

Sixteen

Francis was doing everything right. The problem was, Jim Deeds explained, he was doing it too late. The damage had been done. The breakages he'd been feeling were real. The arterial sclerosis and emphysema were established and both were irreversible. He had a few years left but they might not be good ones. "At least you have family," Jim Deeds said, and for one dark moment Francis actually saw Harry, Mick, Kip, Joanie, and Arlene, "the whole crew" as their father used to call them, lined up with outstretched arms. It wasn't until the next moment he realized the doctor meant Kay and Victor: his frazzle-haired, sharp-tongued, dreamy-eyed daughter and his born-again son. No thanks. They weren't up to this. Taking care of him was going to take a pro. He stood up and shook Jim's hand.

"Nothing like bad news," he said, "to stir the old blood."

The doctor looked at him appraisingly. "You're like Ida," he said. "Brave."

"She was brave, wasn't she," Francis mused.

"She was an amazing woman," Jim said, using the exact words

Francis had heard about Ida so often that he no longer even listened. He had never been sure what they meant anyway. Ida was Ida.

"The thing is," Francis pointed out, "there's not a lot of choice. If you can't go forward and you can't go back you might as well stand your ground and take what comes."

"Yes, but not everyone can do that."

"I'm not sure I can, to tell you the truth." Francis accepted the half-dozen useless prescriptions Jim gave him and walked out to the waiting room where Glo sat, erect in a designer suit, manicured hands in lap, not reading, she never read, not watching the tropical fish in the tank, she never watched anything but him. Her eyes filled with light as he approached. "I have two questions," Francis said, stopping before her. "One: how'd you like to go to Greece?"

Glo, who had been to Greece a dozen times, said, "I'd like that fine." So then he asked the second question and Glo said she'd like that too.

"Adam and Eve and Pinchme went down to the sea to bathe. Adam and Eve were drowned. Who do you think was saved?"

"Not while I'm driving, Nicky."

"Who do you think was saved?"

Kay sighed, said "Pinchme," and held out one arm as Nicky leaned toward her. The euphoria she'd been floating in since finding the ring had not touched Nicky, and the pinch he gave was long, fervent, and vengeful, a three-fingered pinch, which wasn't fair. She yanked her arm away, fighting the urge to slap him. It was April 1, and he'd been "fooling" her all day. "Feel better?" she asked, though she knew he did not. She pulled up in front of the stables to let him off for his day with Neal and kissed him, getting a good loving whiff of his sour-milk boy smell before he wiggled free, slammed the car door, and trudged into the shop with his hood high.

She drove on to the library. As she parked, she realized why she liked this little branch so much. Its mossy roof, knotty pine walls, and misshapen windows reminded her of the forts she and Victor used to construct out of leftover building materials abandoned on the lots of Francis's homes. She unlocked the door for the homeless man waiting patiently on the stone step outside, booted up the cheap computer and retrieved all the files Mrs. Holland had lost the day before, re-inked the stamp pads, watered the plants, tried to scrub a milky stain—grease? vomit? sperm?—out of the oak table in the Reference Alcove, arranged the display of Easter Eggs from Other Lands in the glass case, held a story hour about a Bad Baby Bunny for a group of preschoolers, and settled down to finish reading the sheet music she had ordered for the new Music Section she was assembling. It was a piece by Poulenc, and difficult. Her fingers were tapping invisible octaves on the desk when Mrs. Holland came in, flushed and out of breath.

"I've been job hunting," Mrs. Holland said, dropping her lunch and her crochet bag into a drawer. "How about you? Have you started yet?"

"Yes," Kay lied. "Are you sure this branch is going to be voted out and sold?"

"Sure as sure. Did you see that article on court reporting I Xeroxed for you?"

"I did. Yes. Thanks."

"And the one on becoming a dental hygienist?"

"Fascinating."

"Well it's fine for you, I suppose. You have a rich father. You don't have to worry."

Mrs. Holland's voice was sharp and Kay looked up. She's tired of me too, she realized. Everyone is. "I've applied at the university for next fall," she offered. "I'm going to do what you said, and get my degree in library science. I should whiz through, after everything you've taught me."

Mrs. Holland, mollified, sniffed and rearranged the vase of pencils on her desk. Kay looked at her with affection. This dry, dour widow had been a true friend. And I've had other true friends, she thought. She remembered all the eccentric elderly music teachers she'd studied with as a child—Mrs. Austin, Professor LeBlanc, Miss Poppy—they had all been stubbornly there for her, aware of her lapses, tantrums, and lies, but supporting her anyway. I've had many mothers, she thought. I've been lucky. She spent the rest of her shift feeling this luck—in the smiles and small confidences of the housewives, schoolchildren, and retirees, even from the construction workers who came in from the site next door to use the bathroom and read the sports page on their breaks. Maybe it was the spring weather at last, maybe it was the Poulenc, playing in her head, but for whatever reason, she felt better than she had in ages.

She finished her shift humming and was still humming as she drove to the jeweler's to pick up her ring. She had taken it in to Straub & Levy's a week ago to have it cleaned and sized. Al hadn't been there that day, but he greeted her now, as bald and big-bellied as Francis had described. "So you're the intended?" Al asked, reaching under the counter for the black velvet box.

"Victim?" Kay said. "No. I'm just the daughter." She held out her hand as Al slipped the ring on. It fit. The clunky weight of it settled, hard, and gleamed dark blue on her chewed, freckled finger.

"The daughter? I'll be damned. Your old man bought you a locket from me, twenty, twenty-two years ago," Al said. "Remember that locket?"

Kay looked up, surprised. She had forgotten. Gold, heart-shaped, the locket was the only present she had ever received from Francis. She had disliked it intensely. It had seemed chosen for some small flowerlike sweetheart of a daughter, not her. Still, she had worn it when she auditioned for the conservatory, the night she won the scholarship, and she had worn it again, less dutifully, when she slopped through her first recital there, half-drunk, her lips swollen with Biff's kisses. After Biff left her for the waitress, she pawned it.

"Your father was so proud of you." Al looked at her kindly. "And judging from appearances, I bet he still is."

Kay thanked him, paid him, and, troubled, went into a café next door for coffee. She remembered that scholarship competition, Francis watching her from the audience, calm and attentive, Ida beside him in a neck brace. He had stood up to clap. She reached for her coffee spoon, watching the ring glint as she stirred cream into her cup. I should like this ring more, she thought. And I should have kept that locket. All this time I've been mourning the gifts they didn't give. Why haven't I honored the ones they did?

She set her cup down. It's still possible to start over, she decided. We've had a lot of false starts, Dad and I, but we can begin again. We can still get to know each other. We can be friends. She looked at the clock on the café wall. She was close to Francis's office. She could drop in—other daughters did that with other fathers all the time. It was no big deal. She could just say hello. She would not tell him about losing or finding the ring. She would not mention her separation from Neal. She would stay five minutes and leave.

Francis's office was in a new industrial complex near the freeway on the top floor of a dark glossy building. Kay took the stairs easily, complimenting herself on her wealth of breath now that she had finally quit smoking for good. She hesitated outside the office door, steeling herself for one of his Well, Lookies or Who Asked Yous. He would see her smudged sunglasses, Coco's hair on her sweater, her faded jeans, the strap on her sandal she'd tried to fix that morning with the stapler. So what, she thought. I yam what I yam. She turned the knob and pushed the door open. The reception area was empty. That was odd; it was still early. She tiptoed across the marble floor and around the potted olive trees to peer into Francis's private office. His windows framed a view of the mountain and his huge desk was bare. No photographs of Kay or Victor or Ida, but then there never had been. Nothing but a wall full of awards he had won. She turned to leave and almost ran into

Sunny-at-the-Office, hurrying in from the kitchen area with a bottle of chilled champagne in her hand.

"Oh good," Sunny said, "you're late too. I meant to leave ten minutes ago but the phone's been ringing. Here. Can you take these?" She thrust the champagne and a bag of plastic glasses into Kay's arms. "Give me a sec to powder my nose and I'll follow you out."

"Out where?"

"To the courthouse."

"For what?"

"The wedding."

"Whose wedding?"

"Your father's. Aren't you going to witness?"

"Today?"

"I know. It's ridiculous. It's April Fool's Day. But you know your dad. He said it was as good a day as any. Better, because of the full moon. Come on, Kay. We're going to miss it if we don't get going."

Stunned, Kay drove after Sunny to the town center. She parked illegally under an oak tree in a handicapped zone and followed her into the courthouse, up the stairs and down a hallway to a closed door with gold lettering. She could hear her broken sandal flapping as she walked but it seemed to be coming from miles away. Her face felt hot and wet and Sunny, turning to hold the door open for her, sympathetically touched her own eye. "I always cry too," she confessed. Kay nodded. The small room they entered was rich with dark woods, windowless, and utterly silent. The judge was parting his hands in benediction over Francis and Glo Sinclair while two clerks looked on. Francis, in a business suit, and Glo, in a silk sheath, stood side by side, their heads bowed. Then, on a low instruction from the judge, they pivoted, put their hands on each other's shoulders, and kissed. Kay could hear the click of Francis's dentures. The ceremony was over.

She opened her mouth and a wail came out. "Maaaaa," it said.

Francis turned, astonished, his lips still pursed, eyebrows arcing. Glo turned too, her face white as the orchid pinned over her ear. Kay tried to swallow back the second wail but it ripped out a second later, louder and even more helplessly infantile than the first.

"Do something," Glo said as Kay broke into the third shrill "Maaaaa."

"What?" Francis asked.

"Go to her," Glo said. "For heaven's sake. She's your child. Hug her!"

But before Francis could take a step, Kay was gone. She backed out of the room and ran toward the parking lot. She shot toward her car, threw herself in, started the engine, and peeled out toward the freeway.

She could not stop trembling. She floored the old Lincoln, taking the first exit that opened, blood pounding in her cheeks as she watched the commute traffic part to give way around her. She was so angry she was not even aware, at first, that she was shouting. "How dare you!" she was shouting. She hit the steering wheel and burst into tears. "How dare you, how dare you, how dare you!" She changed lanes, one blurred red tunnel opening narrowly, dangerously to another. "It's only been three months," she shouted. "Who ever heard of anyone getting married again after only three months? It's indecent! And to Glo Sinclair!" She whooped. "Glo Sinclair, dear Dad, is stupid. That's her big secret. She is stupid, stupid, stupid." She brushed her tears off with the back of her hand and sped forward and it was only then she realized where she was headed—she was headed straight to the cemetery to tell Ida about it. She was going to tattle. And that was insane. As insane as shouting alone in a speeding car. And shouting what? Words Ida had used, on her, as a child, *How dare you*—and then the list of petty transgressions: *How dare you go to bed without drying the dishes. How dare you leave the porch light on. How dare you leave the laundry out.* Then that other word: *stupid.* That was Francis's word. Francis owned that word. *Don't be stupid, Kay,* in his light cold voice.

And she had been. She had baaed in public like a slaughtered lamb. What was wrong with her? How could she have made such a spectacle of herself? All her life she had tried to behave, and then, at the worst time, her true self had come out, naked and needy and wrong, wrong, wrong. Whose voice had she cried in and where had it come from? Was that the voice of the "little animal" Charles had talked about? Other people had tigers inside them, dragons, eagles. They roared. They soared. She bleated and bolted. She must be a goat. "Idiot," she said. "Stupid dum-dum idiot." She hit the steering wheel again and sped past the entrance of the cemetery. "I don't care if you get married," she shouted out loud to her father. "I don't care if it breaks your heart," she said to her mother. "I'm sick of you both." And then, a second later, horrified, she burst into tears and another raw "Maaaa" tore out of her throat.

I've lost him, she thought. I've lost both of them.

I never had them, she thought.

She drove for hours. Nothing she passed was familiar but nothing was unfamiliar enough. She turned off the freeway. She longed to get lost but it was hard to get lost, this close to home. Every turn turned her backward; every exit was an entrance to a place she hadn't even left. By the time the sunset faded she was finally off the map, rattling down a rural avenue east of the county lined with walnut trees. She pulled into some farmer's driveway and sat in the green silence watching the dust rise into the new leaves above her. Her eyes fell on the champagne bottle on the seat; she opened it, watched the cork pop out the window, and took a warm draught. It fizzed in her throat and surged unchecked in her empty stomach. So I'm drinking, she thought, so what. It doesn't matter. Nothing I do matters. Which means I can do anything I want. Whether I want to or not.

Another useless rattle of tears shook out of her. She finished the bottle, threw the car into reverse, backed out of the orchard, and sped off again.

She stopped for a bottle of Scotch and a package of cigarettes at a liquor store in the next town. She burned her thumb on the first match and her wrist on the second. She smoked three cigarettes one after the other, then wadded the pack up and threw it into the back seat. What a waste of time that had been, that long hard struggle to quit. Cigarettes weren't important—they were nothing—why had she bothered? Once you made your mind up, quitting was easy. She groped behind her seat, recovered the discarded pack, swerved across the divider line, straightened, and lit up again.

She ran out of gas in a foothill town that smelled like french fries and wood smoke. Salsa music poured from passing car radios and young people gathered on the corners, talking, touching, tapping their feet, full of the same excited secrets that everyone had at their age, that meant nothing, came to nothing, would get them nowhere. She pulled into a service station, bought gas with her last five dollars, and headed toward the mountains. She'd go to Idaho. Wyoming. Montana. Someplace where nobody knew her. Not that anyone knew her. Or ever had.

The old car climbed between high cold granite cliffs like a big-bowed boat cresting easy waves; it cornered and curved without slipping or tipping. The moon rose while Kay gulped the Scotch. The hell with them all, she thought. Mother. Father. Husband. Son.

Son, she thought. She hiccuped, but thought it again: Nicky. My son.

Darkly drunk, she stopped in the middle of the roadway. I am doing to Nicky what was done to me, she thought. I am making myself sick the way my mother did. And I am running away like my father did. And I don't have to. This is my life. Not theirs. She began to pull the car around to go back, get Nicky, and start again, but she hit the accelerator too hard and turned too wide. The Lincoln went into a swift, intractable skid, looping backward so that Kay could have the full horror of hindsight—the white road being pulled out from beneath her—before it bucked at the guard rail, shuddered, and floated forward off an icy cliff. For an instant, she was allowed to feel light and aloft in the pure pale moonlight, and then the car darkened, sank, and torpedoed down. At least, she thought, this will be the last mistake I make.

She awoke on her back. The moon was in her face. It was round and cold as Ida's silver mirror. She heard metal sounds around her, uneven clicking robot sounds, like broken clocks. Looking up, she saw a horse cropping the short grass nearby. She was in a mountain meadow, patchy with snow. The ground beneath her was blue in the moonlight and the horse looked blue too.

She struggled to rise. Blood ran down her leg, filled one of her sandals. Her breastbone felt cracked. She reached for the horse's tail and held on as he slowly picked his way down a path toward a light in the distance. The old couple who opened their door took her in and drove her to the hospital and stayed by her side through the night. They dismissed her gratitude; they would do this for anyone, they told her, as they would expect anyone to do it for them. They were happy to help. But they were confused by her story. They had never—they told her this again and again, amused by her insistence—owned a horse, nor had they seen any signs of a horse when they found her collapsed alone outside their door.

Seventeen

F r a n c i s came back from Greece in September determined
never to get stuck at a banquet table with strangers again. Those
cruise ships had done him in. He told this to Peg Forrest and she
flicked him with her napkin. "These aren't strangers," she scolded,
"these are your oldest friends." Francis shrugged. It was too noisy
in Le Petit Jardin to argue. He and Peg were seated at the far end
of a back room; the Junior Bentleys, wearing tinfoil crowns their
grandchildren had made, were seated side by side on a dais in
front. It was their fiftieth wedding anniversary and they looked as
if it were their hundredth, but that might have been the speeches.
How the old drone on, Francis thought. Ansel Lipscott had been
talking for twenty minutes and every other sentence seemed to
start with "A few years ago" or "A while back." Francis had
heard enough to know that Ansel was talking about the days when
he and Howard and Gil and Francis himself were young husbands
with young families, struggling to get ahead. The car-pool com-
mutes to the city, the Saturday morning tennis games, the drunken
barbecues that ended up with someone—usually Ida—skinny-dip-

ping in a swimming pool while the babies slept under piles of coats and purses in someone's back bedroom. Were those happy days? No worse than any other, Francis supposed. He tried to catch Glo's eye across the table. Still tanned from the islands, she was listening intently to Howard—or appeared to be listening, which was one of her better tricks—and did not look back. If you didn't know her, you'd think she was having a good time. Maybe she was having a good time. He hoped so.

"Wake me if Ansel says anything dirty," he whispered to Peg.

Peg looked into his face. "You all right?"

"I told you, Peg: I'm tired. Been tired as long as you've known me, if you'll recall."

"That's true. Kay told me you used to nap in the garage."

"One thing about Kay: she's a snoop. Another thing: let's not talk about her."

Peg pressed his hand. "She still hasn't called you?"

"She's disinherited me," Francis said. "Boohoo."

"Now don't be like that. You know she's just waiting for the right time to get in touch."

"Timing," Francis agreed, "has never been my daughter's strong point."

"People have to find their own way," Peg said. "You did."

Francis nodded. That was true. And there was no one to blame—or praise—but himself for the way his way had turned out. Again, he looked at Glo and this time, as her eyes at last met his, he saw the miracle—a Chimayo morning, fresh winter air, and a pretty widow in turquoise boots determined to save what was too late for salvage. He had always known, as his idiot ancestor had not, what a treasure was; the trick was how to keep it. He winked, enjoyed Glo's unblinking look back, and mouthed, *Let's get out of this hellhole.* She smiled, polite, not understanding. He sighed and looked down at Peg's hand, still pressed over his, the same warm hand that had nervously picked the gilt letters off the piano the night he told her it was over. She was a good sport, Peg. But not for him. No one for him, really, ever. But Ida.

He joined in the clapping that followed Ansel's speech but when Mimi Johns rose and started to talk, Francis excused himself and slipped outside.

There was an enclosed courtyard outside the kitchen door and he stepped into it with a deep breath, grateful for the fresh air and silence. So this was the *petit jardin* the restaurant was so famous for. He made his way along a brick wall to a stone bench by a lemon tree and sat down. Sunset streaked the sky and somewhere a bird sang. Life is good, Francis thought, in its way. Terrible things happen but they don't happen every minute. He smoothed his linen trousers over his knee. His own hand, he noticed, looked ancient. All wrinkled and splotched. The wedding ring Glo had given him was even worse than the one Ida had made him wear. The diamonds made him look like an old queen. He clenched his fist and suddenly remembered a game he used to play when Kay was a child. He'd put his hand over her knee, say "Go ahead, hit me," and she'd always try; she never said, *No, I love you Daddy, why would I want to hit you?* Not Kay. She'd wind up her little punching arm and let loose. She was fast. But he was faster. He'd move his hand and she'd strike her own leg. Then she'd do it again. She never seemed to tire of it, hurting herself. Still doing it, as far as he could tell. Some things never change, Harry had said, and that was true and that was too bad. But what could you do. People were what they were. He heard another feeble roar of geriatric laughter from the restaurant behind him and rose from the bench, walked to the gate, opened it, and stepped onto the street. No one would miss him. He had to get out.

Kay sat outside on her front porch eating rice pudding warm from the bowl. Ever since the accident she had been craving baby foods, mashed bananas, oatmeal, creamy digestible sweets. It was disgusting fare but it was doing the trick. She hadn't had a drink or a cigarette, but she hadn't had the nerve to confide her "secret"—eat like a baby, be like a baby—to anyone either. Certainly not to her AA group. They were such a sober set. They laughed, big phlegmy laughs between drags on their mentholated cigarettes and gulps from their oversugared coffees, but they never smiled. Saddicts, she called them. Well, she shouldn't joke, she was one too. She turned the spoon over in her mouth and licked it clean. When she graduated from baby foods she supposed she would go on to kid foods, peanut butter and white rice, and then on to adolescent food, french fries and diet Cokes. She would never graduate to the culinary sophistication of Zabeth, who had served black-bearded mussels in something she called "cum sauce" at her wedding shower last week, but she didn't need to be like Zabeth. She could be what she was, a woman on parole from arrested development perched on her half-painted porch with an estranged husband, an estranged father, and a just plain strange son.

She dropped the spoon in the bowl as Nicky came out and sat down beside her by the open bucket of yellow paint. He was listening to a football game on his transistor radio and he seemed at least eight inches taller than the last time she'd seen him, ten minutes ago. "Mom?" he asked. "Are you going to be late?" He sounded worried, and she remembered what Dr. Tamar had told her last week: Nicky was never to feel she was his "job." He was never to feel it was up to him to make her a better person. She reached to hug him, feeling the deep ache in her clavicle where the fracture still had not healed. He tensed against her, giving her the same guarded look Mrs. Holland had given her when she had announced she wanted to stay on at the library until the bitter end— an end which still had not come. The voters seemed to like the West Valley branch as much as she did and had approved the new bond to retain it for another four years. "If you're not careful," Mrs. Holland had warned just before she herself transferred to Rancho Valdez, "you'll stay here forever." Good, Kay had thought. I want to. By forever she would have earned her M.L.S., just in case the county demanded she produce a degree that Charles Lichtman couldn't forge.

She showed Nicky her watch, which, like all the clocks inside the house, was set ahead twenty minutes. Another baby trick that worked. "Honey, I don't have to be at Charles's art show opening until seven and it's only five-thirty. But you're right. I'll look slippy." She covered the can of paint, put the brush to soak, regarded the work she had done so far, which, yellow painted over brown, looked like cold butter over cold toast, told herself it would look better when it was done, and went inside to change. She inched into the seamed hose and red dress Charles wanted her to wear—still dressing for others, she thought as she combed her hair and applied the lip gloss he liked. But if I dressed for myself, she admitted, I'd never get out of my bathrobe. She made a face at her reflection in the mirror. All this recovery work. One step forward, two steps back. And in the end where were you? She set her comb down, noticing with resignation that somehow it was Neal's old white comb again, and glanced at the photo on her bureau. Ida and Francis at an outdoor café in Paris, both in dark glasses, with cigarettes and drinks in their hands. *Toujours gai,* those two. Too bad they had to be her parents. No. Not too bad. Without Ida's hot courage and Francis's cold wit she never would have made it this far. Wherever this far was. She touched their faces lightly with her finger and turned away. One of these days she would phone Francis, introduce herself, and start another stunted conversation. But she needed to wait until she was sure she wouldn't cry, or rage, or expect her basic unalienable daughterly rights. And that might take a while.

"Dad's here," Nicky called. She looked through the curtains and saw Neal walking up the path, his step light and almost springy. Being out of the marriage, losing the stables, and filing for bankruptcy had restored him to the nice gentle bachelor she'd fallen for years ago. He held a bouquet of limp carnations—how could carnations loll like that?—and whistled off-key when he saw her. "Break a leg," he said.

"Don't wish that." Kay grabbed her music and her keys and hurried out to the car Victor had sold her. The first car she had ever chosen, bought, and paid for on her own. So what if it was eight years old, purple, and had two broken back windows? The sound system was great. She put a Glenn Gould tape on, one she had listened to over and over during the weeks of convalescence. She had tried to explain to Dr. Tamar what it had meant to her, lying on her back in the hospital, in pain, truly in pain for the first time in her life, and for the first time in her life understanding a little of what Ida had lived with, day after day, while the perfect piano notes rushed past her. She had not been able to articulate how much she had hated that music. It was like some river of life she was not allowed to ride. And then one day, no reason, no special event, no one said anything to her, nothing in particular happened, the sunlight just moved across the blanket, a hummingbird hovered outside the window, a leaf fell off the weeping fig tree Zabeth had sent her, Gould muttered something ghoulish to himself under the Bach Prelude, and suddenly she was on that river, riding. She was back, intact, alive. That must be what the saddicts meant when they said "Let Go and Let God." That must be what Victor meant when he said "Jesus Saves." Kay did not think she had ever experienced it before. Except once, maybe, years ago, when Nicky was a baby and she and Neal were still being kind to each other and the three of them were floating in her parents' swimming pool on an autumn afternoon. They had heard Ida storming inside the house, something about Greta, something about what Greta had or hadn't done, and then they heard Francis's quiet footsteps, moving away, the garage door closing behind him as Ida's clear voice continued to stab the air with its anger. "Your poor mother," Neal had said. And for no reason Kay had started to laugh, and then Nicky had started, and then all three of them were laughing so hard they had to cling to the sides of the swimming pool, not to keep from drowning but to keep from levitating, to keep from rising like bubbles over the cold glass walls of her parents' house. That had been a moment of grace she'd always remembered. It hadn't lasted long, but while it had lasted she had glimpsed some of the peace she sometimes glimpsed now.

She guided the car through West Valley, past the EVERYTHING MUST GO signs on Neal's stables, past the dark open door of the White Oak. As she passed Le Petit Jardin she recognized the Forrests' car parked outside and slowed. She glanced toward the garden gate of the little brick restaurant, which was open, and that's when she saw him, standing there looking up at the sunset as if he'd been waiting for her all this time, dapper, relaxed, and solitary.

"Daddy," she said.

He didn't turn. Why would he? Daddy wasn't a name he had answered to in years. She drove on half a block, stopped, double-parked, got out, and slowly walked back to where he stood. He turned, unsurprised, taking in the red dress, the lip gloss. "Well, Kay," he said. "What are you doing, streetwalking?"

He was sick, she could tell that, something was wrong. His skin was flushed and pink, his breath was thick. She stopped two feet away from him, feeling the old force field holding her there, repelled, then she took a deep breath and took a step forward. It was like being drunk, trusting like this, stepping into the dark, and, like being drunk, it was easy. She raised her arms, put them around him, let the blue ring on her hand will his shoulders close to hers. "I love you," she said. She didn't care if he said nothing or if he resorted to his standard "Ditto," but when his own hand came up and patted her back, one-two, and his voice, mild, cool, said, "Why, I love you too," she thought she might be excused from the rest of her life. Many things might happen to her in the years to come, but this was as happy as she was going to get. "I was thinking about you," he added.

She sniffled. "You were?"

"The games we used to play."

She nodded, bent her head, took the handkerchief he handed her and blew. She had always blown her nose a little too noisily for a lady. She knew that. She knew too what games he meant. The game where he'd trick her into trying to hit his hand, the game where he'd bet she couldn't hold her breath through the tunnel and then slow to three miles an hour, the game where he'd take giant steps and invite her to match him when they walked on the beach, the game where he'd hold his finger in the candle flame, say "I don't feel a thing," and widen his eyes with amazement when she pulled back, scorched.

"Waste of time, weren't they," Francis said.

"Oh I don't know," Kay said. "I suppose we got something out of them." The word "time" reminded her. "I have to go, Daddy," she said. "Will you and Glo come to the house next week?"

"Whatever for?" Francis asked.

"I don't know. Reconciliation. Redemption. Coffee. Cake." She held him again, the frail collapsed weight of him, stepped close again to kiss his cheek, stepped back, alive, and walked back up the block to her car. As she slipped behind the wheel she glanced at her watch again. Five-thirty. Still? Had it stopped? Her heart sped up, panicked, and for a second she could see nothing in front of her but darkness. The desire never to move again overcame her. She bowed her head and, with effort, began to review the music she would be playing at the gallery for Charles's opening. It was dance music, insistent, inviting, and it nudged her forward, forced her to move. She started the car and put it in gear. If she hurried, she'd make it. She still had time.

About the Author

Molly Giles is an associate professor of creative writing at the University of Arkansas and the author of two short-story collections, *Rough Translations* and *Creek Walk and Other Stories*. She has won several awards for her writing, including the Flannery O'Connor Award for Short Fiction and the Small Press Best Fiction/Short Story Award.

A SCRIBNER PAPERBACK FICTION READING GROUP GUIDE

IRON SHOES

DISCUSSION POINTS

1. *Iron Shoes* deals with characters who are stuck, unable to move forward in their lives. Kay, of course, is the prime example, but Francis, Ida, Victor, and Neal are also weighted down. Discuss their own styles of iron shoes. Did you find that Ida, the only real cripple in the book, is in many ways the freest?

2. Were you impatient with Kay? Could you think of things she could have done to free herself? Could you see why she was unable to do these things?

3. Giles took a risk killing off her most vibrant character midway through the book. How did you react to Ida's death? Did you put the book down? Why did you pick it up again?

4. Were you initially put off by the book's emphasis on physical pain and mutilation? What qualities in the writing helped you get through the first opening pages?

5. Discuss Giles's treatment of male characters. Is she fair to them?

6. What role does Zabeth play in the book? Is she a good foil for Kay?

7. What's your take on the blue horse? Does it work as a fantasy? Can you accept that Ida's hallucination becomes Kay's guardian angel? If so, what does this say about the deeper connection between mother and daughter?

8. Kay feels no one loves her. Is this true? Who does she most want to love her? Who does she most love?

9. The book uses a lot of quick, snappy dialogue. Take any scene and look at the ways dialogue advances toward or skips away from the central conflict. Did you find it believable?

10. Neither conventional religions nor alternate twelve-step programs receive much respect in these pages. Were you offended?

11. The sex scenes between Neal and Kay are some of the saddest in print. Did they also seem realistic? Why do you think bad sex is easier to write about than good sex?

12. What do you think will happen with Kay's marriage? With Kay herself? Where do you think she will be in ten years? Would you be interested in reading a sequel?

13. Giles has described this book as "a comedy about alcoholism, incest, cancer, and death," adding, "I had trouble with the tone." Do you see *Iron Shoes* as a comedy? A tragedy? Neither? Does it seem real to you? Did it make you think about your own life?

A NOTE FROM THE AUTHOR

This book grew out of the title story, "Creek Walk," from my last collection of short stories. The characters stayed with me. I changed them a bit (many have different names) but their essential natures remained unchanged. "Creek Walk" is about grief; *Iron Shoes* is about growth. I wanted to follow the main character, the forty-year-old daughter, as she comes to terms with her mother's death and her father's rejection, and finds her own way at last. I have joked that the book is a comedy about cancer, alcoholism, and incest, but it is, in fact, that, and one of the hardest problems has been trying to maintain a tone that captures the humor and horror without cheapening either. This book took seven years to write, primarily because as a full-time college teacher, I wrote it mainly in Januarys and Julys, but also because I was trying to balance that tone. The manuscript was written on eight different machines (old typewriters and borrowed computers), it was singed in a bar fire, three chapters in a briefcase were stolen from the trunk of my car, it's traveled with me to Mexico and Hawaii in a backpack, it has been with me so long I don't know what I'll do without it. It has been totally rewritten five times and has gone from 417 to 287 pages. The hardest part to get right was the end. In the first version I killed Kay off. It felt great. In the second version I maimed her badly. She would never play the piano again. That also felt great. In the next version I gave her a hit song, a successful romance with a wonderful man, and a good job. That felt, as you can imagine, lousy. The end I have now feels exactly right to me. She is going to be fine. Just not right away.